DAVID S. BRITTON

Ordering Information:

Prime Seven Media
518 Landmann St.
Tomah City, WI 54660

Printed in the United States of America

MESSAGE FROM THE AUTHOR

Hello Reader.

This novel is designed to make you think about something that we often try not to think about – why people hate each other and what the consequences of that hatred can be for the innocent. For a long time, it seems, we have deceived ourselves into thinking, with the end of Apartheid in South Africa, the scourge of racism is ended. As it turns out, we were wrong. It had simply gone underground. We had warnings, of course, with the "race riots" in Britain and the USA in the transition period between the twentieth and twenty-first Centuries, but it only needed an apparent racist like Donald Trump to become President of the USA for the virus to burst out into the open again in its most violent form, spawning movements like Black Lives Matter and Antifa in response. I am a life-long member of the Anti- Apartheid Movement and my late wife was a Nigerian – so my three children and (so far) only grandchild are mixed race. Therefore, you could argue that my position is prefixed – except that it wasn't – it was fixed before I married, and my marriage was only possible because it was. In a sense, the struggle against racism has been my life. It was one reason why I spent six happy years teaching in two African countries (Zambia and Nigeria).

I have written one novel which was based around racism in Britain in the 1960s when it was overt and bad – but not as overt and bad as in the USA and certainly not enshrined in law as in South

Africa – but every bit as devastating for its victims as the more blatant racism elsewhere. The book – entitled "Fifty Years After" which featured a case of injustice being put right 50 years after the event, is still on sale through Amazon. However, to make the pain and horror of racism effective to the majority white community, it needs more than describing what might happen to the black minority – it really needs to strike home by making the majority feel the pains of the minority community in themselves. It's difficult to identify yourself with a person who is different from you. That, for instance, is one of the reasons why Hitler and Himmler were able to inflict the Shoah (Holocaust) on the Jews without any widespread protest from the quiescent German population. This book attempts to address that challenge. In the film, "Titanic", James Cameron asked you to identify with two young people, victims of the disaster. In this book, I am asking you to do the same thing.

I first attempted to write this thirty years ago – but ditched it when I found a scenario needed to create the preconditions necessary for an African nation to seek to enslave their white expatriate workforce too difficult and too implausible, since it presupposed the effective destruction of the European and North American nations. The coming of détente meant the possibility of that happening had receded to the point of near non- existence. Sadly, Vladimir Putin's unsuccessful invasion of neighbouring Ukraine and his Russian cronies' near hysterical demands for nuclear war in Ukraine and, by extension, against the West, has made the possibility only too real again. Hence this book. Using the story of two young British teachers who travelled to Africa to teach, I am inviting you to share in the experience of those millions of Africans who were shipped against their will to work as slaves in the Americas and elsewhere as well as the struggle to liberate them from oppression.

Authors of novels always assure you that there is no connection with any living person. Three historical figures are mentioned, but the context means that there can be no concern over their 'appearance'. On proof reading, I realized it could be possible to postulate a link between two of the characters and two people living today - but I assure you I never had them in my mind, even unconsciously. So, let me repeat, the time honoured formula, 'any perceived connection between any character in this book and any individual living or dead is entirely coincidental.' Finally, to help you, I have listed below, without explanation, the names of the characters with whom you will soon become familiar. I hope you enjoy reading the story, that you come to love or hate the chief characters, and that, if you do, you tell others. I need the cash! But, also, do write to me care of the publisher – you never know – it might persuade them to publish another of my books! I wish to thank Margaret for proof reading this book and for her valuable suggestions and also the publishers for publishing the book.

David S. Britton

London, UK

October 2022.

Named Characters in the Book

(Minor characters in Italics)

1. The Slaves

   Marcus (Mark) and Judy

   Antonio and Maria

   Michael and Marta

   Colin and Chloe

   Jack and Clare

   Bill

   Louise and Marcel

George and Tessa

Reuben and Wanda

Tom and Maisie

Rosalyn

Anna (Browne)

2. *Mark and Judy's children*

   Monica Judy, Matthew Mark, Concordia June and Louis Jake

3. The Austrasians (N.B. Not Australians)

   Matthew and Monica Ngangi

   Josiah Ndenge

   Colonel Musaveni

   Frederick Igbokwe

   Jake (Louis – pronounced Lewis), Longinus, Ade - pronounced Ad-day

   Major General Okpara

   Maritza, Letizia, Daniel, David

   Professor Nwamarkwa, Nathaniel Ajayi & John Okonkwo

   Reuben, Emma, Josiah, Eric, Marta, Micah, Don, Julia, Erica, Lancelot

   Other characters are not named

REVENGE!

CONTENTS

PROLOGUE

Dear Professor Akayi,

I am writing to you to cover a manuscript which I have worked on since my group at the University Geophysical Department completed the excavation and exploration of the Ngugi Falls Cave complex recently. I hope you will find it interesting. My contributions are in italics.

You will know that when we penetrated behind the curtain of water we found a natural cave existed there, but it appeared to have been blocked by some sort of explosion which brought rocks down to block the entrance to the cave system to all but the best equipped individual or team. We cleared the blockage eventually, after a lot of work, only to find a primitive sort of wall across the entrance to the cave. The wall had obviously been forced, but, equally obviously, it had been defended. We found evidence of recent conflict between a community which had obviously lived there for some time and had suffered some form of attack from outsiders and possibly torture. It was then I found the document I have attached to this letter and to which I have added. It is an account of the last few years of our history through the eyes of two extremely significant, but somewhat controversial current figures. I took it with me, did additional research using Government and Military records and have been able to fill in the gaps to the best of my knowledge. I did this because I was struck by the opening words.

"My name is Marcus, but I am known as Mark. I am twenty-six now. My wife Judy is two years younger than I am. We came to this country as teachers. We were enslaved. Luckily, we were fortunate to be freed later. We are now striving for the freedom of all slaves. If you find this, you'll know that we have been only partially successful."

I have written this as a record of these people's lives in the hope of raising the issue of slavery among our people; whether it's moral or ethical to enslave people who are different from ourselves and make them serve us. I hope you will read it and advise me whether I should publish it.

Best wishes

John Okonkwo

CHAPTER 1

Teaching in Austrasia

My name is Marcus, but I am known as Mark. I am twenty-six now. My wife Judy is two years younger than I am. We came to this country as teachers. We were enslaved. Luckily, we were fortunate to be freed later. We are now striving for the freedom of all slaves. If you find this, you'll know that we have been only partially successful.

Neither of us lived exceptional lives in our home country. We were born and brought up in a rural town. We went to primary school in our local community and then to the nearest secondary school. That's where we met. I was in Year 9 and Judy in Year 7. Nevertheless we first became friends and then an item. Eventually we had our first fumbling love making, but, despite its imperfections, it united us, as it turned out, forever. We both worked hard at school, kept out of trouble, and went on to University. Even if any of our teachers survived the war, I doubt if just one of them would remember either of us. We were unremarkable students both at school and at university. Our degrees were reasonable but not brilliant. However they were good enough to allow us to train as teachers. After qualifying I worked for two unhappy years in an English secondary school. It was a real battle to try to persuade reluctant teenagers to enjoy the beauty of English literature! I was, therefore, relieved when Judy qualified, and we were able at the ages of twenty-three and twenty-one to travel out to Austrasia to teach.

We discovered Austrasia is a medium sized African Republic and a former British colony just to the north of South Africa and east of Zimbabwe. It is partly hilly, almost mountainous, and partly savannah. A largish lake, Lake Nduya, lies in the southern half of the country between the savannah and the rising hills. (See the map.) It is one of the tourist spots, as is a one hundred and sixty foot high waterfall on the River Uraya, known as the Ngugi Falls. Its capital is in the southern half of the country and known as Freetown – a name shared with Sierra Leone. The country is divided into provinces, the largest of which is the north western one of Casa Isabella (reflecting the fact that the British had acquired it from the Portuguese at the end of the nineteenth century) and named it after its chief town. The area to which we were sent was in the north and was named after its regional centre, the town where we worked, Concordia.

We had two happy and very fulfilling years, teaching English and History (in my case) or English and Geography (in Judy's) to children who did want to learn and didn't spend every other minute challenging our authority. It was a boarding school so we were all housed on site. We were treated as a married couple and had just begun to think about making it official and becoming parents when the world changed. Most of the staff were young Austrasian men and women. However, there were another three ex-patriots: Antonio (aged thirty-five) and his wife, Maria (thirty-three), both Italian; and Michael (forty-five) (an American) who had married an Austrasian woman called Marta (thirty- eight). Judy and I were British. We six formed a separate group in the staffroom, but, overall, we were accepted by the rest of the staff. For two years we all worked well together. Locals and incomers, we all visited one another and learned to appreciate, and later, to cook, Austrasian, English and Italian food. We even learned to appreciate grits! The Austrasian Government seemed to appreciate our efforts as well. Government inspectors commended us, the local Party officials seemed to like us, and when President Igbokwe visited the school, he made a point of meeting us privately and thanking us for helping the people of Austrasia. My clearest memory from those early happy days was of going down to my form room during evening prep time to tell my form off for misbehaving during the day. As I entered the room there was a tremendous clap of thunder, which caused the boys to laugh, and totally ruined the effect I intended to produce. The result – sudden collapse of angry (but not stout) party!

So, it continued – and we had no reason to assume things would change. But we were wrong. Looking back, certain things that happened to me were warnings of what was to come. During my first year in the school, I clashed with a senior boy who was at that time a Prefect. He was later to become Head Boy. He was known as a bully and I caught him thrashing a first year lad with a cane. I ordered him to stop and asked him what he thought he was doing. He answered sullenly he was punishing a junior. I asked him what the youngster had done, and he told me it did not concern me. When I insisted upon an explanation for his behaviour, he said Prefects controlled the boys and teachers, especially foreign ones, let them do it. I reached forward and seized the cane from him and smashed it across his backside, warning him if I caught him doing it again I would give him a really good hiding. Then I snapped the cane in two and threw it into the Bush. He muttered something in his own language and stamped off. I asked the younger lad what the Prefect had said, and he told me he had threatened that he would get even with me one day and then I would regret what I'd done to him. Subsequently, I, in particular, met a lot of subdued hostility from some of the senior boys – hostility which tended to increase as the months passed.

One event that would later have devastating consequences for us expatriate teachers, changed everything. All the Northern nations blundered into a mutually destructive war with each other. None of us understood the reasons for it then. And we certainly have no idea what or why it happened now. But what we did know is we suddenly had no homeland. We were stateless and helpless in the face of a newly hostile country. We were worried certainly, but more for our families than for ourselves. We saw no change in attitudes towards us at first, unless you consider sympathy for our predicament to be a change. Naturally we were glued to news from the North, which is why we missed what was happening in Austrasia. We didn't listen to the local news, but the two (Government run and therefore printed in English as it is the official language) national newspapers were often found in the staffroom. I did glance through them from time to time and noticed a growing undercurrent of criticism of President Igbokwe together with complaints about the money that was being spent ("wasted") on employing us.

After a month of this, all five of us were summoned to the Head's office. He asked us how we felt about things; thanking us for the work we were and had been doing, he turned to what was concerning him.

"I think you should all, including Marta, consider leaving this country as soon as you possibly can," he said.

I asked why.

"I've heard from Freetown that the situation there is extremely volatile. The Government is in trouble and a Coup seems highly likely. It will change things – and not for the better."

Antonio asked why he thought that. The Head explained there were rumours General Ngangi, an extreme right wing nationalist, opposed to employing foreign workers, was plotting to overthrow the president.

"You're a historian, Mark," the Head said. "You know about Hitler and the Nazis and what Hitler actually did when he came to power. I can see General Ngangi and his followers behaving in exactly the same way, or possibly even worse. Hitler persecuted the Jews. He'll do the same to you. That's why I think it's best you all leave Austrasia as soon as possible."

We thanked him and left. We all went to Michael's house so Marta could be involved in discussing the implications of this alarming news. It was agreed that we could not legally leave until the end of term, which was ten weeks away, but we would submit our resignations immediately. Marta said she and Michael were in a different position to the rest of us and they would wait to see what happened. In the end it was decided everyone would do the same. We thought that even if there was a coup next day, we would have time to make our escape before any sort of crackdown began. We were, of course, totally wrong. Looking back, we should have rushed back to our homes, packed essentials, got in our cars and driven to the nearest border twenty miles away, because even as we were talking, Austrasian troops were moving towards the Presidential Palace. As I learned later, there was a brief fire fight after which the Palace was stormed, the President and his family were marched out into the courtyard and summarily executed under controversial circumstances. Government ministers were arrested over the course of the following days, put on trial for corruption, and hanged within a month.

The Coup had been planned for months. Matthew Ngangi had apparently gained the support of all the senior officers by a mixture of bribery and sharing the resentments of the men involved.* The operation was carefully planned to include what the new regime was intending to *do during the first few months after the revolution. The start of the Great Northern War provided the trigger for these plans at a meeting of the plotters which took place shortly after the war began. They kept minutes which were transcribed later as the first acts of the new Government. The meeting discussed the situation of the fifteen thousand foreign workers ("guest workers" as President Igbokwe termed them). They concluded that they would not let them leave the country, but they would also not employ them under their current contracts.*

After a lengthy discussion, Josiah Ndenge (who became the Vice President after the coup) suggested simply enslaving them all. He said it would be a suitable revenge for what their countries had done to the Austrasian people in the past. Someone objected to this on the grounds that the northern national governments would retaliate. Mr. Ndenge dismissed this argument saying only the American and European nations were affected and they were in no position to do anything about it. Everyone therefore adopted this proposal and agreed to set up a small sub-committee to discuss how this decision could be implemented. The assault on the Palace, as described by Mark, took place about three months later. Once in power, the new regime put the secret plan to enslave the foreign workers (code named Operation Eichmann) into effect immediately.

*Josiah Ndenge came from Casa Isabella. He was a senior member of the United Independence Party (UNIP) and Minister of Defence in President Igbokwe's government. He was an extreme right wing politician who was well known for his visceral hatred of European people and their governments in particular. He had a large popular following which was particularly strong in his own province of Casa Isabella. There was a persistent rumour at the time that he was the real instigator of the coup and he used Matthew Ngangi as a figurehead to ensure he had army support and co-operation.

CHAPTER 2

Captured!

The news of the coup in Freetown and the death of the President hit us like a bombshell. We planned to meet the following morning, but we were awakened early by a heavy knock on the door. I got up and dressed (we slept naked because of the heat) and went to the door. I opened it to find two police officers standing there. I asked them what they wanted.

"We've come to collect your passports," the senior officer answered.

"Why?" I asked.

"We're doing a passport check of all non Austrasian residents on the orders of the new government."

I asked how long they would keep them.

"I don't know," he replied. "We have to send them to Freetown, so they can collate data on everyone."

I asked them to wait a moment and went back inside. Judy had dressed and come into the hall.

"Who's there and what do they want, darling?" I told her.

"We should have run away last night," she said. "Now we can't."

We agreed we had no choice but to do as they asked and handed our passports over to them. I did ask for a receipt and was given one. They left and I found out later they had gone to the other two houses with the same request.

We turned on the radio to try and find out more about what was happening and learnt that all the borders were now closed and all flights had been cancelled indefinitely.

We were now trapped in a country that suddenly didn't want us. This became ever more apparent as the days went by. We even found our lessons being deliberately disrupted by some of the students and parents beginning to complain about our being in the classrooms. Things came to a head one evening when I was on duty. Two prefects came to my house and told me there was trouble in the senior dormitory. They asked me to come and sort it out. I agreed and Judy decided to come with me. When we arrived all was quiet. I commented that everything seemed normal and we turned to go, only to discover our exit was blocked by four senior prefects led by the Head Boy. "You're going nowhere," he said. "I did warn you I would get revenge. This is it." We were seized and stripped naked. Our hands were tied and secured to ropes they had attached to the ceiling in some way we couldn't see. Then our feet were tied together. That's when the serious abuse began. We were taunted and beaten until our bodies were a mass of bruises. When they had finished with us, Antonio and Maria were brought in and the process was repeated with them.

Once they decided they had done enough to punish us, they turned to the clothing they had taken from us. They piled it onto the floor and set fire to it all, rubbing the ashes, as they cooled, over our bodies. "That's what we'd like to do to you," the Head Boy said, "but we can't." He turned to his followers and told them he didn't want us corrupting their environment any longer with our stinking bodies and ordered us to be cut down, have our hands tied behind our backs, be carried out of the dormitory and dumped on the road which ran through the school. "With any luck," he added "someone will run over them." The boys did as they were told, and we were dragged out and thrown onto the road. Luckily for us no one was driving that night and we were found in the morning by some of the younger pupils who reported what they had found to the Head. He arranged for us to be rescued and told us to discontinue teaching because it was too dangerous, but suggested we might work on the roads and paths of the school, cleaning them up.

So, we became labourers! We worked in our pairs and for a while we were left alone. However, one morning, we became four rather than six, because Michael and Marta were taken away. A lorry arrived at their house. They were ordered to pack, and, once having done so, were loaded with their luggage onto the back of an army lorry and driven away. We never heard from them again. Meanwhile, the rest of us also received visits from the Army. We were ordered to pack all our belongings, including the clothes we were wearing, in our trunks, label them, and send them to Freetown so they could be stored against our departure at the end of term.

I protested.

"Do you intend us to be naked?" I asked.

One of the soldiers grinned, but the Sergeant in charge, rebuked him. He handed each of us two pairs of shorts and two bush shirts (army issue), together with a pair of sandals.

"Don't lose them," he warned." Because we can't replace them."

It seemed to us as though we were being treated to death by a thousand cuts. Turned into labourers and now into squaddies. It looked very bad and we remembered, too late, the warning the Head had given us. He, incidentally, had been removed, and an army lieutenant was now in charge of the school. At first things didn't seem too bad as we were allowed to work unmolested. It was very hot during the day, and Antonio and I began to take our shirts off, to be followed by Judy and Maria.

When I asked her about this, Judy answered.
"They're treating us like you men; so why shouldn't we act like you? They don't seem to care anyway!"

I saw her point, even though I didn't feel happy about it. I was sure this could only end badly.

Sure enough it did! Three days later, our shirts were stolen while we worked. We reported this to the lieutenant who simply reminded us we'd been warned there would be no replacements and added that maybe we should have kept wearing them. "It looks as though someone decided you obviously didn't want or need them", he said. When we got back to our homes, we discovered our spare shirts and shorts had gone as well. I realized it would be pointless complaining, but I asked the lieutenant how the thieves had got in. He answered, "I don't know but none of the locks are very safe. Why don't you all move in together?" We agreed to do so.

That evening the four of us discussed the worsening situation. We agreed that things were probably going to continue to deteriorate even further. Antonio suggested we should leave that evening as soon as it was dark and try to walk to the border through the Bush, not using the roads in order to avoid being seen. I was inclined to agree but Maria pointed out that walking through the Bush at night would be extremely perilous. She added it would be dangerous even in daylight because the grass, which is head-high, could be concealing venomous snakes and insects. Judy agreed, pointing out that bare-legged and with only sandals on our feet was no way to tackle such a journey. She went further and told us there might even be lions or other big cats concealed in the long grass and we would struggle to find any tracks in the dark. I looked at Antonio and said, "This journey is so dangerous that in all probability not all of us would reach the border alive. Whereas, if we stay here, no matter what they do to us, we should still live through everything that's happening. So long as we are alive we can always hope that this will come to an end one day. But if we're dead then there is no hope at all." So reluctantly we stayed where we were.

After we moved in together, things calmed down for a while. We all got used to going about topless and hoped the time would pass quickly and we might have an opportunity to escape. Two weeks later, our house was burgled during the night. I heard the unusual sounds and went to investigate. I was seized as before, pushed onto the floor and bound hand and foot. There were about ten of them. They woke the other three and treated them in the same way. All that was in the house were four pairs of shorts and four pairs of sandals. That's what they'd come to take. But, of course, they now had all four of us as prisoners. They began to discuss what they were going to do with us. They spoke in the local language, so we had no idea what was being said since none of us had learnt more than a few words as all lessons were taught in English. However, we knew it boded ill for us all.

I have spoken to the boys. They told me the Army ordered them to enter the house and steal all the remaining clothing so the four foreigners would have to work naked. They were too noisy and woke up one of the men. He was already naked, so they simply jumped him and tied him up. They then did the same to the other three. They were told not to harm them – simply to ensure they would have nothing to wear. They discussed the situation as most of them wanted to march them naked around the campus. Two of the boys even wanted to hang them. (Incidentally, I discovered this happened to the other two teachers because they refused to break up their marriage.) In the end they sent for the lieutenant, who felt he had been put on the spot, so he told them to leave the four of them where they were overnight and he would deal with them in the morning.

They moved us one by one to the bedrooms and tied us face down to the beds with our arms and legs spreadeagled so we could not free ourselves. Once we were tied down, we were each beaten by them before they left us. You should understand that although we had brought the beds together to make double beds, each bed was, in fact, single – so they had simply pulled them apart. Next morning the soldiers found us, and the lieutenant brought us what the Native Americans called breach cloths – one each and the string to tie them around our waists. Our degradation was nearly complete – but not quite.

We were sent out to work and our abusers gathered to tease and torment us even more. There were more than those who attacked us overnight. The number was at least double. Some threw stones at us. Others would suddenly run at us and we would be pushed into the trench we were digging. We tried to ignore them, but we failed miserably. Finally, I turned to face them.

"Why are you doing this to us?" I asked

"Because we don't want you here anymore," one of the boys answered.

The others shouted their agreement, and a volley of stones was thrown at us. As they struck our bodies the stones stung and created small red marks. We tried to ignore it; but it was impossible. We gave up the effort to work and ran back to our house. The boys followed us, jeering at us and calling us cowards. When we reached our house, we shut and locked the door against them, but they began to throw stones at the windows, breaking the glass. Eventually, tiring of this, we decided to face them, and unlocked and opened the door. They rushed in, pushing us back against the wall.

"What do you want?" I asked.

There was a silence which lasted for several minutes as we stood looking at each other. Then one of the boys, who was obviously the leader, spoke.

"Nothing," he said. "You've got nothing to give us except your bodies and we don't need to ask you for those." He turned to his followers. "Strip them and tie them up," he ordered.

They rushed us and pulled us apart. Within two minutes we were lying on our faces, naked on the floor with our arms above our heads and our wrists crossed. They bound them tightly. Within a further minute our ankles were also tightly tied. I felt a foot lever me over very roughly, so that I ended up lying on my back. We were pulled by our legs outside and left in the dirt while our attackers fetched four seven feet long poles which they had obviously cut and stored near our house. We were tied to them. My arms were dragged above my head and a pole was thrust under my ankles and wrists, which were lashed securely to it. I was lifted onto the shoulders of two of the boys. My body sagged downwards so I was hanging from my wrists and ankles. The weight of my head meant that my neck was bent backwards. All I could see were the thighs and buttocks of the boy who was carrying me at the front. His shorts did not leave much to the imagination. Fortunately, there was about six inches of pole between me and the boy. The other three suffered in exactly the same way. We were carried in slow procession out of the school and along the road down into the township. Every so often each of us was deliberately dropped and two other boys would take up the load. Each time this happened, we suffered bruises or grazes to our heads and backs. What with those injuries and the additional bruising from the stones and clods of earth that were thrown at us all along the route, we were already in pain before we arrived at the Town Hall. In this way we were paraded around the town. The crowd that had gathered jeered us and cheered the students who were carrying us. Finally, after at least two hours of this humiliating treatment, we were thrown down on the steps of the Town Hall and the poles were removed. Here the Mayor was waiting, accompanied by an army officer. I looked up at the Mayor's face, as he stared down at me. That image, and the events which followed, has remained with me all my life. Judy suffers in the same way. The Mayor stood with his foot on my chest and spoke to the crowd.

"These foreign parasites came here to steal our money and pervert our youth – encouraged by the corrupt former President. Our glorious new President has ordered they should be forced to pay back to the people what they have stolen. We have already seized and sold their possessions. They thus have nothing left with which to pay off their debts. Therefore, they will pay by their labour. They are now enslaved by decree and will be either allocated or sold in the slave market in due course. To make sure you know them for what they are, we will brand them with the state symbol in your presence right here and now. From then on they are banned from wearing anything at all that they don't own at present. Be it known that it is a serious crime to attempt to give them any of the property or produce of

Austrasia other than the minimum food and water necessary to keep them alive. This is by order of His Excellency President Ngangi."

We screamed as the red hot brand was pressed into the flesh on our behinds and stomachs. Cold water was thrown over us and we were dragged to our feet. Our feet and hands were untied, and metal slave rings were placed around our wrists, ankles and necks. Locks were fitted and sealed shut. Chains were fitted to our wrists and ankles and we were linked by the neck in a slave coffle. Antonio was first, followed by Maria, followed by me, and finally by Judy. We were marched through the town under armed escort and flogged whenever we slowed down as a result of the bruising to our feet from walking on the badly tarmacked road. Finally, we were locked in a cell in the town jail. We were legally no longer human, but animals. Our bodies ached from the bruises and hurt from the branding. We suffered headaches from the times we were dropped on the road. Worse, we realized we were now property, regarded as things and not as human beings. Plainly no one cared about our injuries. Later, we were to learn that this was not entirely fair. They were concerned because a serious injury could reduce our value, as it would with any other item of property. We had acquired economic value, but our emotional state was of no consequence to anyone except ourselves. In the years to come this point was to be expressed forcefully to us by different people several times. We could be bought and sold and now had no rights of any kind. Our degradation was complete. All that remained for us was to wait to see what our new masters and owners required of us.

We soon found out. Next morning, Judy and I were fed with a liquid paste something between mashed potato and semolina but with an additional rather sour taste to which we would soon become accustomed. We were also given water to drink before being taken from the cell and put into the back of an army truck. That was the last we saw of Antonio and Maria. Like Michael and Marta, we have no idea what happened to them. We were driven for several hours until we arrived at a new building in the middle of an obviously large town or city. This was probably the town of Macrone. We discovered it was a science laboratory, part of the local university. We were taken from the truck and marched through seemingly endless corridors and down or up many stairs until we were pushed into a large laboratory. We could see a large number of male and female slaves – all young, all naked and all branded as we were. A female scientist took us into her charge. Judy was taken away somewhere else and I was led into a curtained off area at one end of the room. Two men were there. I was laid across a machine that looked like a bench – with a long handle at one end and a curved area at the other. My neck was fitted into the curved area and I felt a bar shut down across it and locked in place, my wrists and ankles were unchained, and the rings secured to chains at the ends of the machine.

"Is everything secure?" the scientist asked.

"Yes," was the reply.

I felt a hand grasp my penis and a metal rod enter my anus. Someone pressed a switch and the machine and I were both turned on. I felt warmth within myself and my penis begin to grow and thicken – assisted by the squeezing and caressing of the hand. I felt myself coming to a climax quite quickly and simultaneously felt the liquid squirting out of me and hitting a metal object – a cup or perhaps a bucket. I felt a mixture of emotions. I felt stimulated and excited, but also humiliated, angry and ashamed. Most of all, I felt vulnerable and totally helpless. The process continued until I stopped producing semen – then they stopped, and they left me for a few minutes before doing it again. I lost count of the number of times. Eventually, exhausted, I was removed from the machine and rechained before being reunited with Judy who had also been examined – albeit rather differently. She was too embarrassed to tell me what they did to her. We were not told what they were doing – but three days later we were brought back from the holding cell in the basement where we were being kept and laid flat on a table. A complete and intimate physical examination followed after which we saw the three who were processing us in a conversation which ended in smiles and agreement. We were rolled over on the table and a second mark was put on our behinds – this time tattooed on. Rolled back over, they did the same with our stomachs – so we had one branded mark and one tattooed both in front and behind. I saw later it was the letter B. Finally, a number was tattooed on our right wrists – mine was 117M and Judy's was 117F.

Thus labelled, we were enchained once more and sent on to what was obviously the despatching unit. Here we were chained together by our necks and legs before being put in a cage. A label was attached to it and the cage, with us in it, was put on a conveyer belt which carried us out of the building into a car park where a lorry was being loaded with cages like ours. We were lifted up and stowed on the back of the lorry. We were almost the last cage to be loaded, and, once another three cages had arrived, a tarpaulin was draped over us. With cargo secured, we heard and felt the lorry begin to move. Whatever our future was to be, it had been decided and we were being transported to where we were to suffer it.

Three months earlier, Judy and I had been a very happy couple, enjoying teaching and looking forward to getting married. We were liked and respected by those who knew us and we believed we were being useful. All that had now been taken away from us. We were poorer than the poorest Austrasian. All we had left was each other and we suspected even this would be taken away from us. We were naked and condemned to live a life in chains obeying the will or whim of others. We might still be doing something useful and together – but we didn't know what that might be and certainly we would have no say in it. Meanwhile we had been systematically degraded and humiliated. We had been forcibly stripped and paraded in public. Banned from the classroom, we had become labourers. We'd also been beaten, bound, exhibited like animals and branded in the street. I had been milked like a cow and heaven knows what they had done to Judy. Now the two of us were animals in a cage being carried to an unknown destination for an unknown purpose. I wrote we were animals. In fact, we were less than that – because we had no rights whatsoever – whereas an animal is entitled to expect to be protected by its owner. How had the mighty fallen indeed!

CHAPTER 3

The Government's View

I have found several documents that help to explain the last chapter. The first was the report from the sub- committee on enslavement.

"We recommend the process should be gradual and locally based. We do not want to be seen to be actively inciting the process but merely responding to it. We suggest the following step by step approach.

First, secure all the passports, so none can leave the country. Cancel any tickets already issued.

Second, take all their own possessions – say they will be stored in Freetown awaiting their departure. Issue them with minimum new clothing so they become totally dependent on us.

Sell off their possessions in the Government warehouses.

Then slowly strip the foreigners of everything they've been given before publicly exhibiting them naked, chained and branded. Do not interfere if the locals, incited by having power over them, strip, bind, abuse, beat or assault them in other ways including sexually. It will teach them they are now objects of scorn and derision and they are possessions not human beings. This will prepare them for the reality of slavery.

It is important that they should not be aware of what is planned and they should seem to be the victims of local attack.

The whole process should take no more than six weeks."

This policy was apparently signed off by Ngangi – and can be seen to have been worked through in the case of Mark, Judy et al.

The first meeting of the new Government endorsed this process – adding details of the categorisation of the new slaves.

"Reception centres should be set up where the new slaves will be placed into the following categories:

1. Young and sexually active: breeding slaves (B Class). If there's an established couple all the better.

2. Older and physically strong – labouring slaves (L Class) including working in the mines.

3. Others – to be put up for private purchase (P Class)"

There were individual reports. I found the reports on our six cases.

1. "Michael and Marta. (no number)

Mixed married couple (long established). Ordered to break up, they refused, and persisted in their refusal despite continuous torture. After 6 months – taken out and hanged.

2. <u>Mark and Judy. (117)</u>

A young sexually active couple. Category B class.

Sent to St Michael's Island breeding Centre.

3. <u>Antonio and Maria. (3078)</u>

Older married couple. Not suitable for heavy labour. P class. Sold as a couple to the new Foreign Minister at the Freetown Slave Market. Later escaped and not recovered – assumed dead. Foreign Minister was compensated for their loss."

Report on Mark.

"This slave has been thoroughly examined (as has his partner). Both are one hundred per cent fit and highly fertile. Both should be fed aphrodisiac supplements and be regularly harvested. Both are suitable for light farm work in addition. Reports from his former place of work and his arrest suggest he could be a problem because he has leadership ability. He needs to be closely watched and strictly monitored. Any sign of rebellion should be instantly and severely punished."

Addition to the first slavery decree.

All slaves, no matter how they are categorised belong to the people of Austrasia. Accordingly, unless a slave is under the direct control of its owner when on the streets, any Austrasian may use the slave in any way he or she wishes. The slave may not refuse to obey or attempt to resist. It has no recourse to law. No complaint may be made by its owner unless it has been forcibly removed from the owner's control. As no part of the bodies of slaves may be covered, a slave in public must be naked, barefoot and it must be chained hand and foot.

Finally, an extract from a speech by Vice President Ndenge.

"People of Austrasia, President Ngangi reluctantly accepted this position in an attempt to rescue this country from the corruption and failures of the Igbokwe clique. They have been or will be ruthlessly punished and we will rule in the interests of all the people of Austrasia.

"However, we have the problem of fifteen thousand foreigners brought in by the previous Government to milk the country dry. They cannot be sent home, so we have to keep them – but we are not going to pay them to rob us. Instead, we are going to turn them into state slaves. Indeed, this process is already well under way. Their property has been seized and is on sale in the State warehouses in Freetown. They, themselves, are now held, naked, branded with the state symbol, and chained by the neck, wrists and ankles, in centres throughout the country. Some will be sent to the mines and others to slave breeding farms. Many will be put up for sale in the new markets. You may see them on the streets. They have to be totally naked and be chained and they must not walk on the pavements. They have no rights against you, but you can do anything you want with any one of them you meet – except you must not kill them – and only their legal owner, if present, can deny you. Executions of slaves are a Government responsibility. You may rape or force a slave to have sex with you – but you must not establish a relationship with a slave, nor must you put any item of clothing on them. Finally, you will recognise what type of slave it is by the second mark on its body – B – breeding slave; L – Mine or factory worker slave; P – Privately owned slave. Do not think of slaves as humans or even as animals. They are merely property and should be treated accordingly.

"Should you see any foreigner unchained or clothed; or, alternatively, naked but not branded; do not approach them but inform the nearest police post or army barracks immediately."

This is almost the last Government document I am going to add. From now on, the narrative is entirely Mark's, apart from the odd explanation by me. You will recognise these because they will be in Italics.

CHAPTER 4

Captive Journey

The next morning, we were again loaded onto the back of a truck – but this time it wasn't covered. We were in one of thirty cages being carried by three lorries in the convoy which travelled under military escort. We grasped the bars of our cage and surveyed the crowds as they watched us. There was some shouting and booing – but most seemed to be silent. We were taken through the centre of the town and then into the suburbs and here the reaction to us was rather different. We heard jeers and shouts of derision. Some stones were thrown at the lorries and some hit us. When we ducked, the crowd laughed and threw more stones. As a result, we resolved to stand up and accept being a target. Soon enough we were out of the town and passing through the African countryside. We travelled for miles without seeing anything or anyone. Then we reached a village and the convoy stopped. The Captain in charge of the escort spoke to the crowd that gathered.

"We are carrying breeding slaves and work slaves. We also have some slaves available for purchase. They're on the third lorry. The first lorry contains breeding slaves and those on the second lorry are destined for the mines at Loraley. If you're interested in buying a slave talk to the driver of lorry three. If you want to have fun with a breeding slave, go to lorry one."

That's when we knew what we were. One man came and looked at us. He motioned to me to come over to him. Reluctantly, I did as I was told. The driver asked him if he wanted me to be brought out to him. He said yes, so the cage door was unlocked and I was forced out. I was made to stand on the beaten earth of the market, in front of the lorry. He basically fondled me before smiling at the driver and telling him to put me back into the cage.

"He isn't worth bothering with," was his crushing judgement.

I was put back into the cage and the door was locked behind me.

"You're a lucky sod," the soldier concluded.

Judy agreed.

There was some activity around the third lorry. Eventually, the interest became so great that the cages were unloaded, and the ten slaves concerned were put on display in the market area. In the end three male slaves and one female slave were sold and taken away by their new owners. The rest were returned to their cages and we moved on.

At the end of the day, the soldiers pitched camp beside the highway. We were fed and watered, and the tarpaulins were thrown over our cages. The soldiers lit a fire – we heard the crackle of the flames – and sang for a good portion of the night before they settled down. We tried to sleep – but it was difficult in a cage and fully understanding for the first time what our situation really was. We were little better than farm animals. Later we were told what the new Vice President had said about us and we realized it was only too true. In fact, we were worse off than farm animals – even though we realized our function was the same – to produce more "farm animals" in the form of slaves. I noticed something strange though. Every time we were fed, we became much more sexually alive. We'd always been somewhat restrained – but now we felt both free and anxious to enjoy ourselves in whatever way we could. I suppose, looking back, our bodies were the only thing we had, and the only way to find enjoyment was by the most basic means – sex. Only later did we come to realize it was more complicated than that and we were being programmed to fulfil our role as new slave producers. That was still to come. For the moment we were just confused.

Next day unwound much like the first, except the second lorry and its escort left us halfway through the day, turning off to head towards the distant mountains. At the end of the day, which had otherwise been uneventful, we turned into an obvious slave collection point. The lorry was parked up for the night and we were left on it, but we heard some activity in relation to the other lorry and realized they were adding new cages. We also saw a third lorry park up behind us and that too was loaded up. Meanwhile we were fed once more and covered up for the night, except for one couple from an adjoining cage. They were dragged from their cage and marched into the main building where we later heard cheering and it was clear to us the couple were being subjected to some type of abuse which obviously pleased the soldiers. We shuddered as we thought what it might be.

We were awakened the following morning by having a bucket of cold water thrown over us. We were fed and watered. When this had been done, the convoy drove off. We expected this third day would be like the previous two – but we were wrong. Instead of villages we came to a town. This town, whose name we later learnt was Casa Isabella, was apparently known as a rough town. We halted in the market square and the Captain announced we were available for their entertainment, subject to the usual conditions and the others were available for purchase. After that, all twenty of us were unloaded and handed over to the local people for the afternoon. They essentially rented us for a day. Judy and I were separated, but our experiences were similar we discovered when we talked about them later that evening. I was dragged by the chain hanging from my collar into the back streets and there I was raped five times by men and three times by women. I was kicked, spat at, beaten and bent over a table to be flogged by two men and a woman. Finally, I was gang-raped by them – simultaneously entering my anus and mouth and sucking on my penis. The result left me completely shattered. They looked at me and just laughed.

"Send him back," the woman said to the men, "he's fucked."

"That's because he's not one of us," one of the men said, and the other agreed, commenting that my cock was too small to be of much use to anyone – man or woman.

I was dragged from the house and placed on a wheelbarrow like a pile of unwanted dirt. My head was hanging over the wheel and my legs dragged behind the handles. They were pulled together, and lashed to one of the handles, to keep them out of the way. I was pushed down to the square, where I was removed from the wheelbarrow and placed in the cage. Judy was waiting for me. I told her what had happened to me and she told me about her experiences. We now understood, as we were meant to, the full consequences of being a slave. It shocked and frightened us. We had all learnt about slavery, but none of us knew what it actually meant. We thought we knew then – but we didn't. We still had more to learn – and that happened on the fourth and final day of our lorry journey.

The next day we stayed in the town because they had arranged a slave sale for the afternoon. They had different plans for the morning, however. The town square had been arranged into an arena overnight and the centre had suddenly acquired what looked like a boxing ring, but the locals were pouring water into it. We were watching this process when our guard came up and told us we were going to perform on the stage they were creating.

"You're lucky sods," he began, "you've been chosen to do mud wrestling. The winner will copulate with the loser."

We began to object. But he laughed.

"You'll be doing this to entertain the guests at your new place almost every night, so you might as well get used to it."

He removed the chains from Judy's and my wrists and ankles as well as from our collars, then ordered us out of the cage and into the ring. Our feet sank into the mud as we faced one another. Neither of us had any experience of wrestling or had even watched much on TV when we were children. However, we did our best. We grappled with one another and eventually I slipped, and Judy fell on top of me. She made love to me and we were both covered with mud. Everyone was happy. Afterwards we were made to stand outside of the ring and were hosed down with cold water. Meanwhile, another couple were unchained and took our place in the ring. This procedure went on for about two hours until all 10 couples had fought each other. It was then we discovered what was really going on. We had just been the warmup act.

Two men were brought from the third lorry. Both were naked and both had been beaten up. The Captain told us one had tried to leave the country without permission and the other had run away from the police when they had come for him. They had been sentenced to death or flogging. The decision was to be reached as a result of a wrestling match. The resultant fight was vicious and lengthy, but eventually a decision was reached. The winner was tied to a post and whipped so savagely that he died two days later. The loser was nailed by the wrists and ankles to the trunk of a tree and left to die. *It apparently took several days.* We had been shown what would happen to us if we tried to escape. That, at least, was the intention. The result was we knew that if we were to escape we had better not be caught or, if found, not taken alive.

That afternoon we witnessed another example of what our new status meant. The other two lorries were unloaded, and their cargoes of slaves were exposed for sale in the square, which had been turned into a slave market. Stakes were driven into the ground and men and women were chained to them by their necks. We watched as local people and others from further afield came and looked around. We watched them examine the slaves – testing their strength, looking into their mouths and checking the men's virility and the women's sexual potential. We watched the haggling between would be buyer and seller. Finally, we watched the successful purchasers take their new property and lead them away by the chain attached to the slave collar around his or her neck. In some cases, we saw men and women being branded again – presumably with the new owner's mark. The sale went on until the last slave had been sold when the two now empty lorries were driven away, leaving us alone on the edge of the Market Place. It was a very sober lot of breeding slaves who were fed and then covered that night. It had been graphically shown to us that we were no longer people, but objects that could be bought and sold. We had no power of decision and our actions were totally controlled by our masters and owners, but they could not yet control our thoughts. In spite of everything they put us through, we did not think of ourselves as objects or possessions of another: we did not think of ourselves as mindless slaves and we did not want to feel totally dependent for our very existence on our owner. That would come later – our masters knew that. But they also knew that we knew what would happen to us if we tried to rebel or escape.

Mark was, of course, right. The soldiers were teaching them what being a slave actually meant. However, I understand what he meant. They were not truly slaves – merely prisoners who had been forcibly enslaved. The true slaves would be the offspring who were produced from them or by them – or themselves once their thinking had been thoroughly conditioned to slavery.

Next morning there was a significant change. After they had fed and watered us, they unloaded us from the cages and made us form up in a line on the square. A new squad of soldiers from the local garrison, led by a Sergeant, was formed up on the other side of the square. Our Captain walked over to them, accepted the Sergeant's salute, and handed us over to him. The two men walked over to us, and the Captain explained to him who and what we were. He gave the sergeant his orders, which we quickly discovered, and left. A few minutes later the lorry was driven away, leaving us with our new custodians. The Sergeant spoke to us.

"You're now my responsibility. You will be taken through the jungle under our escort to a lake where we will put you on a boat which will take you to your new quarters. You will obey my orders without question or hesitation. If you fail to do so you will be flogged. Do you understand, slaves?"

We answered "Yes, Sergeant."

We were then marshalled into line in pairs, with the man leading his woman. Soldiers removed the chains from our ankles so we could walk easily but attached our neck chains to each other. Our wrists were chained behind our backs. Thus organised, we set off, headed and followed by the soldiers, all of whom carried rifles. Two of them also obviously carried slave whips and had ropes wrapped around their bodies, running from right shoulder to left waist. We understood their purpose was to intimidate us even further.

We were marched for about twenty miles through increasingly wooded terrain, following a narrow jungle track. Every so often we were halted because of a snake on the track ahead. We were not allowed to escape our fate by dying from snake bite! After two hours, a soldier passed along the line giving us water from a bottle which he held to our mouths. After four hours we were allowed to sit down. Our wrist chains were loosened, and we were fed before being chained up again. We were allowed to rest for an hour before we were ordered to our feet and the march resumed. The trees were now very thick on either side of the path and the high canopy meant our way was in the shade. Despite that, it was burningly hot, and we all sweated profusely. As a result, the march became ever more unpleasant as we began to stink of sweat made worse by the stench of urine and undealt with faeces. The soldiers followed the same routine – water after two hours. By this time I calculated we had covered about eighteen miles. The march continued into a tenth hour. We had started about an hour after sunrise, so it was now late afternoon. It would soon be too dark to continue in safety. However, the sergeant had calculated the time exactly, and, as six o'clock approached we saw the glint of water ahead of us in the late evening sun. A few minutes later we emerged from the jungle on the edge of a large lake. In the distance we could see an island, which we guessed was our destination. In front of us was a wooden pier. Beside us were two wooden huts, one on either side of the path. We noticed the windows of one of the huts were barred. The other hut was normal.

As we stood, waiting in line, the Sergeant gave orders to his men, who split into different groups. Some began to cut down or collect wood for a fire. Two, who were obviously the cooks, began to prepare food. Two more dealt with us. We were unchained from each other, our wrists were freed briefly whilst they were moved in front of us and rechained. Our legs were chained back together. We were then ordered to sit down on the grass by the lake and wait. The darkness fell, as it always did, at about 6.45, before the kindling was brought, set and lit. Our food was prepared for us and we were fed. Ordered to eat quickly, we did so. I noticed it tasted different from what we had become used to. The slightly sour taste had gone. None of us appreciated the significance of the change. *The soldiers obviously omitted to add the aphrodisiac.* We were each given a metal mug of water drawn from the lake. As soon as we had been fed and watered, we were ordered into the hut with the barred windows. Once we were inside, the double doors were closed and locked. We were left to our own devices in the darkness. We chatted quietly to each other for a while, talking through our experiences over the previous five days, but not knowing what lay ahead of us. Jack, the oldest among us at thirty-two, had the clearest idea.

"That island is going to be our prison. They're going to take us there and use us to enable them to breed new slaves. The children they make from us in their laboratories will be bred to think of themselves as subhuman slaves, inferior to the natives and destined to serve them."

"And what about us?" I asked.

"When we've ended our usefulness, they'll dispose of us in some way."

"Do you mean they'll kill us?" Judy asked.

Bill, at thirty, average for our group (Judy and I were the youngest), answered her.

"They might, but I think it's more likely they'll either send us to the mines or sell us off.."

Clare, Jack's partner, commented that we would have to try to get away. I reminded them of what we had seen two days before, and added, "If we escape we have to be sure to get away completely – all twenty of us. If they do catch us, despite our best efforts, none of us must be taken alive. If we are, we know what they will do to us."

On that point, we all agreed. Our conversation then became individual as we divided the hut between us by mutual consent rather than as the result of a discussion. Judy and I slept in the far corner. Despite our chains, we kissed, caressed and made love together, before falling asleep. Outside, the soldiers were singing and plainly happy that their task had been successfully completed.

Next morning, we were left alone for some time. We watched the sky lighten and the sun begin to shine. Eventually, after a couple of hours, the double doors were opened, and we were ordered out. We were individually hosed down by the soldiers and then made to sit on the ground to be fed as usual. The sound of an engine broke the silence of the lakeside. A large motorboat came into sight. After twenty or so minutes it was tied up alongside the jetty. The covers were taken off what was obviously a hold used for cargo. We were ordered to our feet and marched onto the jetty and aboard the boat. A ladder had been provided to enable us to climb down with difficulty (because of the chains on our ankles) into the hold. When we were all in. the hold was closed, and we heard the top being locked down. There was a short delay *caused by the completion of paperwork involving the transfer of the slaves from the Army to the Navy*. After a short while, we heard footsteps on the deck above us, followed by the sound of a rope being pulled in and coiled. Finally, we heard the engine being restarted, and the final stage of our journey had begun. If we had any doubt as to the reality of our position – that was finally extinguished. We were being taken away from the surrounding land, where there was a slight chance of being able to escape, to a (probably) closely guarded island facility where there would be no chance of escape. At least, that's what we thought. *And what they were intended to think. It should have been impossible because the island facility – known as St Michael's – was as difficult to escape from for these slaves as Alcatraz in America was for its inmates. Besides, if they did escape, they could hardly hide among the population. Their skin colour alone would betray them. It is clear that they all realized this – but did not see it as a final barrier. At this point they considered it was just another hurdle to be overcome.*

CHAPTER 5

St Michael's Island and Lake Nduya

St Michael's Island is three miles long, running from its most eastern point towards the west, and two miles wide from north to south. It is ten miles from the eastern end of Lake Nduya, twenty-five miles south of the northern side of the lake and fifteen miles north of the southernmost shore. The lake stretches for another one hundred and twenty miles to the west. The island rises from east to west. The landing is on the eastern side where there's a barracks for forty soldiers and a jetty, to which the boat is moored. The eastern end of the island is relatively flat, but it rises to a height of over two hundred and fifty feet at the western end. Thus as you traverse the island the cliffs rise in height until, at the western end, the beach is totally inaccessible from the land. It can only be reached from the lake. A track runs westward from the jetty to a farm surrounded by a five foot tall chain link fence topped with barbed wire. The farm extends for two square miles in the centre of the island (two miles long and one mile wide). There is only one entrance via a gate at the eastern end. The northern part of the farm, to the right of the track, is used for cassava and maize growing. The southern part is used to raise a dozen cattle, used for milk, and a number of pigs, intended for bacon. There is a barn for these animals near the entrance gate on the eastern side.

Six guard posts line the accessible shore at regular intervals, and four more guards patrol the two entrances to the main four-storey building in the centre. There is also a cellar beneath It. The building has its main entrance on the eastern side and a secondary entrance on the west. The top floor is set aside for us slaves. Ten cages line the western end in two sets of five. The eastern end is a large work room which is used to milk us male slaves and harvest the females. The floor below contains rooms for the forty civilian staff. Offices take up the whole of the second floor. The ground floor contains the reception area, a dining room for the staff and the kitchen. There are ten cells in the cellar. These have no outside opening and are dimly lit entirely by artificial lighting. They are intended as punishment cells for disobedient slaves or soldiers. We learnt all this when we arrived. What we didn't learn then is that the main feeder river for the lake enters it on the northern side opposite the island. This was to be important later. *Because it provided the easiest route from the lake to Ngugi Falls.*

To the south, east and west of the lake lie the savannah grassland plains of eastern and southern Africa. To the north lie the mountains. They can be seen from the island and are about one hundred miles away (a five to six day's journey on foot through wild and relatively uninhabited country). There are a number of villages around the shores of the lake, especially on the southern, eastern and western shores. The northern shore has little habitation. The Eastern side, as we knew, has a garrison about twenty miles inland, set in a fairly large town *(Casa Isabella),* which acts as the provincial capital.

The island, were it not for its context as a prison and slave breeding centre, was a very pleasant place to live and work on. The native staff undoubtedly found it so. We found it much less pleasant – but it still had its moments. Government ministers and government officials visited the Centre from time to time, as did local and other national politicians. Whenever there was a visitor, there was a celebration of some kind, as I will describe later – since we were always part of the entertainment. There were four major feast days, when we were locked up and everyone else partied. The staff and soldiers usually ended drunk and incapable for twenty-four hours, as we knew to our cost – since we were not fed during that time! I very much doubt that the other animals were fed either. The four days were Christmas, St Michael's Day, Austrasia's Independence Day and the anniversary of the Coup. Later they added a fifth – President Ngangi's birthday.

CHAPTER 6

"Welcome to the Island"

We arrived at the island after about a ninety minute journey. We worked this out later but being chained and locked into an airless and lightless hold made it seem longer. The cover was lifted off. Two soldiers armed with whips climbed down and we were ordered to climb out. The somewhat clumsy climb was speeded up when a whip cracked across our thighs. Each of us was treated in the same way. The effect was like feeling a line of fire across our legs. Once on the jetty, we were marshalled into a ragged line and found ourselves facing an orderly line of soldiers. An officer stepped forward.

"Welcome to St Michael's Island," he said sarcastically.

We looked blankly at him, and then looked away and down at our feet. The officer ordered his men to march us up to the building and into the dining room where the Centre Governor would meet us later. A liberal use of the whip started us off and kept us moving as we shuffled up the path – hampered by the chains on our legs. As we walked we noticed the island was green but very bare. There were no trees outside the compound. The ground began to slope upwards, gently, but steadily. The wooden building where the soldiers lived disappeared behind us, and, after ten minutes a chain link fence topped with barbed wire blocked our way, with a big building behind it. In front of us there was a gate, guarded by two soldiers. It was opened to let us through and closed behind us. On our left there was a building built partly of brick and partly of wood. We learnt later it was a barn. On our right I could see there was a maize field. A cow mooed a greeting on our left as we passed her. It took another fifteen minutes before we reached the front door of the main brick building, the breeding centre, which stretched four stories above us. It was a plain building, functional in appearance, making no attempt at imposing its authority on us. Once inside, we were ushered into a big room which was obviously the place where they ate their meals. We were made to stand in the middle of the room, waiting for the Governor to arrive.

The Governor was a man in his forties. He was smartly dressed, western fashion, in a suit and tie. He was clean shaven and did not wear glasses. He entered the room briskly, looked us up and down, and then addressed us.

"Welcome to the island," he began. "You are our first batch of breeding slaves and we have been very busy getting ready for you." He paused, turned to our guards and ordered them to remove our chains. They did so. He nodded, and then continued.

"You do not need to be chained. You're not going anywhere. There are rules, and I wish to make them clear to you before you are shown around the building. The most important is you remember that you are simply one of our farm animals, although you are allowed to live in the centre unlike the others. You have no choice in what you do – you simply obey orders. If you disobey, you will be flogged. One of you will be flogged every week as a reminder in any case."

We shuddered at that. He noticed and grinned.

"You don't like it, huh? Good! It will keep you on your toes! You will be housed on the top floor and use the back staircase and the back entrance. This area and the other two floors are out of bounds to you. For your information – the next floor contains offices and the one above, our sleeping accommodation. Outside, you are forbidden to leave the farm, which is surrounded by a wire fence. You will be fed twice a day, be milked or harvested first thing in the morning, before feeding the other animals and then working in the cassava or maize fields. Disobedience will be punished by flogging and/ or imprisonment in the cells in the cellar. Any attempt to escape will fail. You cannot avoid being seen because the island outside of the farm is bare. The only access to the lake is back the way you came, and that's always guarded. However, should you be so foolish as to try, we will first flog you and then hang you – both you and your partner - whether you act alone or together. That goes for all punishments except the weekly example flogging. Any questions?"

He paused. None of us spoke. After a minute, he finished.

"Good. Well, you've had your chance – from now on you do not speak anywhere outside your own quarters unless you are spoken to or given permission to do so."

He motioned to our escorts and we were marched out and down the stairs into the cellar, where we were locked into different cells, and left in the darkness for what seemed like an eternity. It was cold and damp. There was no light and no furniture in the cell except for a stone slab which served as a bed. We sat on it and hugged each other for warmth. Even so, we still shivered. How long we were there, we don't know, but it may have been only an hour. Finally, the lights went on, the doors were opened, and we were taken out. "That's what will happen to you if you disobey," one of the guards told us, as he led us back up the stairs and out of the back door into the rest of the farm, where we could see the cows and pigs on the southern side and the cassava plants to the north. We were told that was where we would be working. Then we were taken back into the building through the front entrance and up three flights of stairs to the top floor. We were warned that we would be punished if we were caught trying to use this stairway again. Our stairs were at the other end of the floor.

After this we were taken into a long room with ten pairs of machines which we recognised from our stay at the assessment centre in Freetown as milking and harvesting machines. The guard told us that was where we would start our mornings and explained what the machines did. The only difference I could see was that whereas the centre had used the human hand to milk the men, this place used a rubber attachment. I remembered once seeing a cattle milking parlour at home where something similar was used. Finally, we were taken out of the room and along a corridor where we saw ten quite large rectangular cages, five on either side. Each cage was numbered. "Those are your future rooms," our guide said, rather unnecessarily we thought. We saw that each was given one of our numbers. "We're going to leave you here to settle in", he added. "You won't be troubled today, but food will be brought to you later. You will also be given milk rather than water. There is a hole in the floor in one corner of your room. It's against the wall.

That is for you to exercise your bodily functions. The rooms won't be locked, unless you're sick or undergoing punishment for some minor offence that we decide. But the doors at the ends of this corridor will always be locked." With that, all the guards left, and we heard the door being locked. We were on our own and guaranteed to be so for almost the first time since that day when we were finally stripped naked, carried through Concordia and branded. That seemed a lifetime ago.

We all entered our cages. They were spaced in such a way that there was a gap between each cage. The cages were a bit more like cells than those we were used to. There were no walls, simply metal columns, spaced too closely together for us to squeeze through if we were locked in. Within each cage was a double sized bed with a mattress, but no pillow or coverings, a table and two chairs. These were plainly designed for us to eat at, since we were never allowed writing materials. The arrangement was completed by a large window which gave us a view over the farm and the island – in our case over the northern side. The windows were barred, and, I suspected, because the vista seemed rather dark, that the outside of the window was darkened so we could not signal outside. The arrangement of the cages was rather odd. There were two sets of two on either side, and a single one in the middle of the pairs along the two outside walls. The cages faced in different directions. The four sets of two were arranged so that they were at right angles to the walls on either side of the room, with their doors facing each other across the aisle between the them. The two in the middle were placed lengthways along the walls on each side and with their doors facing East towards the corridor (where the forbidden front stairs were located) between our room and the workshop where the milking and harvesting machines were housed. Between the two central single cages, within a much wider open area, ten hard double chairs were arranged in a circle. It was obviously designed as a meeting place for us. I looked around for hidden microphones, since everything had clearly been set up so that we would have to talk if we wanted to communicate with each other. I was sure I saw evidence of at least one. I whispered to Jack, "Assume this place is bugged. Tell someone else and get them to share it." He nodded his agreement and set out to do just that. I walked back to the door at the workshop end of the corridor and tried to open it. It was locked, as I expected. We were still imprisoned, but we had the illusion we were free, except that the steel slave collars around our necks and the steel cuffs on our wrists and ankles, as well and the brands and tattoos on our bodies told a different story – as did the fact that we were forbidden to wear any clothing.

During the afternoon we all slept, exhausted after the long journey from the classification centre, with all that went before and all that happened along the way. In the evening we were awakened with our evening meal. It was a pleasant change. It was a fish stew – presumably with fish caught in the lake. It still had the odd taste we'd noticed before, but it seemed stronger here. As promised, the water we were used to was replaced by fresh milk. The two soldiers who brought it to us explained they would be supervising us during the days except on Sundays when we were to be given a free day of rest. I looked at them as I took our plates and cups and wondered. Somehow these two seemed different from the others we'd met since being enslaved. I wasn't sure how, because they had said nothing different and did nothing different from the others. They treated us as slaves – but even so.... . I kept my thoughts to myself, thanked them, and went back with Judy to our cage. We ate and drank, lay down, kissed and made love, and, as the lights went out, fell asleep. That was our first day on St Michael's Island.

CHAPTER 7

Slaves

Our first full day began as the previous one ended. The lights went on, and with them, water sprayed down from hidden inlets in the ceiling, to be drained away down the latrine in our cage. That's when I noticed there was a six inches high metal barrier around the outside of the cage at the base, as well as on the door. This was obviously to keep the water in. In addition, the floor of the cage was slightly deeper than the surrounding corridor and sloped gently towards the wall and the corner where the latrine was. Our food was then brought to us – similar to the previous night. We were given time to eat before being assembled and led to the work room.

We were put on the milking and harvesting machines individually. The controller told us that what was drawn out of us would be piped down to a room on the ground floor, where it would be mixed together and put into an insulated container in the walk-in freezer. At the end of the week, what was collected would be taken by the boat to the west end of the lake and flown by helicopter to Freetown. There they would begin the process of new creation of lives. I can't say what the others thought, but I wasn't impressed.

He then switched on the machines. I felt the usual warm feeling, followed by the sense of tension, followed by release. I felt too the pressure of the prod inside me – forcing me to have erection after erection. The whole process went on for half an hour and left me drained when I was taken off the machine. Afterwards I was given a drink of a purple coloured liquid which acted as a pick me up. We all had the same experience. For Judy and the other female slaves the process was different. Each "girl" was laid on the bed alongside one of the harvesting machines where she was given an intimate internal inspection daily to find out if she had produced an egg. Then, if appropriate, her egg was removed by inserting the harvesting machine into her vaginally and the egg carefully vacuumed out of her. She was then allowed to rest until her partner had been milked dry before we were all collected and taken down to the farm. I have no idea what they wanted or what they did with all the extra sperm. Maybe they just enjoyed tormenting the men and it was only another part of their plan to break us.

Once the harvesting and milking were over, we were escorted down the back stairs and into the farm. Ahead of us were a few trees surrounded by several stumps, which made it clear to us that outside the fence had been deliberately cleared. We all stood still as we saw this, realising what it was. I felt a hand on my shoulder, and I was pushed to the front. My wrists were chained together with a short length of chain. My arms were then raised above my head and the chain fixed to a hook set in the trunk of the tree. My feet were lashed together, with a rope and two men came and stood beside me. Their sergeant provided the commentary. "This is what will happen to you every Monday." I heard the swish of the whip before I felt it crack across my shoulder from the left, followed by another from my right. I jumped with the pain, which felt like fire. The sound came again. This time I was struck twice on the behind. "That's the way we do it," said the voice in unconscious parody of a seaside puppet show or a pantomime act. "Normally it would be much more," he added helpfully. I felt a bucket of cold water thrown over my back. "That's what we do afterwards,' the voice continued. "Then we leave you there to dry out for the rest of the day." He paused, before adding, "But not in this case." I was then taken down. "Don't think this lets you out of the draw for next week," the sergeant added with a grin. I nodded, to show I understood and rejoined the others as we were taken to the barn to milk the cows and feed the pigs.

Judy asked me if I was all right. I told her my shoulders and bum ached a bit, otherwise I was okay. The sergeant heard us and ordered us to stop talking. "If you do it again," he added, "We'll take you both out and flog you properly. Then you really will ache, believe me!" We looked at each other and said nothing. "Good children," the beaming man said sarcastically. He then turned to the two guards and said, "Right, I'm going to leave you two to it. Make sure you let me know if any of this lot disobey and I will see they are suitably punished."

Once the animals had been either milked or fed, we were taken outside and told that for the rest of the day we had to clear the cassava or the maize fields of unwanted weeds. This was back-breaking work. Our bodies ached from the endless repetition of bending, pulling, turning and throwing away of the unwanted weeds. We were given an hour's rest and additional food about midday before continuing our work in the fields. As the day wore, on our backs ached from the effort, our heads ached from the incessant heat of the tropical sun blazing down on us. Sweat poured down our faces, our arms and our bodies. By mid-afternoon we were exhausted and our guards realized we could do no more. We had to become used to this sort of labour. They told us to stop work and sit down in the sun. Then they talked to us – getting us to tell them our stories and sharing their experiences with us. We came to realize that we slaves came from different backgrounds and so did our guards. One pair of us, two twenty-eight year-olds, Tom and Maisie were on honeymoon and were trapped by the closing of the border. Yet we had a lot in common too. Nothing was said about their attitudes towards what had happened to us, but I felt even surer that these two men were different from the other guards – I just could not decide why I believed this. I listened but said nothing – still a little shaken by my experience in the morning.

Suddenly the atmosphere changed. The Guards stood up and abruptly said, "That's enough. You've got to get back to work." We were directed to drive the cattle and pigs into the barn, using sticks to encourage them, before being marched into the building and up the stairs to our quarters, where we were fed and left to mingle until the lights were put out when we went back to our cages to sit and talk quietly for a while about the day's events before lying down to sleep.

Next morning began in the way the previous one had done and continued in the same way too - except there was no demonstration flogging - and we were able to manage to work in the fields a little longer. That pattern continued for the rest of the week. I remember once being asked in a class what a slave's life was like. I tried to answer it by reference to what I had read. I can tell you now that a slave's life is totally boring. Every day is the same – the same meaningless activity; the same threats of punishment; the same tiredness and increasing lack of will to resist. Eventually, you do not know what day it is – only the passing of time by the position of the sun in the sky. The sad truth was that even in that first week we were ceasing to be enslaved prisoners and becoming slaves. We were not, of course, aware of it at the time. Then came our first Sunday – and that was different. The workshop was shut up and some of the staff went out in the boat taking the crates of human "milk" and the plastic boxes of human eggs to the helicopter at the west end of the lake. We were taken outside of the fence to the open area in front of the gate and there given intensive wrestling lessons in our pairs by our two guards. We spent the entire day learning legal and illegal moves and tricks we could play – not on our partner but on those watching and betting on us. After a day of this strenuous activity, we were all sweating like pigs and so the mandatory hosing down with cold water came as a relief to us. We all slept well that night, but not until I'd staged an "accident" and was left alone with one of the two guards who was apparently attending to my injuries. I spoke to him as he "worked on me".

"Are you our friend or our enemy?" I asked.

"I'm neither," he replied.

"What are you then?"

"I'm not your enemy and do not wish you any harm."

"Then why did you hit me with a whip?"

"In order to convince the others that I'm one of them."

"But you're not?"

"No. I disapprove of what's happened, and, at the right time, will help you to show them."

"But that time's not yet?"

"No. Be patient. I'll tell you when we're ready."

During this time, he'd been putting cream on my ankle. He followed this up by bandaging it. He sensed, rather than saw the Sergeant come up.

"What are you doing Davison?" the Sergeant asked.

"Treating this slave, Sarge, He fell and twisted his ankle. I was just checking he's okay to get up the stairs."

The Sergeant nodded. "Okay Davison, carry on."

He walked away and the guard sighed with relief.

"That was a close one!" he commented. "Come on, I'd better get you inside."

He ostentatiously helped me up the steps into the house and up the first and second flight of stairs, leaving me to walk up the final flight. Judy asked me what I was doing. I quietly explained and warned her not to tell anyone what the guard had said to me. For the rest of the evening, in public, I limped a little. When our food was brought we went to our cell, ate our evening meal, and I went to bed as an injured man should.

Next day was Monday, and Monday turned out to be Jack's day. He was the first to be doubly flogged. As we watched, it became clear this was actually a sham flogging. There were marks where the whips fell, and I knew, from what happened to me, that his body would ache from the beating – but there was no blood shed and no obvious bruising – simply red marks where the whips fell. The water splashing was obviously a formality – and Jack was left to enjoy a day in the sun – albeit one tied to a tree. Still, you can't have everything in this life, can you? Otherwise, the day continued as normal – except the Sergeant asked about my accident and the state of my ankle. I told him it still hurt a bit but I would be fine. He said, "Good", and walked away. And so, it went on. By the end of the second week, we were fully acclimatised and able to work the entire day as required. We were also, on the surface at least, fully assimilated slaves. We showed that when, on the third evening of that second week, Judy and I were dragged from our cage during the night and taken down to the dining room where we were placed on an empty table in the middle of the room and made to wrestle each other. We put up a spirited fight until our guard caught my eye and gave the agreed signal. Right hand raised for me to win and left for Judy. It was right – so shortly afterwards Judy allowed me to pull her down, hold her down, and make love to her. The final item, of course, was no illusion!

"Jake," the Governor called out to our guard, "Take your slaves away and put them to bed. Tell them they did a good job." That's how we learnt his first name.

The officials pulled us off the table and handed us over to Jake. At least we knew his name now. He took us up the back stairs, telling us we acted that out very well and he was proud of us. It was almost as though he was our father, and we were his children. We were getting used to that as well. Our official title was either slave, or, if friendly, boy and girl. We were always known by our numbers, which were ultimately tattooed on our chests and backs so we could be easily identified since those who didn't know us said we all looked the same. I remember we used to say the same about foreigners back at home.

On the second Sunday we were all taken down to the cellar, where the lights and the heating were on. Two men, an older man and a younger one, were there waiting for us. Jake's friend, whose name we learned was Ade, introduced them and put our minds at ease.

"You've not been brought down here for punishment, but we need to use the cells to hold you because we have to keep you away from fabrics during this process. These two men are a native doctor and his assistant – you would call him an apprentice. They are going to defoliate you – remove all your body hair. That will make it easier for us to maintain you in good condition. They will leave your head hair though – a visiting barber will keep that cut once its grown long enough. The whole process takes seven hours – one hour to coat you and six hours for it to work. During that time, you may not move so you will be locked down on the bunk in one of the cells. We're going to take you in reverse order of age – so Mark and Judy you're first. The rest can return to your rooms upstairs and we will call for you as we need you."

The others left and we were made to lie on our backs on the central stone slabs usually used for punishment. They began by washing us from head to toe with warm water – a pleasant change from the cold showers and hosing we had become accustomed to. Then they began to coat our bodies with a red liquid, which also felt warm. They started at our hair line and moved down our faces, carefully avoiding our eyes and mouths but covering everywhere else, including within our ears and noses. Our arms were pulled away from our bodies and moved above our heads while they covered our chests and stomachs, as well as our sides, before moving down to our groin areas followed by our legs and feet. Finally, they ordered us to move our arms down to our sides and covered those down to our hands. They did this after the liquid on the front of our bodies had dried sufficiently. We noticed that the warmth remained and seemed to seep into our skins, which began to itch. We were warned not to scratch. I was treated by the apprentice and Judy by the master. We learned later they constantly swapped between our pairs so they each dealt with five males and five females. After a few minutes, when they thought we had dried sufficiently, they turned us over and repeated the whole process on our backs. Once our backs were completely dry, they lifted us by the arms and legs and carried us into one of the cells, laid us on our backs, locked our wrists and ankles into the restraints provided, and left us for six hours, while they dealt with the next six couples. We had no option but to lie still and eventually drifted off to sleep. We were woken up by the Master at the end of the six hours. We noticed the itching and the warmth had both gone and the covering we had seemed to be separate from our skins. The native doctor touched us and smiled. He freed our arms and legs and then gently peeled off the red coloured extra skin we had acquired. As he did so, every hair on our bodies came off with it. He pulled a mirror from his bag and showed us how we looked. "You look just like young children," he said, "and that's how you'll stay because every hair has been taken out by the roots." Then he smacked our bottoms and added, "Now run upstairs and play and tell the next couple to come down."

We didn't know how to reply to this, so just said, "Thank you, Sir," and did actually run off! We were greeted with some surprise when we arrived upstairs. I told Reuben and Wanda they were needed now, and they went down, and then we answered questions from the other four. Food was brought for us, after which we went down and walked around the farm, patting the cows and enjoying the sunshine. We walked up to the gate and asked the guards there if we could go out and explore the island. They were in a good mood and said we could, so we were able to walk around the island and note that what we had been told was true. The only area where you could reach the beach was on the eastern side. The further west we went, the higher the cliffs became until at the western end they seemed positively gigantic. We walked slowly, enjoying each other's company and the rare experience of being alone and the feeling of freedom we had; transitory and false though we knew it was. In all, we spent about two hours in the sunshine, and we returned to the gate as it began to get dark. The last couple did not return from the cellar until midnight and, as a result, we were allowed to rest on Monday and there was no flogging that day. We fed the animals in the morning and put them away in the evening and that was all.

Over the next three weeks everything was normal, except for us, since I was chosen as the Monday victim on the fourth Monday and Judy, on the fifth. Our floggings were not the token beatings the others received. We just suffered from extremely sore backs and sunburn for three days afterwards, but still had to work. We didn't dare complain, but the other slaves showed us real sympathy and we knew they were very angry on our behalf. I was concerned that on both these occasions, our regular guards, Jake and his colleague were replaced by two of the civilian staff and hoped that the two who usually looked after us had not been sacked for letting us outside the fence. We later learned Jake was away on leave for those two weeks. All the slaves were relieved when he was back the following week.

CHAPTER 8

The First Christmas

Time moved steadily on and our now meaningless lives as slaves continued unaltered. There were no more trips outside the farm. Jake told Judy and me that the two guards who let us wander around the island for two hours unescorted were severely reprimanded by the Governor and he had been instructed to warn us that if we tried it again we would spend two weeks in the cellar. So, that was that! We had no idea of time. Eventually, we simply had no concept of what day or what date it was. When all days are the same and you have no hope of ever regaining your freedom, such things don't matter. Although, eventually, we would able to measure the passage of time by the public holidays.

What was clear was that our conversion from enslaved prisoners to slaves was now complete. We had been stripped of everything – even our individuality. We were numbers, not people, and, once they started cutting our hair, all of us had our hair cut level at the level of our chin. Judy joked that they had made me into a girl. I objected. I told her they'd made her into a boy!

"If they dressed us," I said, "they wouldn't be able to tell at a glance whether we were boys or girls."

"No chance of that," Judy said, ruefully looking down at her body and across at mine. "It's obvious to whoever looks at us what we are!"

Our processing as slaves began in June. So, our first Christmas as slaves occurred after we had been captives for six months. Our first intimation of this came one Sunday afternoon, when we were all taken down to the Dining Room. We saw it was decorated for a gala meal. The room was festooned with decorations and it was clear the tables were being similarly prepared. Around the room were twenty wooden columns, ten on each side. We were ordered to stand in line, with the youngest couple (us) first and the oldest (Jack and Clare) last. We were then split into two groups. The older group was sent to the other side of the room. This done, we were ordered to stand in front of the columns – first a boy, and then his partner, starting with us. Each of us was then taken in hand by a member of staff. We were each garlanded with flowers; around our heads, our necks, our waists, our wrists and our ankles. The neck, wrist and ankle garlands disguised our metal cuffs and collars. Thus adorned – I noticed we "boys" wore red garlands and the "girls" wore white ones – we were ordered to stand with our backs to the column behind us. My wrists were moved above my head and attached to a hook in the column by the links on the cuffs and my ankles were similarly attached to the base of the column. The same thing happened to all of us. Finally, tinsel chains were attached to link our wrists to the person next to us all down both sides. We were part of the Christmas decorations! We were privileged to watch our masters enjoying themselves, and, from time to time, we were even given something to eat or drink! At least it was a change from routine – but it made it clear that we were simply property – living and moving property perhaps – but still property; to be used as our Masters chose. It was made even clearer when, at the end of the party, they all left and we were left where we were, with all the other decorations, destined to be taken down next day. By the time this happened our arms, backs and feet ached like hell and had to be massaged by Jake or Ade.

However, it wasn't quite as simple as that. There was a Guest of Honour. She was the Minister for Internal Security (equivalent to our Home Secretary). Apparently, the Ministers had agreed to visit all the slave breeding centres, and she was our guest. She made a long speech to the staff, praising their work and their contribution to the future Austrasian economy. She complimented us on our fertility, hard work and physical fitness as well as how beautiful we looked. It was certainly a mixed compliment. We all thought it would have been better if she'd visited us before deciding to enslave us – but you can't change history. We were what we were, and we were no longer what we had been, nor could we ever be that again. Our future, we now knew, was either that of totally submissive and obedient slaves, or death by crucifixion or hanging. That much had been made clear to us by decisions made by this same woman and communicated to us by the Governor when it became official policy. This woman returned to the Dining Room after the others had left, with the Governor, to inspect us. She walked around the room, inspecting intimately each of us in turn without comment, but asking the Governor questions about us. Having done the circuit, she returned to Judy and me.

"I wish to interview these two tomorrow – privately," she said.

"That's irregular," the Governor protested.

"Perhaps," she conceded – but it's the President's command."

He had no choice but to agree and arranged for it to happen after we were taken down. They fed us before we were taken to her room. That being done, the two of them left and the lights were turned off.

It was quite late when they remembered us next morning and came to take us down from the columns. We were hustled upstairs to be fed and milked/harvested before we were separated from the others who were taken outside to work. Two of the female staff, both looking the worse for wear, scrubbed us with a scrubbing brush, using soap and warm water, before spraying us with some kind of scent and ensuring our teeth were clean and our hair combed and brushed. Then, chained hand and foot, we were taken downstairs. We stopped outside an unmarked door, one of the women knocked and waited for a reply. Told to enter, she did so.

"We've brought the two slaves you asked to see, Your Excellency," we heard her say.

We didn't hear the reply, but guessed she was told to bring us in, because that's what happened. When the Minister saw us, she was angry.

"Why are they in chains?" she asked.

"That's the rule, Minister, when they're outside their quarters. It's a matter of security."

"That may be your rule," she responded, "but it's not mine. Unchain them at once and leave them with me. They pose no threat."

"We can't do that, Excellency," said the second woman. "We have to remain here with them."

"Rubbish!" the Minister said angrily. "The President has ordered me to speak confidentially to them. Go away and wait outside. I'll call you when I want you to remove them."

Their manner clearly indicated they were angry as they grudgingly removed our chains and then left us with the Minister. We both realized we would have a tough time afterwards – to punish us for their embarrassment. We clearly heard their muttered words, "You'll both pay for this," and knew only too well what they meant.

The Minister stood up and walked around to face us. She looked us up and down, walking around us to examine us carefully. She seemed satisfied by what she saw. She returned to her seat and motioned to us to sit down. We looked startled.

"What's the matter?" she asked.

"Slaves don't sit in front of freemen or women, let alone Ministers," I answered.

"Slaves do as they're told," she replied, "and I've told you to sit down. So, sit down!"

She smiled as she said this. We obeyed. But sat up, with our hands clasped in our laps, rather than lounging back in the chair as we would previously have done and as we did when we were with the others. She noticed but didn't comment.

"What are your names?"

"We don't have names," Judy answered. "We're slaves. Slaves have numbers. We're 117 M and F. We're animals or property. You don't name property."

"What were your names before you became slaves?"

"I was called Mark and my partner/girlfriend was called Judy."

"Aren't you married, like some of the others?"

"No," Judy answered. "We were going to get married, but we were made slaves before we could do it and slaves don't marry."

The Minister took this in, commenting that there could always be exceptions. She then started asking us about our lives before we came to Austrasia and in Austrasia before we were enslaved. We told her our life stories and she took notes as we spoke. She commended us for our intelligence and our commitment to the people of Austrasia, before picking up a sheet of paper and asking us a series of what were obviously predetermined questions.

"Can you read and write?"

We both looked surprised and simply answered "Yes."

She apologised and explained she had been given a number of questions to ask and record our answers.

"Do you know any languages other than your own?"

We told her we knew some French, but nothing else. She asked about African languages, including Austrasian. We said we had picked up a little bit of Austrasian, but that was all.

"Have you accepted your present condition as slaves?"

We said we knew we were slaves, understood we were the property and at the disposal of our owners; also we had no choice but to obey them. She asked for a definition of the duties of a slave and we told her it was to do exactly as we were told, to keep our thoughts and opinions to ourselves, not to talk outside our quarters unless we were given permission to do so and only to show initiative if we were expressly ordered to do so She nodded and then asked about a breeding slave's duties.

"I'm like a cow," I said. "I'm milked every day and in the same way as a cow is, except that they take semen from me for the sperm and milk from a cow."

"My womb is inspected every day unless I'm actually menstruating, but that has become rather irregular because of how I'm treated," Judy said. "If I have produced any eggs they are vacuumed out of me."

"I assume Judy's egg is fertilized in the laboratory using my sperm. Our job is to provide the genetic material to enable your scientists to grow new slaves," I added.

She asked if we enjoyed this role. Judy simply said "no" rather brusquely. I held her hand tightly knowing she was both extremely upset and very embarrassed. I answered that it was degrading and humiliating for us both, but it was much worse for Judy because they were not gentle with her and had no need to stimulate her. However, because the only way to obtain sperm from a man is to sexually stimulate him, I did get a perverse sort of pleasure out of it.

"In some senses," I tried to explain, "I feel more alive than usual when I'm stretched on the milking machine being milked like the other animals."

But Judy was in tears by this time. "I HATE the thought that our genetic children are being bred for the purpose of being a slave, will be branded and generally treated as less than human, as we have been. We don't know what happens to our embryos once created. Those children will grow up without knowing what love is and they probably won't know what kindness is either, if our experiences are anything to go by. They will grow up to be hateful and hate-filled people. Ultimately they will rebel with the same sort of brutality they have experienced and probably be cruelly put to death for it."

At this point Judy broke down completely and I hugged her tight until she had calmed down a bit.

She went on, "We've been kept in our pairs, so why don't they let us breed naturally? It does not make any sense."

"I'm truly sorry for the way you have all been treated" the minister replied. "I know it probably isn't worth much to you, but I completely agree – and I know the President does too."

I couldn't say anything, but thought to myself then why the hell don't you stop it?

The minister then asked us, "Are you used to working together as equals?"

We said we'd done so for years, ever since we first met each other in secondary school.

"How do you and your friends feel about being kept naked?"

We looked at each other. Judy answered her question.

"There are arguments that those who work underground in the mines should be naked. There are also arguments that we should be, although I do feel that we could be dressed in breech cloths outside. I don't think slaves out on the streets should be naked. I believe it offends your people and provokes attacks on us against which we are not allowed to defend ourselves in any way.

Eventually some of us are going to get seriously injured or even killed in these attacks. The strict rules forbidding clothing slaves, especially private ones, should be revised and a list of permitted clothing issued. Surely, we could be permitted to wear breach cloths or loincloths – even if we're otherwise naked?"

"Do you agree with Judy, Mark?"

"Yes. Our skin colour, the numbers on our bodies and the brands clearly mark us out as slaves. You could give us a little decency when on the streets or in public. Labourers working on road construction or building sites and in mines also ought to wear basic clothing as a safety measure."

"Do you want to be free again? That's the last question."

We looked at each other and did not reply. She waited and then, when she realized we were not going to answer, she continued.

"It's a difficult question for me to ask you, I know, because you may be afraid of how I will react to your answer. Don't be! I'm not here to punish you – and I'm going to stop those two who brought you in from victimising you when you go out."

"You heard them, then?" I asked.

"Of course I did!" she replied. "I expected it."

I sighed.

"It's a difficult question to answer. Back in June, I would have answered in a word – and that word would have been 'Yes'. Judy would have said the same. Now it's not so easy. We're naked, branded, tattooed with a number and a type. We're foreign. We don't speak the language. We look different to Austrasian citizens. By law, we have no rights, and, outside of the farm any citizen can do what they like to us. In here we're relatively safe, although we are sometimes punished without justification, but life is simple here. What is freedom? If you free us from the Centre – I think you know what would happen to us. If we escape from it and are recaptured, as eventually we would be, we'd be either hanged or crucified."

"Or burnt alive," the Minister added. "That bit hasn't been published."

She turned to Judy. "Do you agree, Judy?" "Yes, Minister."

She told us to remain where we were and asked for the name of our guard. We gave her Jake's name. She picked up the phone and spoke to the Governor, asking for Jake to be sent to her.

Meanwhile she called the women in. They looked scandalised when they saw that we were sitting down in the room in the presence of a free woman. They started to object, but the Minister told them we were doing what she had told us to do. She warned them that there was to be no retaliation against, or victimisation of, us - or the President would be informed, and then dismissed them, telling them she had summoned a guard to take us up to our quarters. They left the room.

When Jake finally arrived after about half an hour, he was surprised to see us and even more surprised that we were drinking tea and eating biscuits with the Minister and engaged in easy conversation with her. She greeted him and got straight to the point.

"Mark and Judy say you get on well with them. Is this true?"

"Yes, Minister."

She then switched into Austrasian and began a question and answer session which involved several exchanges in that language. I was able to pick up enough to know they were talking about us, about the need for us to learn the language, and the possibility of his teaching us. She turned to us.

"How much of that did you understand?"

We gave her a rough synopsis and she was pleased.

"Well, Louis. Will you do it?"

He nodded.

"It would be a pleasure."

"You've already come to love these two, haven't you?"

"They're like my own children, Minister."

"Take them away and begin today. I'll leave instructions with the Governor. After doing their duties as breeding slaves they're to be in your charge every day and all day until they can speak, read and write in our language fluently. They must also be able to understand fully when it is spoken to them. You must tell me if there's any interference in this process – particularly by the two women I've just dealt with - and let me know when they're perfectly able to meet our standards."

She paused, thought a moment, and then added, "Oh. And arrange with the Governor that these two should be legally married. He has the power. He's to use it. I will tell him before I go."

A week later we spent one and a half days locked in a cell in the cold cellar after being flogged until our backs were scarred, cut and bleeding. We knew it was not coincidental, but we also knew we could not complain about it. Later, we learned Jake reported the incident to the Minister, who had spoken to the President. He intervened and ordered the Governor to free us from the cell, arrange for our medical treatment and dismiss the two staff members involved. We were removed to the Centre clinic on the second floor, where we were treated for two days. It was some time after this we learned of the two women's arrest on the President's orders and they were subsequently sentenced to jail terms for assault on two Government employees. Much later, after we had left the island, we learned that while in prison the elder of the two died. Apparently she had cancer which had not been diagnosed due to a lack of symptoms. In retrospect, it was probably after these arrests that our treatment began to get worse and it deteriorated much further after the woman died. The person who ill-treated us the most was Maritza, who became the new head of service. Her replacement partner was Letizia, who happily treated us as badly as Maritza, and in fact she was often far more brutal than her colleague. We could not understand why these two women treated us so much worse than anyone else. Nor could we comprehend why the Governor allowed this brutality to continue.

And so, our lives began to change again, no more field work, no more public beatings – except on that one occasion I've already written about. Just being daily milked in my case and checked and harvested in Judy's. After this, the rest of the day was spent being drilled (not unkindly) in Austrasian by Jake. We asked him why the Minister had called him Louis. He wouldn't explain (although we did learn much later) but warned us sternly not to speak to anyone about it. Meanwhile, we increasingly were picked on by the staff. They picked different slaves from time to time, but they were always the youngest of us. We, however, were chosen far more often than the others. We were roughly handled in the work room and frequently taken down at night to the floor below to be assaulted and raped by members of the staff. They did not actually beat us, since that would have been obvious, but, led by Maritza and Letizia they attacked us in every other way. I remember one night, as I lay spreadeagled on the floor being raped repeatedly, Maritza said to the other officers, "This is all we can do at the moment to any of them. When I'm in charge here, we'll make the lives of all these bastards Hell – but especially these two." We felt helpless in the face of this sustained series of assaults and dared not complain. First, we knew the Governor would not believe us. Secondly, we knew Maritza and her friends would punish us even more severely for daring to complain.

Later I read the report which the Minister wrote about us to the President. She gave our answers to his questions and her assessment of our characters which was very positive. She described her interaction with the two women and her suspicions of what they intended to do to us as well as the instructions she had given Jake. Finally, she concluded her report with these words.

"Mr. President, if you're determined to continue with this experiment, these are the ideal couple to start it off."

A month after we had our conversation with the minister we heard that the President had issued a decree allowing slaves, under certain prescribed conditions, to wear minimal clothing to cover their groin areas, although their brandings and tattoos still had to be clearly displayed.

This is the meat of that Presidential decree.

Slaves in category L and P who are required to go out on the streets of an urban or rural settlement, or who work in a potentially dangerous environment or with dangerous tools are authorised to be clothed in either a loin cloth or a breech cloth to cover their groin areas. Owners of P slaves are permitted to make their own decision about clothing slaves or leaving them unclothed in their own dwellings. The penalties for clothing slaves are rescinded. This relaxation of the rules does not apply to Category B slaves and Category L slaves working in mines, unless, for some reason, they are outside of their Centre or their mine for a legitimate purpose. The President reserves the right to create specific exemptions to the clothing rules for slaves if he personally believes it appropriate in individual cases in connection with tasks that they may be instructed to carry out.

CHAPTER 9

Back to School

Our lessons in Austrasian began the next day. Jake was an excellent teacher who made us use the local language in conversation as much as possible right from the beginning, gently correcting us when we made mistakes and making us repeat phrases again and again until we got them right. Austrasian is a difficult language for a foreigner to learn because the same word can have different meanings depending upon how it's spoken. Of course, these lessons were interrupted by the petty act of revenge on us by the two women who had escorted us to meet the minister. When he discovered we were missing the following day, Jake guessed where we were and came down to the cellar as the two women were flogging us.

"Who authorised you or instructed you to do this?" he demanded.

"It's nothing to do with you, soldier," the older woman replied. "We know they're your pets, but they're ours' now, and we're going to make them pay for humiliating us before the Minister."

She followed this up by smashing her whip across my lower back, causing blood to seep through my skin.

"I'll take this up with the Governor and the Minister and they'll take it up with the President," Jake said. "You'll regret this disobedience."

"Bugger off," said the younger one, as she laid another heavy blow on Judy. "They're ours' and we're going to do what we like with them."

Shortly afterwards, their arms grew tired from the effort of flogging us. We were taken down. Chained hand and foot, and locked into two separate cells, where we stayed until the middle of the next day, when Jake and the Governor came down and took us out. Two more days in bed in the clinic, being treated for our injuries and being investigated in case of internal injuries followed. After this we were returned to the slave quarters, and our lessons resumed. Jake apologised that it had taken so long to free us – but he said there had been difficulties contacting the President. He also told us the two women had been sacked and were now under arrest, facing Presidential charges. That surprised us.

A week after this, we were summoned to go with Jake and Ade to the Governor's office. We were unchained and given breechcloths to wear. The Governor rose from his seat when we entered. After apologising for the "unjustified assault" on us, he asked how we were. We assured him we now felt OK, although still a little bit stiff. He looked at Jake, who nodded in confirmation. Then he asked Jake if we were making satisfactory progress in learning Austrasian. Jake smiled and told him to ask us in the local language, which he did. We both answered in Austrasian that we believed we were doing quite well and Jake said we were doing better than he had hoped or expected. The Governor smiled at us.

"Good," he said. "His Excellency the President will be very pleased."

I put my hand up, as we were instructed to do if we wished to speak without being told to do so. The Governor allowed me to.

"Thank you, Sir,' I said. "Why will the President be pleased that two breeding slaves far out in the country are learning his language successfully? Surely we're not important enough for him to be concerned about us?"

The Governor smiled.

"You're both much more important than you realize. At the moment you're probably the most important couple of slaves in the country. Believe it or not, we're all very proud of you."

"Those two women in the cellar didn't seem to be, Sir," Judy said ruefully and meaningfully.

"They were renegades. We should never have employed them and I'm sorry we did, but we didn't know. Except for your friend and teacher, Jake, here, they would probably have killed you. He stopped them just in time and made sure the President became aware of what had occurred. He then called me and instructed me to make sure the two of you were rescued immediately from the cellar and looked after as necessary. Those two women have been sacked."

"Thank you, Sir," we said in unison.

He smiled at us.

"I've got a pleasant duty to perform, also by Presidential order. But I have no symbol I can use for you. This should be a big celebration and you should be dressed like a princess, Judy. Sadly, all we can do is dress you like a traditional native."

He paused and looked at the two men standing behind us.

"You are the two witnesses, have you brought the special chain I asked you to make and bring?"

Jake nodded and handed a small length of chain over.

"Mark, will you promise to love Judy and stay with her as her husband for your whole lives?"

We were both shocked by this question. "Yes, Sir," I answered, of course I do."

"And you, Judy, will you promise to love Mark and stay with him as his wife for the whole of your lives?"

"Yes, Sir."

"Will you work together in equal and amicable partnership in everything you do?"

We both said, "Yes", in unison.

"Then, by the power vested in me by the President, I declare you to be husband and wife".

He fitted the chain to the cuff on my right wrist and the cuff on Judy's left wrist.

"As you are united by this chain, so you are united by the law."

He then shook our hands and kissed us on both cheeks, before telling me to kiss Judy.

We all signed a certificate, which he said he would send to Freetown for registration – an action we later confirmed he did. Finally, he opened a bottle of sparkling wine, which he called champagne, poured out five glasses, and made us all share a toast to our marriage, before telling Jake and Ade to take us back to the slave quarters where a party had been organised. We were surprised and touched by the enthusiasm and joy of our fellow slaves, who congratulated us and laughed when Jack commented that he always knew marriage was a sort of imprisonment, and now he knew for certain it was – pointing to the chain which still united us.

That night we slept happily for the first time since we surrendered our passports, and the next day, the lessons continued. Importantly, the relationship between us (and, by extension, the other slaves) and Jake and Ade continued to deepen, although we never talked about it. Our lessons in speaking and listening continued for a further three months before Jake felt confident enough to test us. He obtained the Governor's permission, made us put on breechcloths, and took us out of the farm and down to the jetty. Here, he obtained packs of food for the three of us as well as supplies of water and he took us onto the boat for the passage to the eastern shore. He walked us back along the jungle path to the township we had left nearly a year before. We arrived in the evening and entered the main square, noting that the skeleton of the slave we had seen crucified was still nailed to the tree trunk. However, it was no longer alone. The trees around the square contained four more naked bodies of slaves, nailed to them, in various stages of decay or, in one case, of dying. A whipping post had been erected in the square, and was plainly used frequently, because it was spattered with blood. Otherwise, the square was as we remembered it. An army truck containing cages was parked up at the edge of the square. The cages contained pairs of slaves, plainly en route to a new Centre. Jake took us over to them. The officer in charge came out to challenge us.

"What are you doing here soldier – and who are these slaves?"

"We're here with the permission and authority of the Governor of St Michael's Island. These slaves are of special interest to His Excellency the President and we're here to test their ability to understand and communicate in our local language. Perhaps your squad can help us?"

Three soldiers agreed to come and talk to us. Jake told them they had to use only the local language. We were able to conduct a five way conversation with them about who they were, what they were doing, who the slaves were and where they were being taken, that lasted for three hours without a word of English being spoken. We heard it was a consignment of breeding slaves being sent to a new centre to the west, on the southern shore of the Lake. At the end of our conversation, we three were taken in by the soldiers to join their comrades over the campfire, to eat and drink with them, and learn some of their songs. We were allowed to sleep in their tents, and to share their morning ablutions and meal before they left for the west. We were sorry to see them go.

Jake took us around some of the local market stalls, to talk to stall holders there about their wares. We bought fruit and vegetables for our journey back and felt very proud of ourselves. Finally, the Garrison Commander, who had obviously heard of our presence in the township, came to the marketplace to investigate. Jake told him who we were, where we'd come from, how and why. He smiled, happy, I think, that he didn't have a double crucifixion to supervise. He asked us a few questions, at first in our own language. We were about to reply, when Jake asked him to repeat the question in the local language. He did so, and we replied. to those and to other questions in Austrasian. Basically, he asked us about St Michael's Island Farm and Breeding Centre, and we told him as much as we knew about them (from our point of view). Finally, he congratulated us and wished us well. He turned to Jake and advised him not to return to the Lake that day because it was too late and there was a gang of slaves who had escaped from the mines active in the area. He offered to provide us with an armed escort, and Jake was happy to accept. In the meantime, he took us back with him to the garrison – because he was concerned about the effect that two semi-free slaves in the township might have on the local community, especially if they recognised us from our first visit – where we had wrestled for them in the market square.

The soldiers of the garrison were as curious about us as those with the truck, and we were kept in conversation for much of the evening, while they fed and provided us with their local beer. I half expected them to ask us to put on a wrestling match for their entertainment, but they didn't. They were much too curious about us and about what happened in the breeding centres. Finally, we were allowed to sleep in the barracks.

The following morning was a larger scale repeat of the day before. Then, at about 8 am, we left with an escort of twenty soldiers, under the command of a lieutenant. We thought this was excessive, but we were told it was a regular patrol. They would take us to the lakeside and then begin a sweep of the jungle to the north of the track. Our journey back was uneventful. We were not chained, unlike last time, and we were partially clothed. We were always treated with respect, almost, but not quite, as equals. When we were about two hours from the Lake, Jake telephoned the boat crew and asked them to be at the jetty to meet us. They were already there when we arrived. We thanked the soldiers and their officer for their protection and wished them luck on their patrol. We boarded the boat. Seated in the cabin as the boat pulled away from the jetty, Jake commented that surely we didn't mean to wish them good luck. I said of course our sympathies were with the slaves, but we couldn't reveal them and so to wish them good luck was no more than that. Good luck could mean that they avoided making contact with the gang and returned to their base unharmed. Jake grinned, and told me I was in danger of becoming a politician. Judy commented that all slaves had to be politicians and possibly all politicians were really slaves. We all laughed, and Jake called us both cynics. It was fully dark as we crossed the Lake, and way beyond our feeding time when we reached the island. As a result, we stayed overnight with the soldiers of our garrison, sharing the food we brought with them and sharing their food and drink. For the third night we slept in military company and for the third morning shared a military breakfast, before leaving them and returning to the farm. We had passed the test.

Our lessons now changed, and the concentration was on learning to read and write Austrasian. These intensive lessons continued for another three months until Jake was convinced we could be mistaken for natives but for the colour of our skin. At that point he reported to the Governor, who insisted on examining our skills personally. Once he was satisfied, he rang Freetown, spoke to the Minister, who put him through to the President. After speaking for ten minutes to the President, the Governor put the telephone in my hands. He told us the President wanted to speak to us. I took the phone gingerly and trembled as I held it to my ear. I need not have worried. He spoke to me in Austrasian, asking me simple questions about myself, and I answered him in the same language. Then he asked me to pass the phone to Judy and he questioned her too. He was obviously satisfied and told her to pass the phone back to the Governor. The two men talked for a few minutes and when he put the phone down, the Governor looked at us with a smile that was half a grimace.

"The President is coming here next week. He wants to see you and, almost certainly, to take you away with him after he's conducted his own tests. Don't tell the staff or your fellow slaves, whatever you do. Jake don't tell the troops. I will do that."

And so, we learnt that our lives were about to change once more.

CHAPTER 10

Preparing for the President's Visit

The next week for everyone except us was one of hectic preparation. Staff, slaves and garrison were involved in making the place look as good as possible. This included making tunics with the national flag and government colours for us slaves to wear. By the time the President actually arrived, the Centre and the farm were spotless. We were all washed and scented, our hair was dressed neatly and consistently, and our new tunics were clean and pressed. Sadly, they covered otherwise naked bodies. We just had to hope he arrived before the evening winds from the lake revealed the truth behind the façade we were presenting.

For us it was a time of final teaching from Jake and a full revelation of what he expected. Because of our anticipated departure, the Governor waived the rules for us. After our daily stint being milked and harvested, Jake took us, and a picnic lunch, out onto the western hill. Here, alone, he talked openly to us. He told us his father had served in the colonial army and he had joined the army of the newly independent state as an act of loyalty to his father and President Igbokwe's predecessor, who had won the (largely rhetorical) "fight" for independence. It was rhetorical since the colonial power had no desire to hang on to the colony. When the late President was overthrown and murdered, Jake decided to fight back against the new government. He and Ade were horrified by the decision to enslave us, and even more horrified by the heartless way it had been carried out. He told us he had engineered the flight of the so-called gangsters from the mines and had arranged for them to move to a much safer base further away to the west. "You'll be joining them eventually," he told us. We thought he had told us the whole story. As you will see, we later learned he had not been totally honest with us. He told us what he knew we wanted to hear at that stage.

Meanwhile, he warned us that where we were going offered both opportunities and dangers. He told us we could learn government secrets otherwise unobtainable for the rebels. He stressed we must not appear to be anything other than totally loyal to the new President. "If he thinks you're betraying him or deceiving him, his rage will be terrible and his revenge beyond description."

"You have to be very careful," he stressed again and again. "You're no use to us dead – and that's what will happen if he believes you've betrayed him. However, it will be no clean or easy death. You won't even be crucified. I've heard he flays traitors to him alive."

Judy didn't understand what that meant and asked him to explain.

(The reference to flaying prisoners alive was not true – it was like mothers often used to warn their children to behave by threatening to tear their arms off and hitting them with the soggy end!)

"Flaying a person alive," he said, "involves peeling the skin from the body, starting from the top of the head and finishing at the toes. It is done while the prisoner is still alive – and he or she is kept alive during it. If they survive what amounts to the peeling of the body, they will be beheaded. It's not a pleasant death!"

"Tell me about it!" I commented. "Don't worry, Jake.

We'll be extra careful."

"Do you know what we're going to be doing?" Judy asked.

Jake said he did, but he was forbidden to tell us, since the President wished to put it to us himself, so he could judge our reaction.

On a second occasion, he told us to expect to serve the President for about a year before being returned here, but not to expect to be welcomed back.

"The staff will hate you and your fellow slaves will resent you. I will be unable to help you, and you will be made to suffer. The two officers who were sacked and are now in prison were very popular. They have many friends, and they blame you. I suspect you will discover that next week. Don't worry what they do to you – I will find you and the President will deal with your assailants. But when you come back it will be different. You will have to endure possibly unspeakable abuse and suffering until the right time comes to end it all. You will know the day because that's when Ade and I will come to you. It will be on the first festival after your return here"

Later, when it seemed we had been returned to the Island, the two supposed returners were treated as pariahs. At that time Maritza had been appointed as acting Governor, so these two were left without anyone who could protect them. They were left for hours on the milking and harvesting machines until they were almost drained of all energy. They were sent to cut maize or dig for cassava late in the afternoon and left to continue through the night while the others were sleeping. When they were able to sleep, it was in a cell in the cold cellar.

They were regularly flogged and left to hang on the tree not only through the day, but also through the night. Their old cage had been taken over by the two slaves who replaced us, and no effort was made to find them a replacement. Effectively, the cell in the cellar or the punishment tree was their bed. Their food was whatever, wherever, (and whenever) their tormenters chose to give them any. All that kept them going was the hope someone would find a way to rescue them.

CHAPTER 11

The President's Visit: Our Story

We were woken early on the day the President came. Staff members who usually controlled the milking and harvesting machines, instead turned the water sprays on, washed us, scented us to make us smell less like animals and more like humans, in case our smell offended the President, and dressed us in the fancy tunics they had made. Our hair was carefully washed, brushed and combed, and garlands in the national colours of green, black and red were placed on our heads. Our legs were then shackled, and our hands chained behind our backs. All this took over an hour, during which time no thought was given to feeding us.

Once everyone was ready to their satisfaction, we were marched down to the harbour and made to stand, silently lined up at the end of the jetty opposite the island's barracks. The garrison's soldiers were all assembled in two ranks opposite us, and the rest of the staff assembled in a mass opposite the jetty, linking our two groups and making a hollow square. I realized later that they had woken us at 5.30 and we were all assembled, waiting, at 7.30. There was no sign of the boat, which we knew had left the previous day to deliver our products and collect new containers and other supplies. On this occasion the boat would also pick up the President and, we assumed, his party. We had no idea when he would arrive. The Governor was as ignorant of this as we were. He stood in the middle, nervously looking at his watch every so often. The soldiers, used to parades, stood comfortably at ease, talking quietly to one another. We, used to standing still for long periods in silence, did exactly that. The civilian officers, used to neither posture, milled around, talking noisily and volubly complaining. They were eating sandwiches and drinking cups of tea or coffee while we were all waiting, but nothing was brought out for the soldiers (who had probably eaten while we were being made to look presentable for the President) or us. Someone suggested singing the National Anthem – and some of the staff joined in a ragged chorus. We had never been taught it and couldn't join them. The soldiers ignored the request, treating it with something like contempt. I noticed that – I don't think the Governor did. I wondered if there was any significance in that, or, in the fact that Jake wasn't there. He was, apparently, waiting for us in our "room" as he always called it. He knew the President who had been his CO in the days following Independence and so expected he would be very angry at this turn out.

The boat finally arrived at 9 o'clock. The President waited until the boat had been tied up, and then disembarked, shaking the skipper warmly by the hand as he did so. The Governor walked forward to greet him. He had a speech of welcome prepared, but the President stopped him.

"What's going on here?" he asked angrily. "I came here to visit a working farm, not to see this mummery."

"We wanted to welcome you properly," the Governor explained.

"All very proper," the President commented ironically. "I suppose you have a speech there telling me how proud you are I've come to visit you, whereas you've all been swearing about how inconvenient this surprise visit is for the last week! You would then sing the National Anthem – or at least that rabble over there would - and I suppose the troops would join them. I don't suppose for a moment the slaves even know it."

He looked at us, his eyes especially on Judy and me.

We shook our heads.

"I thought so," he commented. "And why on earth would you?"

He turned back to the Governor.

"Why are the slaves dressed in these ridiculous decorations and how much time was wasted in doing all this nonsense? A slave's uniform is his or her body. They need nothing more. Also, Why are they all in chains? Where on earth do you think they could possibly go?" Turning to the troops, "Who's in charge of the slaves?"

Ade and Jake's replacement, who's name we didn't know, stepped forward.

"Remove their chains and all the frippery put on them, let me see them as they are."

The two men worked their way along our line, stripping us and freeing us from our chains.

Meanwhile, the President turned his ire upon the civilian staff.

"Why are you here and not in your workplace?

Who's in charge of you?"

One of the older women stepped forward.

"I am, Your Excellency."

"What are your duties at this time of day?"

"After feeding the slaves, Your Excellency, we take them to the work room where the males are milked, and the females harvested for about thirty minutes. Then we hand them over to the two guards you've met for their field work while we supervise the feeding of the other animals on the farm."

"Have you done any of these things this morning?"

"Er ... No, Your Excellency."

"That's disgraceful! Farm animals need feeding. Slaves are legally property or, in this case, farm animals, but they are also human beings. You have a duty of care for all of them. How on earth do you expect them to perform their duties if they are not properly fed and watered. I notice that you have all fed yourselves! You have failed to do your duty. Go back to the house and do what you should be doing and what should already have been done. I will send the slaves up to you in a while for something to eat and drink. Oh, and don't take it out on them because you've been reprimanded for not doing your jobs properly or you'll regret it."

He turned away in disgust, as they, plainly stunned and angered by this stinging rebuke, began to leave the area and return to the house, muttering to each other as they went.

"I saw no sentries or guard posts along this vulnerable section of coast. My visit was known about and there are some who would like to see me dead. They could easily land an armed party on this shore behind your back. Lieutenant, dismiss the parade and reset the guard posts."

The Lieutenant saluted, and did as ordered, leaving us, Ade, his colleague and the Governor with the President.

The President turned to us and smiled. He walked along our line inspecting us as though we were his guard of honour, passing along our front and then behind us. Unlike almost everyone else who saw us and inspected us, he did not touch us. He asked the Governor and the two soldiers to escort him and asked Ade to tell him our names. He spoke for two or three minutes with each of the slaves in turn except for Judy and me. To us, he simply said, "I'll speak to you two later." Once the inspection was over, he turned to our two soldiers and asked where Jake was. Ade replied,

"Your Excellency. Jake is in the house waiting for his two charges for their daily lesson as he always does. We suggested he should be here, but he said he knew you from the time you commanded his regiment and you would expect him to be at his post, not down here."

The President smiled and told them Jake was absolutely right, before turning to speak to us as a group.

"You all look fine, and I know you do a good job here. I don't blame you for being here instead of where you should be, because you have no say in what you do or where you go. You must be tired and hungry. That is no condition in which to perform your usual role, so I'm ordering these two men who care for you and seem to care about you to ensure the civilians feed you properly and then let you rest before you go to the farm. You two men," looking at the soldiers who had remained to take charge of us, "ensure the civilians do as I ordered without any malice whatsoever towards the slaves and they go and feed the animals. Take your charges back to the house, and", turning back to us, "I'll see you all later." He looked at Ade again. "Tell Jake I'm pleased because he's the only one who did as I expected and I shall speak with him and his charges as soon as they have been fed and rested."

We were led away. Our chains were put in a box, and Jack carried them. We walked slowly and tiredly, back to our quarters, where we were fed by a clearly sullen and disgruntled staff. The woman, Maritza, who had taken the full force of the President's anger, brought us our food. She slammed the bowls and cups onto our table and, despite Jake's presence, spat at us and warned us we would suffer.

"You're his pets, I've heard, and It's because of you he's come. He'd better take you away with him because, if he doesn't, you're both going to wish you'd never been born and that he'd never come!"

With that, she left us to eat, and for Jake to console us.

"Remember what I said," he told us. "You understand now how the civilian staff feel about you. I'll try to protect you today – and – if I can't do that – then to rescue you as soon as possible. But I won't be able to protect you when you return. You do understand that don't you?"

We nodded.

"Good. Remember it will come to an end within a few months. Also, do NOT forget the advice I gave you about your behaviour in the Palace and in Freetown, especially, when you're in President Ngangi's company."

We nodded again.

"Okay. I'm going to leave you to finish your meal and then get some rest. I'll wait for the President's return outside and come and collect you when he's ready to talk to you."

Jake left us. We finished our belated breakfast, relieved ourselves, lay down and promptly fell asleep.

We woke up when a hand gently touched our shoulders. I rolled back from cuddling Judy and looked into Jake's eyes.

"It's time to get up you two. You mustn't keep the President waiting."

We disentangled ourselves from each other, sat up, side by side, on the edge of the bed, and looked at Jake.

"You've got to be good children, not angry teenagers. You have to impress the President. Do you understand? I can tell you he admires you already – now you've got to make him like you."

"Yes, Daddy," we said.

"Don't say that in front of him," Jake cautioned us. "I know I'm not your daddy, but he thinks he might be! Don't disillusion him."

He looked at us and smiled, before becoming brisk.

"All right, lazy bones. Get on your feet and meet your President."

We both stood up and followed him out of the cage into the central area, where the President was sitting, waiting for us holding a small chain. A bowl of fruit, a jug of tropical fruit juice and three glasses were on the table. Jake led us over to the President, who stood up to greet us – an action that immediately threw us into confusion – and then sat down again. Jake saw the expression on our faces and acted to provide a bridge between us and the President.

"Your Excellency, this is Mark, and this is Judy. Mark is twenty-five and Judy is twenty-three. They're the youngest of the slaves and not usually as shy as this. The Governor recently married them, acting on your instructions, and you are holding the small chain represents their union. They're not used to people treating them with courtesy and they won't speak to you unless you tell them they can."

"Thank you, Jake. And thank you for all you've done. Leave them with me. I promise you I won't eat them! Anyway, there isn't enough of either of them to make a good meal!"

Jake laughed, and wishing us luck left us with the President. He spoke to us, to put us at our ease, telling us to forget the rules and to forget he was the President.

"Speak to me as though I'm your father. And, for heavens' sake, sit down – my neck aches from looking up at you both!"

We smiled and sat down opposite him, looking longingly at the fruit and the fruit juice. The President saw it, and, smiling in turn, told us to help ourselves, so we did so. He began the conversation.

"I need to ask for your forgiveness."

We looked startled. That was not what we were expecting to hear. He continued.

"I have ruined your lives. You're both very young and you had a right to expect to live a full and happy life together, following a worthwhile career in your homeland and bringing up your own family in your own home surrounded by your own possessions and with the support of your families. All that has been taken from you – initially by a war which you had no part in and then by actions which you probably think I started. Now you have nothing – except yourselves. You're slaves – naked and helpless before the world. You've been branded like cattle and are treated like the other farm animals – used to breed other slaves, Just like chickens breed chickens and pigs breed pigs, etc. Can you forgive me for doing this to you?"

We looked at one another. Judy raised a finger and I nodded to her. The President noticed this and understood it was our method of communicating with each other. He looked directly at Judy.

"Mr. President, can I speak for us both?" He nodded.

"Many things have happened to us, some good, mostly bad, since we were arrested in June last year and made into slaves. As you said, we now have nothing except our bodies – which don't legally belong to us anymore – and each other. Our entire existence depends on our usefulness to the state and to you, and our future, such as it is, lies entirely in your hands. We don't know what the reasons for the decisions you all reached about us and the other guest workers were, nor do we know whether you all fully realized the consequences of what your decisions would be for us as individuals. We hated all Austrasians after we were carried on poles naked and bound through the town where we had worked so hard for two years teaching their children. The pain of the branding still comes back to us when we sleep and that's why we cling to each other for comfort. Then we met your minister. She stopped some of the abuse that was inflicted on us without anyone except Jake and Ade caring. When the women who hated us tortured us, separated us and threw our naked and chained bodies into two unlit and unheated cells, Jake, she and you rescued us, and you punished the women who did it – although we know more torture at the hands of her friends awaits us when you leave (or when we return). None of that is your fault. This morning what you said to the bastards who treat us all worse than the cattle outside (but the two of us much more cruelly than the others), when you reminded them that, although we are legally farm animals and property, we are still human beings; that showed us you seem to be different."

She paused and looked at me for approval. I nodded and she continued.

"Of course we forgive you, Mr. President. How could we not do so?

"That was some speech, Judy," the President replied. "I feel really humbled by it – and I never thought I would say that to a slave! Thank you – you are both very generous."

The President then switched to speaking Austrasian, as the conversation next turned to more familiar topics and we understood we were expected to make the switch too. He quizzed us about our family history, our history in school and university, our experience teaching in our home country and Austrasia, filling in gaps in his knowledge. We moved on after that to our experience of enslavement and our life at the centre, topics about which I've already written. All that was easy for us. We began to relax. He was being kind to us and somehow he made us forget we were sitting opposite him, immaculately dressed and carrying the power of life or death over us, while we were naked, branded, manacled (though without chains) and collared slaves with no power even over ourselves and totally at his mercy. Somehow none of it mattered at that moment – the huge gap between him and us had been closed by the President.

"What would you say were the strengths and weaknesses of this Centre?" he asked

Again, we looked at each other. This time I decided to answer.

"The Governor is basically a good man, but he doesn't actually know what goes on here. So long as his quota of genetic material is met and there is no trouble from us, he's happy. The soldiers more or less ignore us, except for the two (now three) in direct charge of us, who genuinely care for our welfare. At least, I know Jake and Ade do – I can't speak for the third man because we've never met him before today. The civilian staff are different. Most of them hate and despise us – especially Judy and me. They call us your pets – and hate us for it. Some of them are sadists who love to hurt us. The worst of them is the woman you rebuked earlier and another one who seems to be her particular friend. The symbolic Monday beatings aren't always symbolic. Judy and I were really flogged when it was our Monday."

He looked concerned.

"I've not received any report of this."

"You wouldn't, Mr President," Judy said. "Even the Governor doesn't know."

"He doesn't know, because he closes his eyes and doesn't ask." I added. "He simply doesn't want to know as long as things seem to be running smoothly."

"So, we (and especially the two of us) are left at the mercy of the worst of the staff," Judy concluded.

"I see," the President said gravely; and we realized he did understand.

"I'm so very sorry," he added. "You'll be glad to know I'm taking you away from here. You won't have to endure them for very much longer. Before you return here (in about a year's time) we, (including you two) will try to end this situation."

"Why are you taking us away Mr President?" I asked.

"It's a long story, Mark, and I need to go and see the others and prepare a speech for tonight at the dinner before we leave. For the moment, I'll just say this. I've decided to employ the two of you as my secretaries for the next twelve months. After that, I intend to replace you – but I have already legally adopted you (on my own authority as President) as my children (which is anyway your legal status as slaves now). During that time, Judy I expect you to become a mother of what will legally become my grandchild. I hope he or she will ultimately replace the two of you as my secretary and perhaps even become my chief minister eventually. That's all I'll tell you now. I'll explain everything more fully on the boat." He paused. "Do you accept my offer?"

Judy grinned.

"I hope you'll forgive the question, Mr President, but who will be the Daddy?"

"Of your baby?"

"Yes."

He laughed.

"You're a cheeky young woman, Judy! I know what you're actually asking. But the answer is Mark, of course. I want to have someone who will always remind me of you two. So I can't help you make him or her." He grinned and, winking at her, added, "Not that I'm not tempted!"

We all laughed, as he stood up. We stood up with him.

"I need to get you out of the way and into a place of safety. I'm going to ask the Governor to sign you off and have you sent down to the boat. Wait here. I'll join you this evening on the boat."

He left us.

An hour later the two female staff who were our chief tormentors entered, carrying chains and whips. *Their names were Maritza and Letizia.* They manacled our legs and chained our wrists in front of us, before taking us down and forcing us to march in front of them down to the Lake, savagely hitting us with their whips across our backs and legs every few minutes to hurry us up. Once beyond the gates and out of sight of the sentries, they stopped, shoved me off the path and onto my back on the grass and ordered Judy to kneel on the ground and lick me out. When she refused, she was struck repeatedly by the whips until she obeyed. As she did so, the whip continued to fall on her, to encourage her. When she had finished, they ordered us to stand up. Having done so. I was then flogged for not being more proactive. Normally when we were flogged, the person with the whip divided our bodies into three zones – the area protected by our ribs, our midriff, and our backsides, hips and thighs. The whip never fell on our midriff but was spread evenly between the upper and lower levels. We knew this was because our midriff areas were unprotected and there was a danger of internal injuries, these two women made no distinction, and seemed to concentrate on our midriff areas. (It was then we first felt real pain such as we had never known before. It seemed to come as much from inside us as from the whips.)

"That's a foretaste of what will happen to you if and when you return to us you little sods," the younger of the two women snarled at us. "Now, move!"

We were driven by the whips the rest of the way to the boat, where the skipper sat waiting on the jetty. The older woman ordered him to shut us in the hold.

"On whose orders? he asked.

"The President's", of course she told him.

The skipper said "Okay. I'll see to it." He called two of his crew over to lift the hatch and told the two women they could go back now and leave it to him. The women hurried away without looking back.

As the hatch was opened, he loudly ordered the men to get us down below while at the same time silently indicating to them that they should do no such thing. Instead he pointed them towards the main cabin. As I followed Judy up the gangway, she collapsed forward into the arms of one of the crew. Another man came to help and together they lifted her as gently as possible into the cabin. One of the soldiers came to help me at the same time as another helped the remaining crewman to close the hatch up again. This was when I dimly realized Jake had arrived panting down at the boat. He had clearly been running as fast as he could.

"Where are Mark and Judy? I know they were sent down here by the President for their own safety. I saw the hatch being closed. I bloody well hope you haven't put them down there?!"

The skipper replied, "They're in the main cabin, Jake. The two women who brought them down here told me it was the President's order to put them in the hold, but I knew that wasn't true. Incidentally, they've both been thoroughly messed up."

"What do you mean?"

"You'll see when you go into the cabin. She collapsed as she came aboard and his condition is not much better."

Jake rushed into the cabin. He saw the whip marks all down our backs and thighs, the bruises and the blood from the many places where our skins had been broken by the whips. He was incandescent with rage.

"Was it those two women I passed on my way here who did this to you both?" he asked angrily.

"Yes," I replied.

"Are you absolutely sure, Mark?"

"Yes"

Jake asked me to tell him briefly what had occurred.

"This is unforgiveable," the skipper said. "We should inform the President. He will be absolutely furious. He'd sent them down here so this wouldn't happen to them."

"I will inform the President and we'll get the clinic doctor sent down here at once," Jake said firmly. "You care for them until he arrives. Do you have a first aid kit?"

"Yes."

"I'll leave their care in your hands. I know who the two are. I was meant to bring these two down here. Those two told me the President wanted me, but by the time I found him and discovered he did not want me, those two women had already taken them away. I tried to catch them and I'm devastated I couldn't save them from this."

Jake left us and went on deck where he picked up his phone and rang the President. The skipper treated our injuries as best he could, gave us brandy, which he made us drink, and, finally, made us lie down on one of the bunks and sleep, while he sat beside us anxiously watching us, like a mother hen with her chicks. That, for us, was the story of the President's visit to St Michael's Island.

CHAPTER 12

The President's Visit: the President's Story

(in the President's own words but retold by Mark following later conversations with the President)

My visit to St Michael's Island had two purposes. The first was to check how this, the first of our slave breeding centres, was functioning. I had read Monica's report, and there were aspects about it that disturbed me. I was especially concerned about the fact that she felt the Governor was out of touch and the civilian staff treated the slaves with unnecessary cruelty.

My second reason was to collect Mark and Judy, who Monica and I had identified as being the best couple from that, the first group of breeding slaves to be established, for the purpose she had suggested, and I had approved. I explained this to the two of them on the boat, and what I said will be covered there.

What I saw when I arrived at the island shocked and angered me. I have never approved of ceremonial visits to workplaces. I prefer to see the institution as it normally is – or should be - fully functioning and engaged in its daily routine. That enables me to cut through the official obscuration ceremony permits. That morning confirmed my worst feelings, following Monica's report to me. Later, in my conversation with the two slaves, Monica's report was unconsciously repeated in almost identical words. I also saw the same thing with my own eyes. I hated the dressing up of the slaves to impress me – tinsel and fragile costumes do not deceive – and was especially angry when they admitted failing in their basic duty of care which is to feed the slaves who were totally dependent on them and whose existence and purpose was the reason for their being employed in that place. I watched their body language as they moved away after my rebuke to them and knew Monica was right. That's why I tried to protect my two young proteges later on. What happened to them on the way down to the boat was typical of what I feared. The garrison, too, had obviously become slack. You cannot afford to stand the entire force to in a ceremonial function, while leaving the whole island undefended. It was clear to me the Governor had lost control here, that is, if he ever had it.

After dismissing the staff and the garrison, I reviewed the slaves and was impressed by them – their appearance and their sense of discipline. They were actually better turned out, even naked, than our soldiers. I sent them off to eat and rest and excused them from exercising their primary duty that day. Then I spoke with the Governor. I asked how he organised his office. He answered that he did so through his staff. Asked how he monitored them, he admitted that he didn't. He relied on reports from his Head of Service – the shrewish woman I had sent about her business a few minutes before. I told him that it was not an adequate means of preventing mistreatment – and reminded him that his slaves were a prime target for serious abuse. I asked what procedures he had established to encourage slaves to report any abuse they'd suffered, reminding him that these slaves, especially the females, did need a basic level of care in order to produce the eggs and sperm we required of them. He said there were no such procedures and the law permitted slaves to be abused by citizens at will. Therefore, he had no power to stop it if it did occur. I informed him that as the governor, he did have that power as he was effectively representing me as the owner and owners undoubtedly had the right to stop anyone else abusing their slaves: he should have exercised it.. I concluded he was lazy, basically didn't care and had a "Don't ask; don't tell" approach to cases of abuse. I left him, allowing him to return to his office, only seeing him later to ask him to get Jake to escort my two young proteges to the boat for their own safety. Looking back, I bitterly regret not going to find Jake myself as I now know the Governor sent his Head of Service to inform Jake, but that she deliberately altered the message she was given in order to get her hands on the two of them before they were removed from her reach. The extent of the abuse they subsequently, and totally unnecessarily, suffered on their short journey to the boat appalled and angered me and should have become the subject of an arrest warrant, trial and sentence of imprisonment. The two kids dissuaded me. I was amazed by their forbearance.

Following my talk with the Governor, I entered the barracks which stand by the harbour. I met with the soldiers and found morale and discipline to be poor. The soldiers feel they're wasting their time and that the civilians should be manning the island centre. They despise the slaves and have little time for the civilians. The exceptions to this are the two soldiers – Louis and Ade – who volunteered to supervise the slaves, and, Josiah, who has replaced Louis. I suspect the Lieutenant, whom I interviewed after meeting the soldiers, is disaffected. He was reluctant to answer my questions, seemed unconcerned about the poor discipline and morale in the unit and lacked any interest in the purpose of the island or the welfare of the slaves who were at the heart of that purpose. I came away, deeply concerned, resolved to replace him with a more senior officer, called Longinus, who I knew and trusted. He would perform the function Louis had performed for me. I made my way to the farm, which seemed to be neat and well maintained. The farm animals were in good health and the slave workforce obviously performed their subsidiary task extremely well. I was surprised and gratified at the level of pride the slaves showed in their work.

Next I went to the house and met the staff in the Dining Room. I addressed them, reminding them again of their duty of care for the slaves and telling them I was removing the two youngest slaves and taking them back with me. A replacement couple, I told them, was on their way to the island, and would arrive within the following four days. They were to be treated properly. The two I was taking away would be returned in about a year, and I expected that they would be treated well on their return. As I said these things, I was watching their expressions. I did not like what I saw. My final remark, I was sure, got the words, "No chance," muttered from one woman near the back of the crowd to another. I took the Head of Service aside afterwards and repeated my message, emphasising my anger at the treatment of Mark and Judy in particular, and warning her I would take severe action if the situation did not improve. I ordered her to submit a person by person report on each member of staff to the Governor, outlining their characters, experience and suitability for this work. It should also indicate each individual's attitude to the slaves. The Governor was to take any action he deemed necessary based on the report before sending it on to me. The report never reached me. I imagine subsequent events meant the report was never made.

I then went up to find Louis in the slave quarters. He gave me a fingernail account of his two charges.

"They're intelligent, are well motivated, learn quickly and are extremely sensitive,' he said. "Both would make good army subalterns. They have leadership ability, but they also have the wisdom to hide it. Sadly, I think, they've slowly become slaves, not just physically, but mentally and spiritually too. They follow the rules laid down automatically and without question."

"Have they discretion, Louis? Can they keep their mouths shut when necessary and speak out when necessary?"

"Matthew, they're slaves. They've been beaten into submission. They never complain as they have learned it gets them nowhere and usually makes things even worse. They keep their ideas to themselves, don't speak out of turn and they don't share secrets, except with each other."

"Using these words, how would you describe them: two bodies but one person; two separate entities; simply too crushed to tell?"

"The first Matthew. They are effectively a single person. I've noticed they communicate without words and, when they speak, it's almost as if a single person is speaking in two different voices. They think and act as one."

After this Louis brought them to me. I then sent him away as I wanted them to be themselves with me. The problem is that we've made these young adults into frightened children so they now think and act like frightened children. It took some time for them to gain the courage to let their real selves resurface – but when they did, I found them to be impressive, confirming both Monica's and Louis' opinions of them. I loved the way that Judy had had the courage to ask me if I intended to rape her. I think that was the moment when I decided that I would not return them. Instead I would genuinely make them our children and we would keep them with us. I did not tell them at that time since I first needed to confirm with Monica that she would be happy with this arrangement. Moreover, I also feared for them. The woman I had met a short time ago would never forgive them for being who they were and, although slaves, being so much better than she is. I foresaw trouble for them later and wondered how they would react. Bearing in mind what happened later, I bitterly regret my failure to follow my instincts and instruct Louis personally to take Mark and Judy down to the boat, instead of leaving it to the Governor. We would all have been saved much pain and anxiety if I had done so.

I left them to go down to the farm and meet the other slaves who were working weeding and caring for the cassava and maize plantations. I was impressed by the energy and commitment I saw there, and the careful and sympathetic supervision exercised by the two soldiers. I spoke to as many as I could and found they were resigned to their lot and generally as satisfied by their condition as it is reasonable to expect from people so recently enslaved against their will and treated quite badly by the civilian staff. I was impressed by their rugged good humour, albeit of the bitter-sweet type. It was while I was doing this that Louis came to me to ask what I wanted. I told him the Governor should have asked him to take Mark and Judy to the boat and put them in the cabin. He informed me the Head of Service had come to find him. "She told me that you wanted to see me at once," he said. I immediately feared the worst.

"Get yourself down to that boat in double quick time, Louis. Those kids are in trouble. Rescue them and ensure they're safe. Then return here and report to me."

I continued to meet, talk to, and work with the eighteen slaves in the cassava field. I listened carefully to what they were saying and gained a clearer understanding of the extent of the brutality they were all experiencing. I now knew how serious a problem I had. I realized I ought to close the Centre down and move the slaves to another centre, but did not wish to do so since it seemed that they had formed a community and were settled. The Centre was actually working well, despite everything. However, this conversation was causing me to begin to wonder what exactly we had unleashed when we had enslaved our white "guest workers". I remembered then that Louis had already warned me that enslaving these people would be a huge mistake. It's a pity I didn't take his advice rather than listening to everyone else, but I couldn't change things now – or could I?. I knew I needed time to think about it and decided to talk to my new son and daughter. I realized then, if I hadn't fully realized before, they had both become very dear to me. They have that effect on you. It also struck me that before I allowed slavery to be introduced, they were two delightful young people it would be almost impossible to hate (unless you were jealous of them or resented them for some other reason). But now they were in a situation where it was very easy for some ill-disposed people to hate them, because the government sanctioned it. I had made our guest workers into people on whom Austrasians could take out all their resentments (even if they were completely unjustified). We have demonized them and stripped them of their humanity. That is why the civil workers in particular treat them so cruelly. Oh, Louis, why, why, why didn't I listen to you! With these thoughts running through my mind, I turned to speak to Ade, planning to ask him to gather the slaves together so I could discuss with them all about what I had learned. It was then my phone rang.

It was Louis. He described what had happened to Mark and Judy and how serious their injuries (especially Judy's) were. He asked me to bring the Centre doctor to the boat as soon as possible. I asked him how he would describe Judy's condition. He used the word, 'critical'. That was enough for me. I rang the Governor and instructed him to send the Doctor immediately to the farm gate where I would meet him and then we'd go down to the boat together.

I met him ten minutes later. We hurried to the "Macrone". I'm afraid I'm fitter than the doctor and I hurried faster than he did, arriving on board the boat about five minutes ahead of him . He found me sitting beside Mark and Judy. It was only then I remembered I hadn't told the Governor I was ending my visit to the Island and therefore would not be attending the evening dinner. I rang him to say that under the circumstances I was unable to continue with my visit and asked him to apologize to the staff. I also ordered him to suspend the two women who assaulted Mark and Judy, pending an investigation. Then I telephoned the governor of the neighbouring Centre I had planned to visit the following day and apologized that due to unforeseen circumstances I had to cancel my visit.

CHAPTER 13

On the Boat

The boat was officially known as a motor vessel and her name was the *MV Macrone* – named after the first President of Austrasia. It was one of two sister boats based at Port Franklin. It had four sleeping cabins – usually used by the skipper, and his three crewmen - a small wardroom and a much bigger common cabin. There was, as we discovered, ample hold space for cargo. Her maximum speed was ten knots, but she normally cruised at between 6 and 8 knots. She also carried passengers. That night she carried four crew and eight passengers – the President, Judy and me, Jake, and four members of the President's bodyguard (who had remained aboard the boat during the visit.) The President liked to visit unaccompanied, but he had left a small staff (as we were to find out) at Port Franklin. This was the main town on the lake, but there were a number of villages of varying size dotted along the shore, especially on the southern side.

Jake and the skipper were watching over us when the President returned to the boat at 17.00 hours and immediately came to the main cabin, where Judy and I had been half-asleep on one of the long cushioned seats that lined the room. He felt our foreheads, noting that we seemed to be sweating more than we should do, and asked the skipper whether he had taken our temperatures. He said he hadn't because they lacked the means. Their thermometer had been broken on their last visit to Port Franklin and they had been unable to obtain a replacement.

"I think they're feverish," the President said.

The doctor arrived and came to our side. He also felt our foreheads and agreed with the President. He took our temperatures and agreed they were both high. Seeing we were conscious, the doctor spoke to us.

"How are you feeling?" he asked.

"I hurt all over," I replied. "It's much worse than last time."

Judy said the same.

"I feel both hot and cold," she added.

"Is your pain outside of you or inside of you?" he asked.

That confused us.

"What do you mean?" Judy said. "We don't understand."

He thought for a moment, trying to think of how to express it.

"Where is the pain?" he finally began. "Does it seem to be on the surface of your body – on your back and down your legs, or does it seem to come from inside you? Or is it both?"

"It's both," I answered for us both.

"I see," he said gravely, "that's what I thought."

The doctor turned away from us to speak to the President and Jake who were hovering impotently behind him.

"I can't deal with this. I'll stay with them and help you keep them comfortable. However, we must get them to Freetown University Hospital as soon as possible if not sooner! It's really that urgent."

Jake came back to us while the doctor and the President walked away towards the skipper and the three of them discussed matters in low and obviously urgent tones. The skipper hurried off. I saw the president make a phone call, but could not hear to whom he was talking nor what they were talking about. However, the crew had disappeared as the call was being made and within five minutes the boat was under way. The doctor and the President returned to us. The President asked us how we were. .

"Don't try to get up," he added hastily as we struggled to sit up. "Stay where you are."

"Can we have something to drink?" Judy asked. "I feel very thirsty."

"So do I," I added.

"Of course," he said – and nodded at a soldier who went to get a couple of glasses of water. The President put his arm behind Judy's back and Jake behind mine. They lifted us gently so we could drink. "Not too fast", the doctor warned us before allowing to us to sip the water. Then we were gently laid back down and they sat down beside us, just like our mothers would have done.

"You're acting just like our mother," Judy whispered to the President.

He smiled and reminded us he was now legally our father.

Judy looked up at him and asked him why he chose us.

"We won't sleep now," she explained. "Talk to us and the pain might go away."

He told us a doctor would be waiting for us when the boat stopped shortly at the nearest village on the southern shore of the Lake.

"You ask why I chose you. I have reports on all those who were enslaved, together with photos of each individual. They have been divided into groups, depending on how we categorised you and where we sent you. You were in the first group of B category slaves to be sent to a centre because St Michael's was the first to open. Tomorrow, incidentally, I was due to visit the last one to open. I believe you met the slaves destined to go there, three months ago."

"Yes, we did, when we went to Casa Isabella for our speech trial," I said.

"That's right. Well, I pulled out the twenty reports from St Michael's and studied each of you in turn. I liked the look of you two – physical appearance is important to me. I like being surrounded by beautiful people – and you're both beautiful, even if you don't think you are. I was stunned this morning when I saw you both in the flesh, if you'll forgive the term, in that line up. I could see why the female staff have targeted you both – it was simply jealousy.'

"I'm not beautiful," Judy murmured. "My Mum always said she should have called me Jane, not Judy."

"Why Jane?"

"Because Jane is always called plain Jane, Daddy."

The President leaned over, gently pulled her head towards him, and kissed her.

"Beauty lies in the eye of the beholder, and to me you're both beautiful. I've always wanted a daughter – and now I won't get rid of you after a year. You'll stay with me for two. You'll need to, to wean your baby."

"Do we have to go back?" I murmured.

"You'll understand the reasons eventually, but the answer is yes, reluctantly." He paused, regretfully, I sensed. He added, eventually, "but perhaps not. What happened to you this afternoon frightens me because of what they might do to you when I'm not there. I have to talk to Monica first before finally deciding what to do with you." He looked away from us before continuing, apparently talking to the wall of the cabin.

"Any way, I chose you because of your appearance and your characters. Everything I've heard from Monica (the Minister) and Jake plus everything I've heard from and seen of you confirms that. I'll talk to you when you feel better and stronger and answer your real question, as to why I chose two slaves at all. But you're not able to take it in yet. Just understand Monica and I have good reason. By the way, I think I should tell you Monica is also my wife, and, therefore, your new mother."

"She never told us," Judy said.

"No, she wouldn't. I don't think anyone out here knows that – because she was announced under her maiden name. Don't be mistaken, she's a very shrewd politician. It's dangerous to try to deceive her!

It took about ninety minutes for the "Macrone" to reach the lakeside village fifteen miles away to the south. In those ninety minutes, in which we were constantly sponged with cold water to bring our temperatures down, we could see the three men constantly, but furtively, looking at their watches. This was when they weren't talking to us, making sure we stayed awake. Sometimes, they were making phone calls which seemed to us, even in our semi-conscious state, to be becoming more and more frantic. Whenever Judy or I closed our eyes, one of the three men would say something designed to make us laugh, cry or argue against them. We guessed they were trying to stop us falling asleep, but didn't understand why. It's all we wanted to do. We realize now they were fighting a desperate battle against time to keep us alive during that crucial ninety minutes voyage.

The "Macrone" came alongside a wooden jetty normally used for fishing boats which had been moved away to make room for us. Another doctor boarded the boat and examined us. He nodded gravely when the centre doctor gave him what I understand is called a "handover report" about our condition. We were lifted gently from the couch and laid on two stretchers on trolleys. They laid a blanket over me and wrapped it under my legs and somebody did the same with Judy. This was to keep us warm. In this way we left the boat, which subsequently returned to the Island to drop off the doctor before continuing to Port Franklin to take the four soldiers to rejoin the rest of the President's party for the flight back to Freetown.

CHAPTER 14

Freetown

The details of that desperate flight are still vague and shadowy in our minds. We remember being taken from the boat and wheeled to a helicopter, followed by the doctor, the President and Jake. We were wheeled up a ramp into a large open space. We remember Jake and the Doctor and several other people in overalls, clustering around us and attaching us to various machines and bags of blood. We can remember the incessant bleeping of a machine near us, not realising it was bleeping our lives away. We could hear and feel the sound of the engines as we were wheeled aboard. I can remember, although Judy says she can't, the sound of them fixing blocks against the wheels of the trolleys we were resting on. And I can remember the sound of the engines as the helicopter took off.

After that, everything became increasingly vague and distant, as I seemed to become detached from my body and begin to drift away. I saw Mum and Dad and my brother and sister holding their arms out to welcome me home - but it was not home, because it was bathed in a brilliant light. I looked around for Judy, and she was following me, a little way behind. Then I heard a voice cutting through the image from outside – "Mark, Judy, don't leave us. Come back. Stay with us. We need you." The messages were repeated and were insistent. We looked with longing for our parents, but they had disappeared, and we fell back into our bodies, where our saviours were cutting away the bracelets and collars that were marks of our slavery. We were barely conscious when the helicopter finally landed and were only vaguely aware of being transferred from there to an ambulance or arriving at the hospital. My last memory, and Judy told me it was hers as well, is of being rushed into the hospital entrance hall and from there into a lift. Then everything went dark. We knew nothing of the desperate fight to save our lives that day, nothing of the initial scans, or of the subsequent operations, nor even how long we were actually in the hospital. We did not know where we were or that the President, his wife, and our friend Jake, divided their time so one of them was always at our bedside for when we recovered consciousness, neglecting their duties to do so. We did not know how long it was before we opened our eyes and saw our new mother sitting beside our bed.

I murmured, "Is that you, Mummy?" and she looked startled. She had been looking wistfully out of the window. At the faint sound of my voice, she shot around and bent over me.

"It is you. Thank God," she said. "You're alive."

She pressed a button, and a nurse entered the room. She looked at Monica, and then at me and at Judy, who was also showing signs of stirring.

"I'll call the doctor," she said to Monica. "Stay here with them until I return."

She left the room, returning a few minutes later with the doctor, who looked into our eyes, took our pulse and temperature, followed by our blood pressure and then asked us some simple questions:

Question: What's your name? Answer: Mark or Judy

Question: How old are you? Answer: twenty-six or twenty-four

Question: What or who are you? Answer: The President's son or daughter.

Question: Who is this woman? (Pointing to Monica) Answer: Our mother.

Question: What's the relationship between you?

Answer: We're married to each other.

Then he smiled. "Welcome back among the living," he said. "Now we've got to get you fit enough to go to join your parents in the Palace."

With that he left, and the fight to rehabilitate us began. It was nearly a month before we were discharged – a month when we were made to realize just how important we had become to our new parents and their friend, Jake/Louis. It was during that time we came to understand we had changed our legal status as well as our relationships. It took us a while to come to terms with our new situation. Also, it slowly dawned on us that the cuffs and collars that had defined our captivity were gone. The tattooed numbers and letter Bs had been excised from our bodies too. The brand marks were still there and would always remain – just as our experience of slavery could never be forgotten – but we were now free. The only bonds which held us were the human bonds of our new family. We asked the President and Monica about that and they confirmed that our understanding was right.

"You are our son and daughter – you cannot also be our slaves. So – we've freed you. When you go back to the Island, it won't be to stay, it will be as my emissary, to inspect it and report on progress there," our new father informed us.

"But daddy, we have to go back – or at least appear to, because it's necessary for us to do so for Jake to be able to free the other slaves," I said.

He smiled. "It may also be necessary for you to die, to enflame them – but that's not going to happen to you. I will find, among the slaves, two volunteers who look very much like you and who are prepared to risk their lives in exchange for their freedom. There's bound to be someone."

"If you're going to do that, they must also act as our doubles," Judy pointed out, "and do visits to other places in our name, including the Island. Otherwise, they'll notice the difference."

He nodded and agreed Judy was right, before smiling at us and producing two packages and giving them to us.

"Put these on," he said. "You're coming home with us, and you can't do that naked!"

We opened the packages eagerly, and found appropriate underwear, a pair of shorts, a bush shirt, socks and sandals inside. We dressed and were clothed completely for the first time since early June in the previous year. Monica told us we had other clothing waiting for us at home. With that, they led us out of the hospital room which had been our home for six weeks (we were told this because we only knew about four of them) and walked us out of the hospital, past a line of clapping nurses and doctors, whom we all thanked individually, to a large official limousine with the national flag on the bonnet. Once we were seated together at the back, it drew away from the kerb, preceded and followed by a police motorcycle escort on the way to the Presidential Palace. Our new life had begun.

CHAPTER 15

Our First Day in the Palace

The Presidential Palace was, our new parents explained, the former residence of the colonial Governor. It was set at the end of a long straight drive within a large park-like garden. In some ways, I thought, it resembled the White House in Washington DC; the same appearance with the fountain in front of the building. It did not have the two wings of that building, but it was higher and, we soon saw, an extension had been built at the back. The car drew up in front of the main entrance, and the chauffeur opened the doors to let us out. His lips curled, I noticed as he bowed his head and handed Judy out, as protocol demanded.

We entered and were greeted formally by the Palace staff. Our parents introduced us. We were politely, but not warmly, received. I sensed there was tension in the air and our presence there was almost certainly the cause of it. The President either did not notice it or chose to ignore it. Instead, our new parents led us up the stairs into the residential area, and took us into a suite of rooms, which constituted a flat.

"Welcome to your new home," Monica said. "Explore it and settle in. When you are both ready, come out of your front door, turn left along the corridor and the next set of rooms are ours. You don't have to knock, now, or ever, just open the door and come in. We'll call for tea."

They turned to go, but Judy stopped them. Surprised, they turned around and came back in.

"What's the matter, dear?" Monica asked.

"They don't want us here, do they, Mummy?"

"Their opinions don't matter!" the President answered. "We've made the decision. You're our children. Presidential families always live here. You're no exception. If they don't like you or don't want you here, they have two options – to swallow their feelings and get on with it or leave. There are plenty of suitably qualified men and women looking for work in Freetown. We can replace them easily. Don't worry about them."

"But, if they insult you or do anything to upset either of you, tell us at once: and we'll deal with it," Monica added.

We nodded and they left us.

We looked around our flat. It consisted of a reception room, living room, private dining room, a bedroom with built in wet room and a spare room that would in due course be used as a nursery. We were not surprised to find Jake sitting in the Living Room. He greeted us, saying how good it was to see us again and looking so well. He escorted us around the flat, showing us where everything was. We felt overwhelmed. Our last "home" had been an open barred cage with basic furniture, and our "clothes" had been our skin, cuffs, collar and chains. Our "jewellery" had been a brand, a tattooed letter and some tattooed numbers! Now we had a complete wardrobe of clothes, a comfortable bed, a private bathroom, and our own living, eating and entertaining spaces. Judy found earrings, necklaces, bangles and rings. We even had a range of bottles of spirits and other drinks provided as well as a refrigerator and a microwave oven. Judy went back to the wardrobe and found a red dress for herself and a light tropical suit and shirt for me. She looked at Jake and told him that she suddenly felt shy.

"Jake, I know you're used to seeing us naked, but you haven't seen us dress or undress, and we feel very shy about doing it here. Could you please go into the living room, pour yourself a drink, and give us a chance to change in private?"

Jake smiled and said he understood perfectly and left our bedroom. We changed out of our travelling clothes into the ones Judy had selected, found suitable shoes and socks, and I waited while she fixed her hair. I refused to wear a tie. Thus equipped, we rejoined Jake. I told him we were invited to join our parents in their apartment. "I know," he said, "I've been invited too. He told us Mum and Dad thought it would be easier for us to overcome our shyness about intruding on them if he was there. So we all left together.

We walked the short distance along the corridor to the next door, noticing that the building had obviously been extended further very recently, or, had at least been redecorated, because we could still smell the fresh paint, and the carpeting looked new. I asked Jake, and he told us that my first suspicion was correct.

"They made the decision about you six months ago, and the extension was built in that time. It also allows accommodation for the additional staff needed, which includes me."

We did as we were told, opened the door and walked in. We were warmly greeted and welcomed to the Presidential flat. Our parents thanked Jake (or Louis as they called him) for encouraging us and, when they knew it was Judy who had chosen our attire, complimented her on her choice.

"I wanted to be a girl again," Judy explained. "I haven't worn a dress for nearly two years."

"You look beautiful in it," our father said. "I congratulate you."

"Mummy," Judy said. "I assume it was you who chose our new clothes. We love them all and can't thank you enough for the time and care you took in choosing everything."

We all sat down and our father picked up the phone that lay on the table and ordered tea to be brought in to us. He specifically asked the butler to bring it.

I asked him about Jake …

"Daddy," I said, "We're really confused. We thought that Jake was an ordinary soldier who was a rebel against your government. But we're plainly wrong. Who and what is he?"

The President laughed. "I'm not surprised you're confused!" he said. "He confuses me sometimes too! Explain yourself, Louis."

Jake explained he was really Louis and was a very old friend of our father going back to their school days – in fact they were best friends. He was not a private soldier, but a full colonel. "I'm surprised you didn't realize that" he commented, "but I suppose you can be forgiven since you were never in the army." Our father commented that it was just as well we hadn't realized, because if we had then others whom they didn't want to know would probably have done so too and that would have made things impossible. I told him I'd thought there was something not quite right about him and Ade.

I asked what his role was now, and he replied he was a senior intelligence officer. We were his most recent assignment. "I was already there on another assignment which we won't talk about today. A short time after you arrived I was asked to first check you out and confirm your suitability and then to train you – which I have now done. My new role is to act as your ADC and advisor when your father sends you out on your own, as he will. I shall also sit in on cabinet meetings in that capacity. By the way, now you know my real name is Louis, please try to remember to use it when we are on official business."

I commented that he was very convincing, and our parents concurred.

Father then said, "Tomorrow, son and daughter, I am going to spend the day with you both – and answer all your questions about why we've done what we've done. I warn you we're all going to be very unpopular in certain quarters – but we'll ride it out. One thing I must stress – although we're speaking in Austrasian here, when anyone enters or in public like at the Cabinet meeting in two days' time, we speak English. If anyone speaks Austrasian keep a blank face as though you have no idea what's being said. It is crucially important. You'll understand after our talk tomorrow."

There was a deferential knock, the door opened and the Butler entered, carrying a tray. He laid it on the table, with a stiff bow, and was about to withdraw, when the President stopped him.

"Jason, why were the staff so standoffish when my son and daughter entered the building?"

"Some of them feel offended that you've brought two slaves to lord it over them, Mr President."

"They're no longer slaves. They're our adopted son and daughter and should be given the same respect and care that we are given. Make it clear to all the staff that any discourtesy to either Judy or Mark will be met with instant dismissal. I can't demand that they love them, or even like them, but I do insist that they show them every respect and courtesy. They should also make an effort to get to know them and be friendly towards them. They are people, orphans both of their family and their country. They are now part of our family, even though they don't look like us. They must be shown warmth, sympathy and understanding - not coldness, hostility and resentment. They are no more responsible for what happened in the past than we are. Do you understand?"

"Yes, Mr President."

"Good, Jason. Make it so. Dismissed."

The Butler left. I could see that he was embarrassed and unhappy at being carpeted in front of us. I said so and Father smiled, saying that he intended that reaction. We then shared the cakes and drank the tea, and we were encouraged to talk about our experiences, both as teachers and as slaves, and our parents told us about the debates they had had about us and how they finally made their decision. I asked about our treatment by the doctors, and, for the first time, sensed that none of them wanted to talk to us about it. In the end, Jake told us that the doctors on the helicopter and in the hospital had to fight to save our lives. He refused to tell us what the doctors and surgeons did to us, but simply said this, "You were both less than half an hour from death on the helicopter. You both had to be put on life support machines at the hospital in order to keep you alive long enough for you to be operated on. I don't know how much blood was transfused into you both – but I do know that, in the English idiom I learned at school, you both had 'one foot in the grave and the other on a banana skin!'"

"That's enough, Louis," Father said sharply, "They don't need to be told more." He turned to us.

"You're both well now," he said to us. "Nothing else matters. You're going to have to take it easy for a while, but then we'll set about making the people love you. Never fear."

That ended the discussion. For the rest of the evening and over dinner, we learnt about the customs and routine of the house and they gently probed us to find out our likes and dislikes, our hobbies, interests and what we wanted to do now we were once again free to do it.

The grandfather clock in the hall struck nine and mother was telling us we should go back to our flat and go to bed. "You've only just left hospital," she was saying, when the door was thrown violently open and a very angry man in a suit and tie stormed in.

"What the hell do you think you're doing, Matthew?" the man began, speaking in Austrasian. "Why are these wretched slaves here, dressed up and poncing themselves about like people of importance?"

"Watch your language, Josiah," the President replied, "and don't forget who you're talking to!"

"You should remember who you are, Matthew! You're the President of the Republic – or you were six weeks ago! For the last six weeks you've been wasting precious time M.I.A. – mooning around in the hospital over the probably deserved fate of these two subhuman animals."

"I have NOT been missing in action for six weeks, Josiah. I've been at the hospital worrying about my son and daughter and working from there as necessary."

Father turned to us.

"Let me introduce Josiah Ndenge, my Vice President. You won't understand his tirade, but you have probably guessed he doesn't like you. Mr Vice President, it behoves you to show some decorum when you are talking about my son and daughter. At least speak in a language they understand."

The Vice President then exploded, using a stream of obscenities about us in the vernacular that, had they been stated in English, would have made us both blush. Instead, as instructed, we kept a stony face. Father was about to respond, when I raised my hand in a clear signal to him to say nothing. He looked surprised and stopped. I spoke instead.

"Mr Vice President, I do not know your language, but I did go to school in England, as did my wife, Judy. We both heard language used against and about us, such as I suspect you've been using tonight. I've been called a bastard, a wanker and a cunt (mutually exclusive adjectives you might think), a cretin, several kinds of idiot, and much worse. So has Judy. I'm shocked to hear the second most senior member of the government using such language and being so rude as to speak about us in a language we don't understand. However we can interpret from your uncouth manner and lack of self- control, that the gist of what you were saying was both diabolically rude and insulting. You plainly don't like us. That we understand, and I assure you, the feeling is mutual. However, we are the President's and the Cabinet's secretaries. It is our job to know what the President knows. So, if you came here for some purpose other than to malign us, tell us, in English, what it was. If you merely came here to insult us, then you had better leave now – before my Father has you thrown out."

"You little jumped up, white bastard!" the Vice President yelled. "How dare you speak to me like that! Who the hell do you think you are, you piece of no- good, white shit? If I had my way, your rotting bodies would be hanging from a tree and not poncing around like pampered princelings."

"He's just told you, Josiah. 'He's my secretary and he speaks with my voice. I couldn't have expressed the feeling of all five of us at your outrageous behaviour better if I tried. How dare you come barging in here uninvited and without knocking? Mark asked you to leave, I repeat the request as an order plus this, tomorrow I expect a written apology to me, Monica, Louis, and to both of them, together with an explanation of this outrageous outburst. Now go, before I call the guards and have you thrown out."

The Vice President looked shocked, seemed about to respond, changed his mind and left without another word, slamming the door as he went.

"I think I've just made an enemy for us," I said. "I'm sorry, Father, I should have kept silent."

"Not at all, son. You handled the situation in a masterly way. He already saw you as an enemy and wanted to destroy you or at least undermine your confidence or my confidence in you. He failed absolutely, and I'm proud of you both. Now, Louis, take them away and make sure they go to bed. Then return here – we need to talk. Good night you two. Tomorrow come here after you've bathed and dressed, and Judy's done her hair, even if it takes till lunchtime!" he said with a grin, " We'll have breakfast after which we can discuss the current situation and where we go from here. Louis will join us."

We kissed them both and left. Jake took his instructions seriously. He marched us into our bedroom, before going outside and letting us get ready for bed. It felt strange putting nightclothes on again. When we called him in, he had made us a drink of warm chocolate and he sat with us while we drank it. Then he tucked us into the bed, before walking to the door, switching off the light and wishing us good night. The last thing we heard before falling asleep was the outer door closing.

CHAPTER 16

Our New Role

Next morning, we were awakened by Jake bringing in a tray with a pot of tea, two cups and saucers, milk jug, sugar bowl and three teaspoons. We sat up, looking somewhat dishevelled and disarrayed. He looked at us and grinned. "I guess you didn't go to sleep immediately then!" he commented. We blushed and looked shy – which was odd considering the circumstances under which we had previously existed. He poured out two cups of tea and sat on the edge of the bed as we drank it.

"I took the tray from the servant," he explained, "because I want to explain something to you both before you meet your parents."

"Okay," I said, "Go on, we're listening."

He looked a little surprised.

"My goodness, you've changed over the last few days," he said. "The Mark and Judy I knew were demure and reticent. I never thought that was the real you. Now I know it wasn't."

"We were slaves, Jake," Judy explained. "The real us was beaten out of us and we didn't dare show it. Things are different now and we can be ourselves."

"I'm glad you realize that, because it's why you met the reception you experienced yesterday. It's also why your parents changed their minds. You were to remain their slaves and secretaries for twelve months and then be sent back into captivity and replaced, but you did what I told you to do. You made Matthew love you and want to keep you, but as free spirits not as chained and caged parrots. What you did and said to the VP yesterday, Mark, both surprised and pleased him. That's what he wants from you. He learnt to value your judgements at St Michael's; he saw how you could respond to threat and pressure yesterday. He will expect you to carry on in the same way. Call him Father and Monica, Mother. Be open with them, and, as I told you before, never lie to them. And you'll be fine."

"Why won't they tell us the truth about what happened to us in the hospital?" Judy asked.

"That's because of how close they came to losing you both through his and my error. It's not something they want to think about or speak about. They still don't know whether there was any permanent damage done to you. You will all find that out when you go back for the follow up visit in a month's time. Meanwhile, you have to rest and recuperate. My advice is that you should be nice to the staff and try to win them over. Just remember they're afraid of you – and you'll be okay."

He stood up and spoke briskly in his familiar way.

"Now, get up, both of you, get your arses into the bathroom and get ready for breakfast. It doesn't do to keep a President and his wife hungry waiting for you to get dressed and for Judy to fix her hair!" He smiled and moved to leave us.

"Yes, Daddy," Judy said.

"I've told you before not to call me that," Jake said.

Judy grinned mischievously, "You're just like our Daddy. Do you want to come in and bath us?!"

Jake laughed, "Get along with you, you little hussy, before I put you over my knee and spank you."

Judy stuck her tongue out at him and ran into the bathroom, leaving Jake laughing again. I followed Judy into the bathroom and told her, "Be careful, Judy, you can push Jake too far, you know." She just laughed and splashed water at me. Half an hour later, we rejoined Jake in the living room and the three of us left to join our parents for breakfast.

After breakfast, we gathered in the presidential living room. Father telephoned the receptionists' desk, telling them that neither he nor his wife were available that day. They would not accept any phone calls and receive no visitors. He added, that if the Vice President should come with a letter addressed to him, it should be received and brought up later. "However, determined he is to see me," he concluded, "the answer is, 'NO'". Then he began to give us a potted history of Austrasia. We knew much of it already because we had attended a conference at the International Briefing Centre at Farnham Castle before we left England for Austrasia. That had included hour long lectures on its history and geography. This was subtly different. The Farnham lecture had been impersonal, almost clinical and very scholarly. It was scrupulously fair and lacking in any human interest. It was lifeless, like so many school history lessons. This lecture was full of life and very personal. We learnt more than he told us, because he conveyed their love of their country as well as their dismay at how things had turned out – especially the inter-tribal civil war that had wracked the country ten years before, a civil war in which both men had fought on the Government of the day's side. Former President Igbokwe had been the Army's commander in chief during the war and took power immediately after it.

I asked why President Igbokwe was deposed and killed. Father explained that he mishandled the economy, permitting corruption to flourish among his ministers and handing over too much control of the economy to western multi-national companies – especially mining companies, which controlled the gold, silver, copper and coal mines where many of our fellow countrymen were now enslaved.

"I did not want Frederick Igbokwe killed," Father said, "But Josiah went behind my back and issued a secret order to that effect. He had a special grudge against him."

"You should sack him, Father, and replace him with Mother," Judy said.

"If only I dared," Father replied ruefully. "He's my enemy, but I believe in keeping my enemies close to me where I can see them."

"Not if it's a venomous snake," I commented. "You can watch them, but make sure there's a thick sheet of glass between you and them."

Father looked surprised. "Why do you say that Mark?"

"Because the man is a snake and a very dangerous one."

He asked how I knew, and I explained I recognised the type because I'd experienced something similar at university. He agreed with my description and said he needed hard evidence before he could act.

"Father, tomorrow, before people come into the cabinet, have each one searched for weapons. Order any weapons to be surrendered at Reception. Josiah will not hand his revolver in and will try to bring it into the room. That's all the evidence you'll need."

"Make sure there's an armed guard outside the door, covering the person doing the search," Judy added.

"I'll do that," he agreed, thanking us for our suggestions.

That brought him on to the reason why we were there. He explained the fissures in the cabinet and how attempts had been made to isolate him, but also to get him blamed for decisions which were never agreed but sent out under his name, like the one permitting any slave to be interfered with in any way by any citizen if they felt so inclined without the slave having any recourse to law.

"That's why we were assaulted in Casa Isabella," Judy added, "when we were separated and dragged off to be gang-raped and beaten. At the end Mark was triple raped simultaneously by two men and a woman. The woman sucked his cock, and the two men thrust their cocks repeatedly into his mouth and arse until he was physically sick and drained. It's why the two women you imprisoned did what they did to us and why those other two tried to kill us."

"What do you want me to do to them?"

"It's not what you should do, Father. I know what I want to do. I want to place my hands around the older woman's neck and strangle her."

"Judy!" a shocked Monica said, "That's scarcely Christian! Aren't you supposed to forgive?"

Judy turned around to look at our mother.

"You do not know what you're asking, Mummy," she said sadly. "Should we forgive those who caused the war which destroyed our country and our families? We know they're all dead because they were waiting for us to join them in Heaven when we were in the helicopter. We saw them and were running towards them when we were dragged back. In the end we forgave those who first harassed and stoned us and then stripped us naked, carried us tied to poles by our feet and hands through the town where we taught for two years, dumped us on the town hall steps and watched us scream in agony as we were branded. We have forgiven those who transported our naked and chained bodies across the country, those who processed us, those who made us wrestle in the mud and rape each other, those who assaulted us that day, those who put us on the machines every day making us into simply another farm animal, those who flogged us as an example and the ones who assaulted and imprisoned us illegally in the cellar. We cannot go on forgiving. Those who tried to kill us are beyond forgiveness from us – because they still want to kill us and will try to do so if they can. Why should we forgive them? Tell me! Would you do so in our place?" Then she burst into tears.

Monica took Judy into her arms to comfort her, wiping her tears with her handkerchief before cradling her head on her shoulder. "There, there, darling, of course we understand. You've been through so much – no one can ask more of you."

"But I'm afraid we're going to," Father said. "We need your help to break a conspiracy that we believe is brewing against us. Also, when you're both fit enough to travel and before you become too pregnant to travel, Judy, we need you to visit all the places where state slaves work …"

"Except St Michaels Island", I interrupted.

"Except St Michael's Island," he agreed, "we want you to report on the conditions there and suggest any improvements which need to be made. Be aware though, we will have to take things slowly and carefully. It takes a lot longer to repair damage than it does to cause it."

He then went on to issue our instructions and we listened carefully. Judy recovered her composure and listened as well. After he'd finished, she looked at him in the cheeky and pert fashion she used to keep for me.

"Daddy, you said that we had to do these visits before I got too pregnant, has Jake (or Louis) been telling you things about us as we say, 'out of school'?"

Both men laughed.

"We're both sure you have…, if you know what I mean?" Father said, still laughing.

"British girls asked that question by their dads used to say, 'That's for me to know and you to worry about!' Our comment, Father," I said, "is that's for us two to know, and for you three to wonder about!"

They all laughed, and we began, once again, to talk about other things until lunch was served.

After lunch we became more official as Father, presidential now, went through the next day's Cabinet agenda with us and gave us a list of cabinet members and their responsibilities together with a seating plan, explaining the places were fixed and unalterable. Before we could break up, however, there was one final incident that pointed towards the dangers ahead. A messenger brought in a sealed envelope which, on opening, turned out to be a letter of complaint demanding we should be stripped of clothing, rechained and sent back to an establishment set aside for foreign slaves. It was obviously prepared and signed by the Vice President and it was counter signed by five other ministers. He read it grimly and passed it to us. "Note the names", he said. "Those are our enemies." We ticked the names off on our place list and handed the note back.

"I'll deal with this tomorrow," he said. "Meanwhile, you two go and rest and forget about this rubbish – it will come to nothing. We'll see you for dinner at seven." We thanked them and left with Jake – us to go and lie down and Jake to do whatever he had to do.

Judy swiftly fell asleep, but I couldn't. My mind was too alive with thoughts of what I'd heard and seen over the previous thirty hours. Eventually, I got up and looked at my Cabinet file. I read the standing orders and looked at the seating plan – and a thought came to me. It grew and grew until I felt I had to share it. I left our room, leaving a note for Judy in case she woke up and wondered where I was. I went back to Father's office and knocked on the door before walking in. He looked up, intending to rebuke me for intruding, saw who it was, and gently rebuked me for being disobedient instead. I said I was sorry, but I couldn't sleep because of what I'd learned. I told him I had developed a plan that could resolve the issues which had arisen. He looked at me, saw I was holding my Cabinet file, smiled, and put the papers he was reading to one side.

"You're a live wire, aren't you, Mark? I see I'm going to have to watch you, or you'll be after my job."

"No chance, Father. I've been a President and a Secretary. I'm a much better Secretary than a President. You're the other way around. Together we're unbeatable."

"That's a bold statement, Son. What's your plan?"

I explained. He listened. He said he liked it but would like to get Louis' opinion. He summoned him, and, ten minutes later he appeared. Father explained that I'd come in with what seemed to be a workable plan – and he wanted me to run it past him.

Given the go ahead, I drew out my seating plan – which showed the six signatories of the letter grouped around the end of the table, with three to the left of the Vice President, one unticked on his immediate right and then the other two. I asked about the seventh person. Father said he was the VP's brother-in-law. I then asked about where the Palace Guard and the Palace staff came from and who appointed the latter. The answer was, as I expected, the VP. It also transpired that the VP had laid out the seating plan.

"Everything is in place for a coup attempt against you, Father. I think we are to be the trigger point and tomorrow's cabinet meeting the occasion. So, I propose the following actions:

1. We postpone the Cabinet meeting for twenty-four hours 'for operational reasons.'

2. General Ngangi invites two hundred officers and men from his former regiment to come for a festive dinner at the Austrasian White House tomorrow evening. They should be joined by the Palace Guard – and we should ensure each guardsman is made paralytically drunk. Once they are, they should be stripped of their uniforms, piled into the coaches which brought your men here and carried out to the far south of the country and dumped there. Your men will

switch their uniform jackets for Palace Guard jackets and assume their duties. Subsequently you will, as Commander in Chief confirm and make permanent the new status of your regiment, Father.

3. Judy and I will undertake to create new Cabinet Standing Orders, and you, Father, will create a Government Secretariat under our control, with, say three trusted people working under us, give us an office and order that all papers for the cabinet, all intended press releases and all government decrees and cabinet papers have to be passed through our office after consultation between you, us and the originator.

4. The cabinet meeting will be short and will simply confirm our appointment and duties and authorise our redrafting of the standing orders. It will then adjourn until next Tuesday when those orders will be approved. The next full Cabinet will be the following week.

5. We will look at the seating plan and rejig it in order to break up the VP's block.

6. Father, you will appoint Jake as Minister of Justice.

7. Jake, in your new role, you will prepare arrest warrants for high treason against the VP and an open one for whoever accompanies him.

8. In a moment I am going to call our receptionist and tell her that you have ordered the VP and a friend to come to a meeting with you in 2 hours' time.

Finally, 9. You will ensure that what happens when the VP arrives is recorded."

"You've obviously been thinking very hard young man when you were supposed to be sleeping! What is your intention?"

"To force a premature attempted coup, Jake."

"I see – then we can get rid of the whole awkward squad."

"Not only that, but Father here can actually become the President, rather than the figurehead he has been."

They looked at each other and, after a moment, nodded.

"Okay, Son, what do you want me to say to him?"

"Nothing, Father. You'll be having an urgent meeting with the Minister for Internal Security, checking that the country's tea and cakes service is still acting efficiently!"

At this, they both laughed uproariously.

"And who's going to break this unwelcome news to him, Son?"

"Judy and I are, Father. And we are going to goad him and his friend into making incriminating comments in Austrasian which you are going to record, and Jake is going to use as a reason for arresting them both. After which you are going to appoint Mother as acting VP, to be confirmed later, and Jake's friend Ade, who I suspect is no more a soldier called Ade than Jake was a soldier called Jake, to replace the missing minister."

"You have really thought this through Mark. I thought I'd got to know and understand you – but I appear to have massively underestimated you! Does Judy know what you've planned?"

"No, I don't," the female voice came unexpectedly from the now-open door. We were too busy talking to notice her come in. "My beloved husband let me go to sleep, then got up and left me a note. I hope Dad gave you a good telling off."

"He put me over his knee and spanked me," I said, laughing.

"So he should!" she replied, also laughing.

"I wish I had," he confessed – and we all laughed.

At this point, Mother came in to ask what all the laughter was about and what we were doing up when we should be resting. Father told me to go over it all again for the sake of the two women, after which I picked up the phone and contacted the receptionist, having asked her name.

"Marta, this is Mark, the President's Secretary. He has asked me to ask you to ring the VP and instruct him to report to the President's office at 17.30 hours for an urgent discussion. Tell him he can bring a friend."

"And if he says he's too busy?"

"Advise him to put his affairs in order, because, if he's not here by 17.45, a military detachment will be at his door by 18.30 to arrest him for high treason, and he'll face a tribunal before 20.00 hours and a firing squad before midnight."

"He can't do that!"

"Marta, the President can declare a State of Emergency and, under such a decree, his will and the law become the same thing. As a result, he has the power of life and death over every citizen, however high they may be. We are ready to declare a state of emergency at 17.50 if the VP isn't here by then."

The President took the phone.

"You heard him Marta. Get on with it."

We looked over the seating plan and, with the President's approval and the benefit of his knowledge, rejigged it. Judy suggested printing named place cards so they would all know where to sit, and our parents divided their forces – Mother to go down to the kitchen to break the bad news of the sudden celebration dinner as gently as possible and Father to send out the e-mails to cabinet members of the changes to their scheduled meetings and, at his suggestion, to invite the leaders of his supporters to meet him and us next day. He also issued a decree announcing Jake's appointment with immediate effect. His final job was to send e-mails to his regiment summoning them to Freetown for the following evening and then to set up the recorder which would start recording automatically at 17.30. I suggested to Jake that his second duty as the new minister was to approve and organise the fitting of bugs to phone lines in the homes of the seven members during the cabinet meeting. Then we waited. Jake came back to say he had everything in hand. I asked him to stand by the door when the VP came in. He was to be prepared to shoot the VP if he tried to draw his gun and to disarm him if he didn't. He should be prepared to do the same for both visitors. He agreed and went out to prepare himself.

Judy and I went through what we were going to say to the VP if he came.

"I only wish we had another soldier we can trust," I said.

"We have," Judy said." "We have Dad." She went out, spoke to him and he said he would come in as soon as he heard on the monitor (always set up in the cabinet office) that he was needed to give Jake armed back up. We continued to wait. 17.30 came and went. So did 17.45. It was at 17.49 precisely Marta rang through to say the VP and his brother-in-law had arrived. I told her to send them up.

Their entry was dramatic. The study door was thrown open and the VP stormed in, followed by his sidekick.

"What the Hell do you think you're doing, Matthew to send me such a message?" he began and stopped when he saw it wasn't the President but Judy and I who were there.

"I've come here to see the President, not a couple of slaves," he growled, "Where is the bastard?"

"I'm afraid he has been called away to another meeting; an urgent one with the Minister of Internal Security. He asked us to deal with you. Sit down, Josiah. You're late."

"You filthy little swine," he began, and his hand dropped to the gun at his side.

"I wouldn't touch that if I were you," Jake said. "My gun is in my hand, fully loaded and is pointed at you. I will shoot you if you try to pull out that gun, and that goes for your brother-in-law too."

The VP turned around and saw that the threat was real. He moved his hand away.

"Good, now pull the gun out slowly with the barrel pointing down, drop it on the floor and kick it over here; and you," speaking to the VP's brother-in-law. They both sullenly obeyed. Jake picked the guns up and remained with his gun in his hand.

"That's better," I said. "Now sit down."

"I prefer to stand."

"You were told to sit," Jake said. "Do it or you'll lie down permanently." He knocked off the safety catch with a loud click. The VP sat down.

"What do you want?" he said sullenly.

"We want to know what you mean by this letter," Judy said. "It hasn't been given to the President because it was incorrectly addressed. It should have been addressed to us, for the attention of the President. Accordingly, technically it is undeliverable and won't therefore be delivered. What do you mean by it?"

"That you're a couple of jumped up, dirty, thieving slaves, and the sooner you're disposed of the better."

"How do you intend to go about that?"

"We have our ways. Certainly you'll both regret ever having engineered this meeting."

"Is that so? Presumably you planned to bring this issue up tomorrow," I said.

He didn't answer. Instead, he spoke to his brother- in-law in the local language.

"Micah, call your friend and offer him ten thousand dollars to kill these two vermin in the next two days."

"Sure, Josiah. I'll do it now." He began to get up.

"Stay where you are, you murdering swine!" The President's voice was powerful with anger.

"Minister of Justice, you heard the treasonous order. Do you have the warrants for their arrest?"

"Yes, Mr President."

"Carry out your duty then."

Five minutes later it was done. On a previously agreed signal two of the security police entered the room, arrested and handcuffed the two men and took them away. Ten minutes later, the new Minister of Justice declared a state of emergency. One hour later he placed an order for the execution of the two men before the President, who signed it. The two men were taken to the firing range outside the city and, at 23.00 precisely, shot by a firing squad commanded by Jake and watched by the President. Their bodies were removed and buried in an unmarked and unrecorded grave. The counter coup had begun.

Next day saw part two of the operation take place. The various loyal ministers invited by the President all turned up at 10am. Father and Mother introduced us and explained what our role was to be. We were invited to speak and explained the nature and reason for the changes we proposed to introduce next day and outlined why three new ministers were being appointed, including a new Vice President. They were both surprised and pleased. All had been afraid of Josiah Ndenge. After that the meeting was transformed into a cocktail party so we could meet and talk to ministers individually, since Father had proclaimed to anyone who would listen that "we could charm the birds from the trees." Well, we did our best to live up to our billing. The 'critics' (the three in the White House) seemed content. In the late afternoon, four coaches full of troops arrived from the north. A huge marquee had been erected in the grounds, and, after we had explained fully to the newcomers what we wanted them to do, the resultant party went off with a bang. Much alcohol was consumed by all the palace guards and, apparently, by their guests. But you can't always believe your eyes, can you? We sat with our parents, presiding benignly over the apparent chaos below. Eventually, when some of the palace guards seemed more resistant to the effects of booze than the others, we assisted them with carefully selected strong sedatives. Eventually, the Palace Guards each succumbed to the combined effect of drink and drugs. They were stripped of their uniforms and carried away by two soldiers each, to be loaded onto the coaches. As each coach was fully loaded, it set off on its night journey, each to a different area of the far south, where they dropped their unwitting passengers, a few at a time, in the ditches beside the road, and left them to recover in due course. That night a new guards' regiment took control, and no one noticed the difference.

In the morning, the cabinet met in its new seating plan, and with three new ministers. Monica combined her old role with the new. We were introduced and our role and some of the new rules explained. The five remaining rebel ministers complained and asked where the former VP and his in law were. We could honestly say we didn't know. Our appointment and that of the new ministers was confirmed, as was the definition of our role and the programme we had outlined, by twenty votes to five each time. Finally, Father adjourned the meeting for a week so the new rules for procedure and the new standing orders could be drafted for approval at that subsequent meeting. Stage two was over. Incidentally, we both began to earn a salary from that point.

After the cabinet members left, we five plotters met for lunch and a bottle of champagne (more accurately Austrasian sparkling wine). We toasted our success and Father said he was glad we were on his side and not on that of the former VP.

Jake added, "If they were, Matthew, we three would be dead, rather than the other two!"

We kept our thoughts on the subject to ourselves.

CHAPTER 17

The Failed Coup

There are three stories of this event. I will describe them each in turn.

The Conspirators' tale

Their story began on the night of the counter coup. Quite suddenly, they realized that their leader and deputy leader had both disappeared. They planned to raise it at the cabinet meeting next day. However, it was postponed for no good reason, as they saw it. They contacted each other and tried to piece together the events of the previous day. They called each other frantically, as well as the unanswered numbers of their leader and deputy leader. Neither turned up at the Cabinet meeting. No explanation was given, and, because of their separation, which came as a surprise to them, they were unable to communicate with each other at the meeting. After the meeting, they heard the homes of the two missing members of their group had been raided and searched by the security police. They also heard that various members of the two families had been arrested. All this, and their anxious debates about the events as they learnt about them, were discussed in lengthy telephone calls. They realized they were being watched, but plainly did not realize we were also bugging their calls.

After three days had passed without any information about their leaders or any attempt to contact them by the two individuals concerned, they concluded they were dead. They could not understand how or why. All they knew was the two of them had responded to a Presidential demand for a meeting and had not been seen or heard of since. The general opinion was that there had to have been an accident because "the General was too stupid to realize how close we were to overthrowing him and his wretched wife." That statement, incidentally, infuriated all of us because of its sheer arrogance. They chose a new leader and decided to continue with the plan, but based around the next meeting of the cabinet, and using the Presidential Guard and staff, as planned. The problem was their original sources seemed to have dried up and all attempts to contact the Guard failed. Puzzled, they fell back on plan B; using the Palace staff. They tried to contact the Butler, but without success, because we had given him leave to go home for a month, together with many of the staff and had recruited local replacements on a temporary basis. After what we learned we made all the changes, including a new butler, permanent.

Finally, in desperation, they decided to contact us; in an attempt to win us over to their side. We were interviewed (I'll describe the interview later). As a result, they concluded we could not be trusted. In any case, they finally dismissed the idea as preposterous. How could we be used by them when our ultimate fate, if they succeeded, was to be hanged, burnt alive or shot? They decided the only option was the desperate one of taking their guns with them to the next cabinet meeting and shooting us all down in cold blood there. They confirmed the plan on the Monday evening.

The Guardsman's tale

The former Palace Guard, geared up for an assault on the evening after the Cabinet meeting, did not know what hit them. They thought it wholly appropriate that they should drink the President's wine and eat his food, the night before they killed him and his friends. They had a great time and didn't mind falling on the tables, drunk. They knew the Russians used to do that. They thought the example a good one to copy. None of them knew what happened later. Therefore, it came as a shock when they found themselves stripped to their underpants and lying in a ditch beside a lonely road somewhere deep in the countryside. As they recovered, so they gathered into small groups, and tried to make their way back to civilisation, following the main road in both directions. Sadly most of them had little knowledge of the countryside in that part of Austrasia, and, one by one, they died. I only know of one, a southerner, who was strong enough and knowledgeable enough to make his way to his native village and eventually back to Freetown. He arrived after the coup had been attempted, failed, and the plotters executed. There was no way back to favour for him and so he turned to begging.

Several years later, we met him on the street near the Palace. We were walking with our three children and passed him. He knew who we were and called out to us. I saw him and walked over to him.

"Why are you here?" I asked.

"I'm an ex-soldier," he replied.

"Oh yes! Which regiment?"

"The old Palace Guard. I'm the only survivor."

I stopped and asked him to tell me his story. Judy and the children became impatient and called me to come, but I told them who this man was, and they came over to listen. I asked his age. He told me he was fifty; or, at least, he thought he was. I wrote down his name in a notebook I carried and details of his military service and asked the Minister of Defence to arrange a pension for him, signing it Marcus Ngangi. I tore the page out, gave it to him, and told him what to do. Later, I went to the Ministry where I was told he'd come and they'd agreed to pay him a monthly pension. I was pleased we could help one of the accidental victims of the intended coup at least.

Our Tale

For us, it was a waiting game. The chips were down. The first moves had been made and clearly won by us. The chess pieces and board of the plot had been rearranged. The odds had been reversed. Now they were overwhelmingly in our favour. The plotters would have been advised to desist and change sides. They dared not do that and so we expected some attempt. We continually monitored their phones. Therefore, we knew as much about their plot as they did. I was surprised, however, when one of them came to our office. He asked to speak to us. He tried to impress on us that our Father was a vicious tyrant who would wreck the country and, once we were no longer of any use to him, destroy us and our people. I smiled and said we did not share his analysis. Our experience of him and his wife was very different. The ones who wanted to destroy us were the Vice President and his friends, including himself. He persisted, asking us if we would support him and his friends if they decided to take action to save the country. We said a firm, 'No'.

The day before the second cabinet meeting I sent an e-mail to all cabinet members that handguns should not be brought to the Palace, and that, if they were, they should be handed in at Reception. We gave Marta a holiday and replaced her with a girl soldier, out of uniform. We provided her with a warning button, and each time a cabinet member refused to hand in his handgun, she pressed it. One by one, they were stopped by armed guards at the entrance of the cabinet room, body searched, disarmed, and arrested. We arrested all five plotters. The meeting unanimously accepted the new appointments and the new standing orders, as well as the new arrangements as described in the previous meeting. They also voted through the President's nominations of five new cabinet members, to replace those under arrest. Then the meeting was adjourned until the following week and I asked for agenda items for the next cabinet meeting to be submitted to the Secretariat before midnight on Saturday. The meeting also approved of the appointment of three additional members to make up the secretariat office.

Searches of the homes of the five plotters, carried out at the same time as their arrest, produced irrefutable evidence of their guilt, and, as a result, they were given a formal trial that afternoon and were executed by firing squad the same evening. Their bodies, too, were buried in unmarked graves.

Next day the five of us met to celebrate. I warned Father that the problem was not solved yet. We still had to deal with discontent in some areas, but I thought it might be a political rather than a military or legal problem, except for the vipers' nest on St Michael's island. I asked that the island should be effectively isolated until the evil there could be cauterised. I said it was the responsibility of Jake and the two of us. They should deal with the other areas but leave the Island to us. They agreed.

CHAPTER 18

The new Government

The day after we crushed the plot, our parents brought the axe down on us. "You've had enough excitement", they ruled. "The doctors ordered you to rest, and rest you will, if we have to lock you in your flat to make you do it." Jake joked that we could probably escape out of the window if they did that to us, but we told him that we were not that desperate or even ingenious enough to attempt it. He looked at us disbelievingly. We still had our meals with our parents and, after a day or two, I told them that they would have to find us something to do to keep us occupied that would not involve exercise, or we would die of boredom. They both laughed but promised to think of something.

Two days later, Father came to our flat, carrying seven boxes of financial documents. There seemed to be hundreds of them. He explained that they came from the seven executed plotters and represented their financial dealings since they came into government eighteen months before. In the case of Josiah Ndenge it was considerably longer than eighteen months since he had served in the Igbokwe Government. He asked us to audit them and give him as accurate an accounting as the documents permitted. We said we had never done anything like that before, but we would try. He promised he would ask the Government's Chief Accountant to make herself available to us if we needed any help, especially in regard to laying out the information and interpreting it. It was a very big job and proved to be a very difficult one, particularly as there was a lot of cross checking between the various accounts. It was a bit like doing seven different jigsaws with the pieces mixed up and no picture to guide us. In between working on these documents we also had to supervise the working of the secretariat office. We took that in turns, me doing the mornings and Judy doing the afternoons. With the troublemakers out of the way, the work of the cabinet became much simpler and Father began to be a President in fact as well as name and showed himself to be a good and determined one. Given firm leadership, the cabinet settled down, and began to develop clear policies aimed at ending the tensions between tribes and areas, developing agriculture and industry, improving communication infrastructure and ending unemployment. The areas which were untouched were education, still suffering from the forcible removal of so many foreign staff, and the slavery issue. Both seemed to be waiting for us. We did look at maps and begin to plot our journeys and visits for when it was possible for us to do so. For that first month, however, a "visit" involved going for a walk in the extensive Palace grounds. We knew (because we tried it) that if we ventured to the gate, the police officers or the soldiers on duty there would turn us back and tell our parents, who would, in turn, rebuke us (the verbal equivalent of being put across their knees and spanking us) all in our own interests of course. But we knew that. Suffice it to say we only tried it once. The next day, we were locked in our flat without breakfast all morning. The point was made! We did not do it again.

Slowly the picture we were seeking emerged as we uncovered evidence of a huge, interlinked, systematic and highly organised fraud. Once we began to pick up the trail, we were able to follow it, see how and where it was carried out and how the seven men were jointly involved. They were almost a joint stock company – but in a massively illegal enterprise. Eventually we were able to get to a point where we asked the Chief Accountant to join us. She spent an entire day with us, examining the documents and testing our conclusions. Finally she told us she agreed with us.

"I have to congratulate you both," she said. "This fraud would have defeated most of our investigators because they simply wouldn't have had enough time to tease out the strands and deal with the cut outs. I will, if you will permit, take these documents and your analysis of them, and write the report up in the correct manner, so you can sign it off and we can take it to the President. Remember, you've only done half the job. You've found out how much money was involved. We've still got to try to find it. That's a professional job – way beyond your knowledge and ability – but you have done the spadework without which the experts could not do what they have to do. That's what the President hoped and he will be very pleased with you both."

The investigators ultimately discovered that the seven men and their families had defrauded the nation of over twenty million dollars, most of it irretrievably lost as a result of the Northern War. In all, up to now, over thirty years later, they've only managed to claw back two million from investments made, and a few surviving and functioning foreign banks. They had also, by various means, acquired control of the mining industry. They had begun siphoning off profits from the mines, reducing their overheads by sacking the workers, thus saving their wages, replacing them with unpaid slaves (hence the L classification which the VP created) and employing family members to supervise them, who took their wages from selling gold, etc., on the market.

The main changes which Mark and Judy introduced to cabinet involved fines for the use of local languages at meetings, a clarification of the Secretary's role, and tightening of the procedure for the publication of decrees, cabinet decisions, cabinet minutes and public statements — written and oral.

Once we had got as far as we could on the fraud investigation, and, still subject to our parents' and doctors' restrictions, we turned our restless energies to the Constitution. We read through it together and drafted the changes we thought were necessary to prevent the abuses previously experienced from being repeated. Then we took them to our father. We walked into his office, where he was closeted with Jake and Monica. He looked up at the interruption, and his face softened as he saw who it was. He saw the sheets of paper in my hands and rolled his eyes theatrically.

"What have you two miscreants been up to now? Don't you ever just relax and read a novel?"

"There's no chance of that, Mr. President," Jake added. "Those two are always up to something. They're a couple of twenty -something years old teenagers!"

They all laughed. We grinned, we thought, mischievously. Father became serious.

"What <u>have</u> you been doing, children?"

"We've been reading the Constitution," Judy said.

"Heaven help us!" Jake exclaimed. "Is nothing sacred to you?"

"Not much!" I answered, to general laughter.

Father put his papers to one side.

"All right, you two. What have you got for us?"

The Civil War

to Concordia

2nd Corps
Jakes

R. Ngola

2nd Corps

Engadi

3rd Corps

R. Montoya

Cuet

Ngugi
Falls

1st Corps

3rd Corps
Okpawan

to
Freetown

Sta Isabella

Rebel Province of
Casa Isabella.

L. Ndugu

Port
Franklin

1st Corps
(Longinus)

⚑ Rebel Surrender
✕ Battle
→ Gov't Advance
⇒ Rebel Retreat

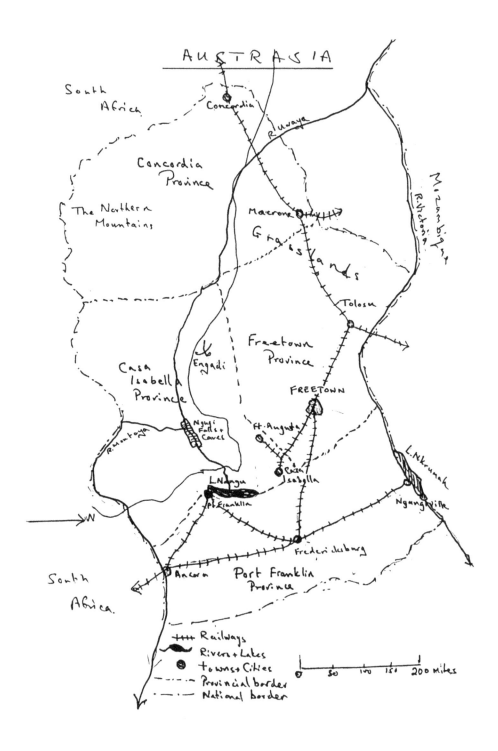

AUSTRASIA

South Africa

Concordia
Concordia Province

The Northern Mountains

R. Uvaya

Macrone

Grasslands

Mozambique R. Victoria

Tolosu

Engadi

Freetown Province

Casa Isabella Province

FREETOWN

Nguli Falls + Caves

R. Montoya

Ft. Augusta

Casa Isabella

L. Nangu

L. Nkrunah

Pt. Franklin

Ngangville

W

Fredericksburg

South Africa

Ancora

Port Franklin Province

┼┼┼┼ Railways
〰 Rivers + Lakes
◉ towns + Cities
–·– Provincial border
–··– National border

0   50   100   150   200 Miles

St. Michael's Island

→ N

Lake Ndwgu

Cliffs

trees

Cassava

Maize

Animal Grazing

Breeding

Barn

Fence

Path

Gate

Barracks

Landing Stage

250 200 150 100 50

Legend:

~~~ Contour Lines (feet)
* Guard Posts
☐ Buildings
— Farm Fence

Miles
0   ½   1   1½   2

Floor	
3rd	Slave Quarters + Milling Room
2nd	State bedrooms
1st	Offices
G.f.	Public Rooms
under ground	Punishment Area

Plan of the building (not to scale)

FORESTED

Casa Isabella Province

Lake Ndugu

Port Franklin

PORT FRANKLIN

AIRPORT

N

Port Franklin Province

Grasslands

R. Lister

R. Umoru

2nd Cataract

1st Cataract

St. Michael Island

Exitoca Landing

Trail to Ndugi Falls & Caves

Trail to Citadelle

0   25   50   75   100

miles

Lake Ndugu

Lake Ndugu

"We've come up with some changes we think are necessary to prevent what happened before from happening again. We've written them down."

He asked to see them – and read them out, one by one.

"The President of the Republic is the executive head of state and commander in chief of the armed forces. He or she is the final authority in all political and military matters. He or she appoints and dismisses ministers, initiates and approves all decrees and policy statements with the advice of the secretary or secretaries and Vice President, and the assistance of the appropriate minister(s). He or she gives his or her approval to all government statements before they are issued. He or she, on the advice and with the approval of the senior ministers and Vice President, can declare a state of emergency for one week, subject to any further declaration of emergency being confirmed by Cabinet. During a state of emergency, the President, advised by the Vice President and the senior ministers, has absolute power over all the organs of state and every citizen and resident. The President shall normally be elected for a five year period by a simple majority of the votes cast by Austrasian citizens aged over eighteen, all of whom are eligible to vote. He or she can be elected more than once."

He looked at us and asked who the senior ministers were. Judy told him they were defined in a later article. He looked at the other two and asked them what they thought. Neither saw any problem – subject to agreement on the senior ministers.

"Okay," father said, "provisionally approved."

He turned to the next article.

"The Vice President assists the President in the operation of his or her duties and may represent him or her if so requested by the

President. He or she may also be given specific responsibilities and can hold another cabinet office. He or she is the direct appointment of the President and is merely confirmed by the Cabinet."

"No problem," father said. "Next?"

I handed him the third sheet. He read it.

"The Cabinet shall consist of the President, Vice President, Permanent Secretary or secretaries, and the following ministers: Foreign Minister, Home Affairs Minister, Finance Minister, Minister of Defence, Minister of Internal Security, Minister of Trade and Industry and Justice Minister (the senior ministers) and such other ministers as the President shall determine are necessary. Their term of office and the details of their responsibilities shall be determined and laid down in a job description which shall be prepared for each minister by the secretary or secretaries, acting on the instruction of the President. Their activities and behaviour shall be determined by the Cabinet's Standing Orders. Cabinet Ministers shall present to the Accountant General a statement of their business holdings and assets and their tax returns at the end of each financial year. This rule also applies to all senior military officers, judges, senior civil servants, and (if they exist) local and national Party officials. Such individuals are expected, unless specifically permitted, in writing, by the President of the Republic, to own only one property or business."

"Hmm," father mused. "This is a mixed bag – but I think I know what you are trying to achieve, and I agree. I think you should have included agriculture among the senior ministries."

"It is," I said. "But we need to clarify it. Add 'including agriculture in brackets' after industry.

He did that – and they agreed to all three, obviously linked, clauses, with the observation that they needed to be properly and clearly laid out.

I handed him the final paper which was a definition of the nature, purpose and operation of the Secretaries and secretariat. He glanced at it, observing that it had already been approved by Cabinet, and asked if we had anything else. Judy said we hadn't.

"Good," he said. "Now, both of you go back and read something short. How about 'War and Peace'? I don't know about you two, but you exhaust me just trying to keep up with you."

Judy grinned.

"That's because you're so much older than us, Daddy."

He laughed, called her a minx, slapped her bottom lightly; and gently, but firmly, pushed us out of the office.

"Madam VP," he said, "under the new definition of your office I'm requiring you to assist me by ensuring these two reprobates stay away from Government papers for the rest of the day. Take them away and fill them with tea and cake until dinner time."

She laughed, saluted and said, "Certainly, Mr President!" before turning to us and adding, "Come on you two. We know when we're not wanted!"

As we left, we heard Father say to Jake, "Kids and wives, Louis. You can't live with them and you can't live without them. You're better off staying single!"

As we walked away, she said to us, "He doesn't mean it. You know he's as nervous about next week's appointment at the hospital as I'm sure you are." We told her we did know that and that we loved him as much as we loved her, and we knew they loved us.

That's how we spent our first two and a half months as the son and daughter of the President and Vice President of Austrasia.

CHAPTER 19

Return to the Hospital

The next week we consciously behaved like the children they kept telling us we were. We talked, we made love (often), walked in the grounds and played football with the off duty soldiers. We chatted up the house maids and kitchen maids and ate and drank with our parents. We talked about, in the words of *Alice in Wonderland*, 'shoes and sticks and sealing wax, and cabbages and kings.' We were happy – actually happy – for the first time in two years; and we felt safe in the loving care of our new parents. Yes, we were young adults in our twenties, but, looking back we realize that, after the bitter experience of slavery, we needed loving and cherishing. We didn't realize it then, but thinking back later, we realized that Matthew and Monica Ngangi did – and they gave us what we needed. We responded, especially in that week, in the way they wanted us to. Their great grief was that they could not have children of their own. We were their answer – and, for four years, we have been both adults and children for them. But we've actually been far more than that. We have been their sharp sword and shield. They both knew that a debt owed to them by us – for our lives – had been cancelled out, because we had undoubtedly saved theirs. Had we never met, we would have been dead on St Michael's Island and they would have died in the Palace in Freetown, just like President Igbokwe did, and Josiah Ndenge would now be President. The result would have been hell on earth for both slaves and ordinary citizens. People, seeing the changes we caused to be made in the Constitution and the Cabinet Standing `orders criticised us for creating a possible monster – a President with no limits on his power or time in office. We know that's possible, but we also know we stopped a real monster (not a potential one) in his tracks and eliminated him and his supporters from the scene. When we visited the north west later, the former VP's fellow tribesmen asked us if we regretted our roles in the destruction of their heroes. We told them we didn't. It was necessary for the good of the country as a whole, even if they suffered in consequence.

"In the end," I said, "you should be grateful to us. Josiah Ndenge would have eventually been overthrown in a bloody coup and your people would have been massacred by an angry nation for supporting his excesses and making them possible."

You, the reader, might feel that's not very Christian. I answer we're not Christians, but that, even if we were, what Ndenge had caused to happen to us could only be forgiven by a man with the stature of Jesus of Nazareth or God – and we did not and could not claim to be the equal of either. No human being can. My only regret is that I did not possess a gun and, therefore, could not shoot him myself after I heard him order our assassination. If that's not Christian and if I'm destined to go to Hell (if it exists) for it, then so be it. I am who I am, and it is what it is. In the words of Martin Luther, "Hier stehe ich, ich kann nicht anders; Gott hilft mir. (Here I stand, I can do no other; God help me.)"

The week passed eventually, and we returned to the University Teaching Hospital and the surgeon who had saved our lives. Once more we lay naked on a table, and once more hands roamed over our bodies. However, this time they were gentle and caring. He pressed our stomachs and midriffs and asked if we felt any pain or had seen any bleeding. We said we hadn't. He looked directly at Judy and asked if she was sure.

"Not even period blood?" he asked.

She said she hadn't seen any blood. He was surprised.

"When did you last see your period?" he asked.

"Not for at least three months," she answered.

He was surprised and he asked why. She told him what had been done to her over at St Michael's Island, and he understood. He nodded, but also looked meaningfully at Monica. Then he turned back to us and told us to roll onto our stomachs. He felt the right cheek of my behind, touching the brand mark. He moved over to Judy and did the same. He made us roll over again and repeated the action with the second mark. Then he told us to get dressed, while he spoke quietly to the attending nurse. She left the office, returning later with a small medical pack in her hand. When we were dressed he spoke to us.

"I noticed that neither of you have any body or facial hair, including pubic hair. That's unusual to say the least in people of your ages. What happened to you?"

We explained about the native doctor and his defoliating potion. His eyes showed his understanding.

"That explains everything," he said. "Did you notice anything about the after effects, other than the removal of the hair cells?"

We told him about how the liquid seemed to penetrate all our skin cells. He nodded and explained that it meant that our skins and our bodies would heal more quickly.

"That's one reason why you're still here to talk to me," he added.

He went on to explain that the brand marks had faded and were being closed up by the quickly growing skin. He told us he could quicken the process by performing two skin grafts on us. He explained that he would take some skin from the other side of our bums and graft it over the brand marks on our stomachs and bums. The skin would cover the brand mark and eventually both areas would return to how they were before. He looked at the four of us, told us he was prepared and able to do it, and asked if we agreed. We said, "yes" immediately. Our parents thought about it and said the same. The doctor then said that, if he was right about Judy, he needed to do it as soon as possible because it would be better not to operate on her too late. Father and I didn't understand, but Mother plainly did and said she agreed. Judy simply looked confused. They looked at the diary and it was agreed that we would come in as day patients the following week.

"Now young man," he said seriously, "what have you been doing to this young woman over the last four weeks while you were supposed to be resting. And you, young woman, what have you been doing with him?"

"That's for us to know and you to figure out," she replied grinning, while Father later said I merely looked embarrassed and actually blushed. At the time he remarked that now he understood why it had taken us so long to disentangle the plotters' finances. "What else do you think we had to do, Father?" I asked by way of an answer. The doctor smiled, and said, "I thought so," and you do too, don't you Mama?" Mother nodded. "I think I know," she said, "even if she (and they)" – looking at Father and me – "don't". The doctor looked at the now equally grinning nurse.

"Take Mama and young Judy to the WC. You know what to do. When you know, come back here with them."

The three women went out, two grinning broadly, and the third, Judy, merely looking confused.

Father and I looked at each other in a state of mystified confusion, which the doctor did nothing to dispel, except to say that we should not worry, there was nothing wrong with Judy. He began to talk to us about other things as we waited. The three returned about half an hour later. Monica looked happy, and Judy looked at me triumphantly. The nurse spoke.

"Judy has something she wants to tell you."

We looked at her, and I suddenly realized what she was about to say. I began to get up to go over to her, but Mother motioned to me to sit down.

"Let her tell you," she said. "Then you can kiss her!"

Judy looked at us and giggled. She made us wait.

"Darling," she said eventually when she decided she'd made us wait long enough, "you're going to be a daddy. Daddy, you're going to be a grandad."

We jumped to our feet and ran over to embrace her. Father picked her up and swung her around like a small child to express his joy. When he gave her back to me, I almost crushed her because I hugged her so tightly and kissed her a dozen times, before kneeling down, pulling up her bush shirt – we were wearing shorts and a top (so we could dress and undress easily and quickly) and kissed her stomach, telling her I was kissing her and our future child.

The doctor went to his fridge – used to keep certain drugs cool, but also used by him for liquids that were drugs of a different kind! He drew out a bottle of French champagne produced before the Northern War and obviously kept by him for a special occasion, found six glasses, asked Father to pull the cork, and emptied the bottle into the glasses. We drank in celebration, to our health and to the health of the baby.

We were about to leave after this, when Father, turned back.

"Doctor," he said, "we didn't come here to celebrate Judy's pregnancy. We came here to find out if there was any lasting damage done to them."

"No. Not that I can see. The native doctor's potion may have saved them and probably made it possible for Judy to conceive. I can't say that for sure, but it does have a strange and strong power. I've read about it and spoken to someone who claims to be able to make it, and he told me no one really knows what it does do."

He paused. "I think you're all very lucky, and especially these two. I'll see you next week."

Mother and Father turned to go. We didn't move. When they saw that, they turned back in surprise.

"What's the matter, son?" Father asked.

"Are we legally children still or are we legally adults? I don't know. We're your children now. That I do know, but we're confused, and we need to be clear. We want to ask the doctor something and we don't know whether we're allowed to?"

"You're our son and daughter, and, in our eyes, our children. But you're legally adults. What do you want to ask him?"

"We want him to be our doctor, to look after us if we're sick, to take Judy through her pregnancy and later on. We want him to be at the delivery of our child, and to be our family doctor thereafter. Will you allow it, Father?"

He smiled.

"Certainly," he said. "In fact, Doctor, we haven't appointed an official Presidential doctor, which is remiss of us. Will you accept an appointment as doctor to the Presidential family?"

He agreed. We left happily to break the news to Jake and the staff at the Palace. Later I asked Judy if she had known before we went to the hospital and she said she didn't know and had no reason to suspect it, in view of all that had happened to us before.

"It looks like we're back to normal physically as well as socially," I commented, and she agreed.

That night, the staff put on a celebration party. Next day, the press were invited to the palace and the President introduced us as his adopted children, full citizens of the Republic and his official secretaries. Having done that, he also announced we were the parents of his future grandchild. Asked when the baby was expected, Judy told them that we didn't know yet, but expected to do so in a month's time, when we would inform them. After that we had to pose as a family and as a couple for the photographers, knowing we would be on the front pages of the next day's newspapers and the lead story on the news. The press conference went on to discuss what the reporters referred to as the purge of the cabinet and we referred to as an attempted coup that was scotched.

That evening, as we sat after dinner chatting as we always did, Judy looked very pensive. I asked her if anything was wrong. She said that nothing was wrong but a thought had just occurred to her. Father looked at us quizzically.

"I don't like the sound of that," he began. "When either of you two have a thought it normally means yet more work for me! What is it this time?"

Judy grinned at him.

"Dad, you've told everyone I'm pregnant haven't you?"

"Yes, darling. Of course I have. Are you upset about it?"

"No, Dad. But it's made me think. There could be many slave girls in private houses who are also pregnant. What are you going to do about them?"

"I'm not going to adopt them! That's for sure! What do you want me to do about them?"

Judy and I looked at each other, wondering how to answer this, but it was Jake who answered. He pointed out that the child of a slave is a slave by definition. He said that could cause a problem. I asked him to explain. He did so.

"There are four types of slaves. There are dedicated breeding slaves. They will not, because of the nature of their work, produce pregnancies. Mining slaves are all male, so there can be no problem there. The remaining two groups comprise the largest number of slaves and that's where the problem lies. They're the slaves who work in shops and factories or in private homes. The birth may be welcome because it produces more workers eventually, or it may not be welcome because it immediately involves more cost for the owner. Either way we need a solution."

We talked about this for some time before eventually deciding to set up a small committee, chaired by Mother, to look into the issue and come up with solutions.

The committee met several times and took evidence from experts before coming up with proposals which were accepted by Cabinet three months later. This rules that the decision lay with the owner. If he or she wished to keep the child there was no problem. If, later, the owner wished to sell the mother, the child had to be sold with her if it was under the age of sixteen. If the owner did not want the child it had to be placed in an orphanage. Each province was ordered to build an orphanage in the provincial centre as a matter of urgency. Later that was extended to the children 'born' as a result of the Slave Breeding Programme, resulting in the construction of more orphanages. Most of the original five were completed within a year.

The following week we were taken back to the hospital, put under anaesthetic, and the last evidence of our former status as slaves was expunged from our bodies. We were ordered to return to the Palace and rest for an additional week before taking on our full duties. Judy was cautioned to remain careful. Mother was instructed to ensure Judy did as she was told. It was a very happy (if somewhat sore!) party that returned to the Palace. We behaved ourselves like good children should during the next week. At least we let our parents think we did! We spent the week closeted with Jake and a map, plotting our programme of visits to the mines and breeding centres of Austrasia. Meanwhile, Ade and Jake began, with Dad, to work through the catalogue of photos of the slaves, to find two individuals of the right age, body and hair colour and shape, to be our doubles. It was during this week, too, I, on behalf of us both, began to write this account of our lives before and in Austrasia.

Just before our rest time was up, Jake brought two naked slaves in to meet us and speak to us – male and female. The female had blond hair and blue eyes, the male had brown eyes and hair. They were in their twenties, branded and marked with a B. They looked enough like us to be taken for us. We asked their names. They were Colin and Chloe. We asked whether they had been or were in a relationship with each other. They were. We asked if they knew what we wanted them to do. They said they did. We made them repeat their instructions and warned them that they would meet a very hostile reaction when they arrived and urged them not to rush into the visit but to wait for instructions from Jake or us. Finally, we told them our names and enough about our history to convince anyone who doubted them. I asked Jake for a map to show them where the island was, and they told us they didn't need one because they had been at the new centre which we were supposed to visit with Father when we were attacked. Chloe said, "We've met you before." That surprised us and we asked when and where. She answered it was when we visited Casa Isabella with Jake and that they were part of the consignment of slaves on the lorry. We pretended that we remembered meeting them, thanked them for volunteering to be us, and wished them luck. "You're going to need it!" I concluded. Jake nodded his agreement and took them away to continue the briefing. Events were to prove that the timing of this meeting was both premature and unfortunate. I sent him a note, later, warning him he needed to get them defoliated by the native doctor, as we were. It came back, annotated that he knew and had it in hand.

CHAPTER 20

Our First Mine Visits

Once our period of renewed purdah was up, the three of us met for a morning conference with Dad, to organise our tour. He asked what we needed and wanted for our trip. I started the list with two items that surprised him.

"We need a letter of authorisation from you to permit us to leave the grounds of the Palace, and a second one addressed to whom it may concern confirming that we are your son and daughter and are calling to inspect the premises on your behalf. The recipient is to give us access to all staff, including slaves, and every area of his or her institution without let or hinderance."

"I understand the need for the second, son, but why the first? You know you can go in and out as freely as Mum and I can!"

"The guards at the gate must be instructed to ask us for the letter if they think we're trying to leave the Palace; despite any objection we may make. This is to stop our body doubles visiting the city and being photographed there while we're photographed somewhere else."

He nodded and commented that it was sensible.

Judy asked for the Governor of St Michaels Island Centre be recalled and assigned to our team. Dad was surprised at this – but she explained that there would almost certainly be violence in the near future at the island and we wanted to spare him that because he had been kind to us. We also felt his advice and experience might be useful to us when we examined the Slave Breeding Centres.

I asked for a doctor and nurse, an engineer and an accountant to be added to our team, to which Jake added a dozen soldiers. Additionally we requested twenty experienced mine supervisors to be put on standby, so we could always take two with us. Judy said we also needed a large helicopter or light aircraft to transport us and an ambulance or ambulances on standby wherever we visited, fully equipped as the one that carried us from the airport to the hospital was. Dad asked about the ambulances because every other request made sense immediately to him, but he wondered who the intended patients for the ambulance crews were. We said we didn't know, but we were aware that one or more slaves could need emergency treatment, or, at least, hospital treatment.

"Finally," I said, "we need the financial records for the last ten years from each of the mines. They had to be submitted to the National Government, but only you can release them, Dad."

"I wish I could, son. Sadly, I can't! Ndenge took them and said he dealt with them. I expect they're at his house, unless they were collected when the house was raided. I'll have a search made, and if we didn't collect them, I'll ask your Mum to order a second visit."

The papers we wanted arrived three days later. In the meantime we turned our attention to private slaves and prepared a policy statement to be sent out to all owners of such slaves. We also included one rule for all slaves. This is what we prepared and what was sent out.

"Slaves in private ownership are the legal property of their owners, but have the same legal status as children, with this caveat: the body of a slave, in its entirety, belongs totally to its owner, who, within reason, can do whatever he or she wishes with it, except that they may not cause the death of the slave by any action of neglect or deliberate harm thus making it illegal to inflict unreasonable physical punishment. Owners who break this rule will have the slave confiscated and the slave will be resold without any compensation being due to its previous owner. No physical punishment may be inflicted other than for a legitimate offence. The clothing of a slave indoors is entirely at the discretion of the owner. There is no stipulation except that the slave should wear a collar, and cuffs on its ankles and wrists, and be marked with the owner's brand, the letter P, and the slave's number, each of which should be clearly visible at all times.

"It is an offence for a slave to be in public naked. If found, the slave will be taken into custody and the owner summonsed. The owner will pay a fine of one hundred dollars for the offence plus the cost incurred for feeding and housing the slave while waiting for it to be collected by its owner. The slave is not to be punished for this offence as it is deemed to be entirely the responsibility of the owner. Any other offence committed by the slave will also cause a fine to be levied against the owner. The fine will be commensurate with the slave's crime. The owner will also be obliged to inform the courts, in writing, what punishment the owner has inflicted and what steps have been taken to prevent a further offence.

"The slave shall wear basic and minimal clothing that leaves clear vision of the slave's upper body – this applies to both male and female slaves. They should wear either a breechcloth or loincloth which should he held up by a light chain around the slave's waist secured by a lock, so the chain fits tightly. They should wear sandals and be cuffed (ankles and wrists) and collared. A disc should be permanently affixed to the collar giving the name and contact details of the owner. The slave's identity should be clearly displayed on the front and back of its body. If the slave's identity and the identity of the owner is not clearly displayed, the slave will be put up for sale in the market as will happen if a naked slave is not claimed within three days of being taken into custody.

"The public are reminded and warned that for anyone, not the owner of a slave, to interfere with or molest in any way a slave who is out in the street on its owner's business is a crime and will be punished with either a heavy fine or a term of imprisonment, depending on the nature of the offence, when such is reported by the slave's owner to the police.

"All new-born slaves must be registered within a week of being born. No slave under the age of sixteen is to be branded in any way, this includes any created by the breeding scheme. Junior slaves may have a tattoo placed on their right wrists showing the number allocated to their mothers (if known) but with the letter 'C' replacing her 'F'. Each breeding centre will be allocated a code consisting of one letter and two numbers. Where the mother is unknown, the tattoo will be the code which applies to the breeding centre where they were created. Any owner who brands a slave under the age of sixteen will have that and all their other slaves confiscated and sold off. They will also be penalised in line with any person convicted of causing grievous bodily harm to a non-slave child."

We were criticised frequently, and still are, by historians, for using the pronoun "it" of a slave, rather than "him or her". We had no hidden message here. We were simply trying to save space. Later, when we heard the complaints, we changed the wording accordingly.

We could not do a general visitation of privately held slaves, but Judy and I visited six households in Freetown who were slave owners and spoke with both the slaves and the owners. We presented them with our first draft of the above document and amended it following their comments. By and large, we were happy that the slaves were being treated well and saw no reason to interfere further.

In view of what we had already learnt, we decided to visit the twenty mining establishments before we began on the twenty-five slave breeding centres. We felt this was where slaves were most at risk, and we were concerned about the misuse of moneys earned from the sale of coal or ore. There are three mining areas in the Republic. Coal is mined in the mountains of the north, gold to the east of Lake Nduya, and silver and copper in the south in the plains around the town of Fredericksburg. We decided we would not take one area at a time, since the mine owners would warn their colleagues about us, and we wanted our visits to be unexpected and without warning. So we deliberately planned to criss-cross the country, visiting the different types of mine and mixing up our times and days of visiting. We wanted to finish this aspect of our work in ten weeks, doing two visits a week, but events outside the control of our team forced a change of plan.

It took three weeks for our team to assemble fully. When we were assembled we gathered them together for a day conference, to be opened by the President, but to be held in camera. He spoke to us briefly, explaining how important our role was, and introducing Judy, Jake and me as the leaders. He ended by wishing us luck and left us to get on with it. We explained in detail what we were looking for: the treatment of workers; both paid workers if there were any and slave workers; and what happened to the income from the mine.

We explained that each of them had a task to do:

The medical team were to examine every worker (and especially every slave worker) and compile reports, deal with injuries, and try to trace evidence of deaths and their causes. They were also to examine what first aid facilities were available on the site.;

The engineer was to examine the structure of the mine, and especially the safety aspect of the mining area;

The accountant was to secure the financial and production records of the mine and compare them with the records recovered from the VP's house and the "official" returns from the mine;

The two supervisors were to come with us to their allocated mine, including the cutting face. While we interviewed the workers, they were to look at the condition of the workers, the system of control, and what safety features were in play. They had to be ready to replace the existing supervisors immediately;

The soldiers were there to provide back up and security for the team.

We handed out the financial records we had for each mine and the matching official returns for each mine to the accountant and as many records as we held for each mine to everyone else. We had secured the official records relating to the allocation of work slaves to each mine – photographs and details *(like the ones I quoted earlier in the book which related to the six slaves taken from Concordia school in the early days)*. Finally, we gave the supervisors details of the mine they were going to take over and the dates of the intended visits.

Jake then spoke to them. He explained he was in charge of the security of the Party and of the itinerary which we were to follow. What we were going to do now, he said, was role play a visit, so we would be ready to move like a well-oiled team as soon as we arrived at a mine. "The first half hour is vital," he stressed. "Speed is essential to secure the area so that no cover up is possible."

The meeting then broke up into three assorted groups, each led by one of us. The discussion was serious and intense. When we each reported back, we found there was almost complete unanimity in our approach. We reconciled the slight disagreements between groups, and we felt we were good to go. I concluded the conference by thanking everyone, and revealing the name of our first mine, a gold mine near Casa Isabella, and the date – two days later. We set the take-off time at 07.30, in the Palace forecourt. For everyone, the next day was one of intensive study of their documents.

Two days later, everyone assembled on time, boarded the helicopter, and it took off for the one hundred and twenty mile journey to the Eldridge Gold Mine. We arrived at 08.30 and landed at the entrance to the mine, behind the fence and men guarding it. They turned in alarm, drew their weapons and ran towards us, to face a line of soldiers holding modern machine guns aimed at them. They halted. Jake ordered them to lay down their weapons and sit on the ground. They obeyed, and two men left the ranks and collected up the weapons. Jake ordered them to return to their posts, which they did, but covered by the troops as they did so. Meanwhile our team raced to their designated areas as arranged. I waited for the Manager to come to meet us, as he did, ten minutes after we landed. He was in a fury.

"Who the hell are you?" he demanded, "and what the hell do you think you're doing?"

"Before I tell you who we are, tell me who you are," I replied calmly.

"I run this place."

"I see. I am Marcus Ngangi, the President's son. The people who've just entered your mine and associated buildings are members of the President's Commission on the use of slave labour and the finances of the organisations employing them. My wife (the President's daughter) and the Minister of Justice and I are leading this group, and we are carrying out a snap inspection of your premises. Here is my letter of authority." I showed it to him. He glanced at it and pushed it back in my face.

"This mine does not belong to President Ngangi, but to Vice President Ndenge. You and your so-called Dad have no business here. He's President in name only anyway, Josiah Ndenge is the real President. We all know that. I'm going to my office to contact him so he can order that stupid President of your's to behave himself and call you off."

I turned around.

"Did you hear that Louis? He called the President of the Republic stupid and stated that he's not the President at all, but Josiah Ndenge is."

"I did, Mark. I gather he expects to phone the VP. Shall we let him? I suspect he'll get a shock."

We laughed and followed the irate manager into his office and watched him pick up the phone and dial a number. There was, of course, no answer - simply an unobtainable sound.

"Try the official number," Jake suggested. He did so, and a female voice answered.

"This is the office of the Vice President, Vice President Mrs Ngangi speaking. Who am I speaking to?"

He put the phone down hurriedly. "What the hell is going on?" he asked.

"The ex VP and his six friends tried to mount a coup. Sadly for them, we anticipated them, knocked away their supports, arrested and shot them all after a formal appearance before a judge. Their bodies are buried in unmarked graves. Yours is likely to follow them, unless you change your attitude."

"Louis is much too diplomatic," I said. "What he means is that you're under arrest for treason and removed from your post. Two soldiers entered the hut used as an office, seized the manager, cuffed his hands behind his back and bundled him off to the helicopter, where he was chained by the ankles and left under the armed supervision of one of our men.

We entered the mine, following the path taken by Judy. We walked for about half a mile before we came to the active face of the mine. We passed two naked slaves dragging a heavy truck of minerals, to which they were tethered like horses. We noted they had no protective clothing and both had new cuts and bruises from a whip. They were also so dirty it was impossible to tell whether they were white slaves or black workers. However, we knew what they were from the job they were doing. As we got nearer to the cutting area, the smell composed of human sweat, faeces, urine and blood grew overpowering. We both had to cover our mouths and noses with handkerchiefs, to be able to breath comfortably at all. At the face we saw naked men, without a stitch of clothing, protective or otherwise, helmetless, covered with dirt, their own filth, and running with sweat, often mingled with blood which was obviously the result of severe floggings from the whips of the two men who were supervising – or at least they were supposed to be supervising. The slaves were swinging pickaxes at the wall, liberally encouraged on by the lashing of the whips across their backs. Judy had hung back, waiting for us, afraid to enter that scene of violence. I looked around for Jake and saw that two of our men had followed us, Jake strode forward, drew his handgun and spoke in a loud commanding voice.

"Hold! Put down those whips and move back from those men."

"Bugger off!" one of them said.

Jake raised his hand and a machine gun clattered from behind us. The speaker looked surprised, suddenly grasped his belly with his hands, and fell forward onto his face, not to move again.

"Do you want the same treatment?" Jake demanded of the other man.

He shook his head.

"Fine, drop your whip, raise your hands above your head, and walk towards me slowly."

He did so, and one of the soldiers seized him as Jake pronounced his arrest, handcuffed him and led him off.

The workers dropped their pickaxes and turned around to see who their rescuers were.

"How many of you are slaves? And how many are paid workers?" I asked.

"We're all slaves," a man answered. "Who's asking?"

"I'll tell you later," I answered. "What we want you to do now is to make your way out of the mine. At the entrance of the mine there is a fully manned and equipped First Aid post. We want you to report there to be checked and treated, and then have a bath, before we talk to you individually."

"You're joking in bad taste, whoever you are. There's not a fucking First Aid post here – never has been. Ain't no baths, neither"

"There is First Aid for you all today, because we've created it. We'll also set up some sort of shower arrangement if there are no baths. Please do as we ask, because we're limited for time and we have much to do."

I don't think they believed us, and I understood why, but they did as we asked anyway, and I'm sure, were amazed when they saw I had told them the truth. We followed them out, leaving the corpse of the dead supervisor to be recovered later.

We found the Accountant in the main office, going through the filing cabinet, securing as many financial documents and letters as he could find. He said there seemed to be gaps – but he hoped he might be able to close a few before we left. We nodded, and left him to it, speaking instead to the engineer, who was deeply concerned about the structure of the mine. There had been insufficient time and money spent on maintenance, and no concern for the safety of the miners. Those were the issues he pinpointed. I nodded. I thought the same. "The mine's essentially unsafe," he said. "I've spoken to our two new supervisors and they agree. Production will stop, and they'll start on restoring the mine. There's no evidence of any safety equipment, except that worn by the two supervisors. We have already indented for personal safety equipment and modern steel pit props to be sent over."

We walked over to the medical unit. They were horrified by what they saw, and they told us no records had been taken of injuries. I looked around and found the slaves' spokesman.

"Come with me," I said to him. I called to Judy, and she found a hose pipe, attached it to a standpipe, and hosed him down. We found some soap and a cloth and let him wash himself in the cold water, before finding some dry towelling which he could use to dry himself. The slaves were similarly cleaned up while we took their spokesman into the manager's office and sat him down in the only chair. We sat on the table.

"You have probably guessed,' I began, "that we were slaves like you. We've been very lucky. The President discovered us, liked us, freed us, and adopted us. I'm Mark and this is Judy, my wife. We are here, at the President's request to investigate how you are all being treated and to see what we can do to improve things."

"You can free us, that's the only thing we would accept that would help us."

"Officially the President dare not do that – not yet anyway, but we can change things here so that you are effectively free workers, although, to the natives, you'll still look like slaves."

"What are you saying?"

"Mark is saying that you will become paid miners, wearing protective clothing and being paid a wage. You'll be given proper medical support, and, if we can find a way to do it, breaks from work and from the mine."

"What's in it for you?"

"Nothing," I said. "The one who was making money from you was the former Vice President. He is now dead and his cronies are dead as well. All seven men have been executed having been tried and found guilty of treason. Now we're bringing these mines back under Government control. But we do want something from you in return."

"What?"

"Information. We don't need to ask about how you've been treated – we've seen it for ourselves. We were both enslaved for nearly a year, so we know enough to understand what we've seen. We want to learn two things from you."

"Go on."

"First (a yes or no question) have there been any deaths or serious injuries among your number?"

"Yes. But I can't tell you who or how many."

"I have the list of names of those who were sent here. What I want you to do is take it and go around all the men who are here, ask them their names, and tick them off. Don't forget to tick your own."

"Okay."

"When you've done that. There will be a number of unticked names. If you can remember for sure what happened to them write D for died and I for injured. If you're not sure put a question mark. Will you start to do that now and give me the completed list before we leave this afternoon?"

He nodded, took the list and a pencil, and set off to fulfil his task. One of the supervisors heard us.

"He seems a good man," he said, "I'll make him works foreman."

"Good idea," I said. "You need to think of means of building these men's morale."

"Don't worry, Mark. We know. When you come next year, as I'm sure you will, you won't recognise this place. I promise you."

"You'd better be right, Don, because the President will probably come with us."

"No pressure, then!" he said, laughing, as we left the office.

Finally, we walked over to the First Aid Post. I spoke to the doctor, who told us they had referred six men to the local hospital. I asked if he had the names, and he said he'd given them to the man with the list. He said the helicopter had ferried them to the ambulances. I asked about the provision here, and he laughed. "What provision?" he asked. I nodded. "I've contacted the local hospital and arranged for a flying clinic to be established here and for it to be provisioned. We will try to get a barefoot medic here to man it." I sighed. "You know, David, I expected this to be bad; but it's much worse than we could possibly have imagined. I fear the other sites will be the same."

"They may even be worse," he replied.

I nodded. "Sadly, yes," I said, as I walked away. It was mid-day. We had been there two and a half hours and we were still uncovering atrocities. I walked over to where the men who had been treated, had washed and were sitting waiting to be fed. I saw Judy sitting apart on a rock, her head in her hands. I sat beside her, placing my hand around her waist and hugging her. She turned and looked at me and I saw the tears in her eyes.

"It's horrible," she said. "St Michael's Island was bad enough, but this – this is – I can't describe it – it's so brutal! It's unimaginable that anyone could do this to another human being – let alone so many."

"It's been done before, darling. Hitler did it to the Jews. Our ancestors did it to the Africans. In the United States before the Northern War many white Americans were still doing it to Black Americans."

"It doesn't make it right," she said. "Two wrongs don't make a right."

"I know, but this was not a simple matter of revenge. This was crude exploitation of one race by another in the interest of one man - Josiah Ndenge. We were supposed to be his latest victims. However, we are far from his only ones. Remember, this is only the first. We have nineteen more to go yet."

"Don't remind me."

"You don't have to come, darling. You know that. No one will blame you if you stay at the Palace . Certainly, our parents won't."

"Do you really expect me to let you face this alone, darling? Of course I'm coming with you! I will become hardened to the sights, believe me."

She stood up and wrapped herself around me. I pulled her close and let her head rest on my shoulder. Then I pulled her head around and kissed her. She kissed me back. "I do love you," she murmured. "That's all that matters now." "And I love you," I answered. I kissed her again. There was a cough behind us. We separated and turned around to see Jake standing there grinning and holding two hot bowls of soup. "I thought you might be hungry," he said, "and I'm obviously right, but really, children, there's no need to eat each other!" We laughed and took the bowls with thanks. He took two spoons from his pocket, rubbed them against his uniform trousers and passed them to us. We thanked him and cleaned the spoons with our handkerchiefs before eating a very warm African version of tomato soup. I asked Jake how we were progressing. He told me that they were feeding everyone at the moment, but he thought we were where we wanted to be at this time. The helicopter had refuelled and returned. Jake said that we had the problem of what to do with the guards who were presently being held in their barracks. We both thought about it for a moment, Finally, I suggested we dismissed the present guards and left our twelve men here to take their place until we could find a fresh garrison. Jake thought I was wrong. He suggested leaving just four men as a training force, and arming and training some of the slaves. With improved equipment and greater safety standards, the actual mining workforce could be reduced, and so the men could be spared. Judy and I agreed and left it to Jake to organise. We planned to spend the afternoon talking to the slaves, now the medics had finished with them.

We found some resentment among the slaves at what they rightly perceived to be our good fortune. We pointed out that we had not cheated and lied or manoeuvred to get where we were. It was providential in that we were now able to ameliorate their suffering. We listened to their stories and told them what we planned to do and reassured them that the men who had done this to them were now dead, and the ones here would probably follow them. The stories they told us confirmed what we thought and what we had seen. In this way, the afternoon passed quite quickly. One by one the teams packed up. Finally, we gathered together and addressed the workforce. I spoke to them.

"Julius Caesar once wrote of a military campaign he conducted, 'I came, I saw, I conquered.' We can say, 'we came, we saw, you conquered.' What has happened here is inexcusable and indescribable, although we will find words to describe it. The man who has done this to you. Indeed he has done it to fifteen thousand of us, including us two, is dead. We were saved by the President, who was already also his victim and destined to become a dead victim. He saved our lives, and we saved his and his wife's; and our own. Now we are set on saving your's. We have set in train changes that will alter your condition, your status and, with it, your lives. You will get back your pride in your work. This is now your mine. You are working for the Government and People of Austrasia; but also for yourselves. Officially you will still be slaves. However, actually, from this moment you are paid employees of the mining company and the government. From tomorrow, you are going to start making the mine safe. You will receive safety clothing and better equipment. The supervisors have been replaced; as has the manager. We will appoint a new manager, but for the moment, the two new supervisors, and Don, are in overall charge here. We have dismissed your guards. They are being replaced by four of our men, who are here to train a number of you to take their place. They will be suitably uniformed and equipped. That will be sorted out tomorrow. In a year's time we will be back, with the President probably, to see how you're getting on. We wish you luck. If you need anything more, remember, you only have to ask. If there's any delay, ring the Presidential Palace and ask for Mark or Judy. We will sort it for you as quickly as we can. Remember the old railway slogan – See it; Say it; Sorted. Au Revoir and Bonne Chance! See you later and Good luck."

They clapped and cheered as the team left them and made their way to the helicopter, which was loaded with boxes of documents gathered by the various teams. They waved to us as we took off – and we waved back. It was 17.30. We landed at the palace at 18.30, to be greeted by Dad and Mum. Before going to join them, we informed the team we would meet there again in two days' time for a visit to the Waranga Coal Mine in the Northern Mountains.

That visit, as we expected, set the pattern for our remaining visits. What we saw there was repeated time after time. It didn't matter where or what type of mine it was, we found the same abuses. The overall death toll continued to rise. By the time we had covered half the mines, and our progress was altered by events elsewhere which I will shortly describe, we counted forty-three deaths and sixty-seven serious injuries among the slaves, representing just under ten per cent of the work force at the ten mines. We counted eleven hundred named slaves working in these ten mines and one hundred and ten were no longer there. Subsequently, we were able to establish that, of the sixty-seven, only twenty- three returned to work, fourteen survived but were too seriously injured to resume work, and forty succumbed to their injuries – making a death toll of eighty-three. It was with grim faces that we were contemplating the second half, when the news from St Michael's Island hit us like a sledgehammer.

CHAPTER 21

Back to the Island

We had just completed our tenth inspection visit and dismissed our team until after the weekend.

The three of us were in the process of analysing our findings from the first ten visits. We were intending to begin the process of drafting a report on the mines when we were disturbed by an obviously distressed Guards officer. He was the one sent out to escort Chloe and Colin. Seeing his state, cold fear gripped my heart. Jake spoke to him.

"What's up, Eric?"

"Chloe and Colin have been kidnapped and taken to St Michael's Island," he answered.

Jake swore volubly. "When and how?" he asked sharply.

"They insisted on going to Casa Isabella."

"You should have stopped them," I said. "You know how dangerous it is, especially for them (pretending to be us)."

"I really tried, but they refused to listen to me. They would have gone on their own, so I decided it was best to go with them. I assumed the garrison would respect who they thought they were. I was wrong!"

"Don't worry about it, Eric, we would all have thought the same. What happened in Casa Isabella?" Judy asked at the same time as I demanded, "When did this happen?"

"We went there two days ago."

"And you only reported it today?" Jake interrupted angrily.

"The Garrison CO met us, with the appearance of correctness. I was taken to the officers' mess and entertained. They became his guests. From what happened, I believe all three of us were drugged. When I finally woke up around mid-afternoon yesterday, it took me a while to remember where I was: I had evidently been heavily sedated, presumably to make sure Chloe and Colin's capture was a fait accompli by the time I did.

I went to look for the kids. When I asked where they were, one of the garrison guards told me that my two charges had been taken, under escort, to St Michael's Island."

"What did you do?" Jake asked angrily.

"I went to the airport and found my pilot and helicopter. He flew me to the village opposite first thing this morning. I requisitioned a motor boat from one of the villagers there and made my way to the island. I told the boatowner I would probably need to get back in a hurry: he agreed to wait for me. I spoke to the guards' CO there and he told me the two kids had been brought in, stripped, chained, hooded and unconscious, and handed over to Maritza, who is now the Acting Governor. I was horrified and immediately made my way back to the helicopter to fly back here and report. I couldn't go in on my own to try and bring them back as I don't have the authority and I could hardly expect the guards there would support me. All this took time."

"How the hell did that bitch get to be Governor?" Judy asked incredulously. After a moment's pause she went on, "Oh my God, it's my fault! I asked for the Governor to join our team. I should have known she would take over."

"We should all have thought of this", I told her putting my arm around her consolingly.

"It's all right, Eric," Jake said, "we understand. Leave it to us, we'll take it from here."

"One more question before you go," I said. "What was the reaction of the CO and the garrison on the island."

"Shock and real anger. I was told they have already been ill-treated."

"Okay," Jake said. "It's a pity its's happened, but it is what it is, and we will have to sort it out before those two youngsters are seriously hurt."

After Eric had gone we discussed what he had told us. We were all absolutely furious that this had happened, especially as we had predicted, warned about and tried to guard against it. We realized immediately that we would have to postpone our inspection programme for at least a fortnight, so we sent messages to the team, explaining what had occurred and giving everyone involved two weeks leave while we dealt with the issue which had arisen.

We were all interested in Eric's observation of the attitude of the St Michael's Island garrison CO, Longinus. He and Jake were old friends, so we agreed that Jake should speak to him on the phone. It took two hours of continuous phoning, but eventually Jake got through and talked to him. Jake asked what had happened to the two youngsters who had been brought to the Island.

"Those who brought them said they were the President's adopted son and daughter. I looked closely at them, realized they looked very much like them but were in fact not them. I guessed you were involved in the deception, but didn't know how or why. Maritza was so determined on revenging herself on her perceived enemies, that she failed to see what I saw. She has been very pleased and smug believing that she now had the two of you completely under her power. She took total charge of the two youngsters, since she is now acting Governor and has the power to decide on the supervision of the slaves. She has always hated white people for some reason and has let her feelings get control of her actions. Until Chloe and Colin arrived, every slave had been beaten every other day as a result of her orders, but she appears almost to have lost interest in all the other slaves at the moment. The two youngsters are in the personal control of Maritza and Letizia, her sidekick. No one else is allowed to go anywhere near them. I think she's determined to kill these two, but very slowly, causing them as much agony as she possibly can."

Jake asked for details.

"They were immediately taken to the cellar. There they were subjected to electric shock treatment so severe that we could hear their screaming from the courtyard. That night they were made to work in the cassava field.

Next morning they were each tied to a tree, flogged and left there until this morning. Following that, they were thrown into separate cells in the cellar and permitted to sleep after being given the minimum of food and water needed to keep them alive. The two of them have to work in the maize field all night and are left in the cellar all day. I've been told tonight she plans to leave them on the milking and harvesting machines all night. I imagine tomorrow they're destined for another day on the tree or in the cellar followed by another night working in the fields."

"What do your men think about all this?" I asked.

"The men know she thinks they're the two of you. They are all absolutely appalled and exceedingly angry"

"And the other slaves," Judy asked. "They were rather resentful when the President took us away. What are their feelings?"

"Much the same. I think they share our feelings."

"Has no one objected?" I asked.

"I've tried – but she told me to stick to my job. 'You're responsible for the troops, I'm responsible for the slaves. It's very simple! Let's keep it that way. I won't tell you how to do your job and I sure as hell won't let you tell me what to do. I'm in overall command here not you and don't you ever forget it. Those two were responsible for the death of my lover (Josiah) and his brother-in-law.

Their blood calls for the blood of those two. I intend to let them have it – but very slowly and as drawn out and painful as I can make it. I intend those two murdering bastards to regret the day they were ever born. I want them to pray for death, before I permit them to die. If I have my way, they'll be burnt alive.'"

"Bloody bitches!" Jake exclaimed before asking him to take the "Macrone" to Port Franklin as soon as possible, requisition a flight on a military plane to Freetown, and report to us at the Palace sometime on Sunday afternoon. It was Thursday night, and we knew the "Macrone" sailed to the west every Friday night, arriving at Port Franklin around midday on Saturday and usually leaving again in the evening, so as to be back on the island during early Sunday afternoon .

We discussed what we had learned grimly, realizing that, had we travelled to the Island, trusting in the protection of the President's name, everything Longinus had described would have happened to us. We agreed we would have to send troops to the island and Maritza and her staff would have to be removed (either from the island or from life itself). We also decided the troops of the garrison were likely to support any action we took and this action had to be taken as soon as it was practically possible in order to preserve Chloe and Colin's lives. Jake told us that when he met with Longinus, they would plan the operation, and he would inform Dad what had happened. We left him to it and returned to the work on our interim report. A thought struck me, and I shared it with Judy.

"All this means Casa Isabella is a centre of rebel sentiment and the garrison CO is a Ndenge man."

Judy concurred.

"That means we have to be very careful when we visit the mines near the town" she commented."

I agreed and added that we were very lucky Chloe and Colin had made the mistake of trusting the garrison CO because we could have easily done the same, especially after our experience with him earlier, on our local language testing visit. That thought chilled us and we turned back to our work.

(This is a reference to Colonel Musaveni, the commander of the garrison at Casa Isabella, a distant cousin of Josiah Ndenge and one of the leaders of the coup against President Igbokwe. It was the Casa Isabella troops who stormed the Palace. When Louis (Jake) took Mark and Judy to Casa Isabella to test out their ability to communicate in Austrasian, Musaveni took the three of them to the Barracks, entertained them during the evening and provided them with an escort for their return to the Island next day. It is interesting, in connection with the plot against Igbokwe, that Ndenge's six supporters later put on the post-coup cabinet, were all likewise related to him in one way or another. Mark and Judy would not discover this until later.)

We presented our interim report to Dad and Mum at dinner that evening. He was pleased at how far we had got, angered by what we found, and distraught about the news Jake had broken to him from St Michael's Island. Judy asked him if he could appoint a new acting governor to replace Maritza. Father explained it was not as easy as all that because of the need to find an appropriate person to control Maritza. I asked him why Longinus didn't simply order his troops to take over the centre and assume overall command himself. Dad said it would set a dangerous precedent. He believed there was sufficient time for us to plan a military raid by the Palace Guards to achieve the same result. Jake agreed, but we were not convinced. Judy was especially worried for Chloe. After her own experience of Maritza's malice, she had serious concerns for Chloe's safety. I shared those concerns – but said I believed Colin was equally vulnerable. Jake told us that he had carefully explained the risks to them, and expressed his frustration that Chloe and Colin had plainly disregarded his warning. We both gave up at that point and changed the subject.

We realized we were investigating the state of a minority (under three thousand out of fifteen thousand slaves). I asked Dad about the other twelve thousand. He told us they were mainly either in private houses, factories or small businesses. These had not been touched by the Ndenge clique because they did not provide as great a source of income as the mines. The two of them had ordered a parallel enquiry into the business sector and had found a different picture from that in the mines. Slave workers dealing directly or indirectly with the public or working for families or individuals were generally much better treated. There had been a few exceptions and they had used the powers we had given them to remove the slaves involved and find them new and better owners. Dad showed us a decree which the two of them had worked on and which had been fine-tuned by our secretariat team. It represented some tweaking of our earlier draft for private slaves and had been prepared to go to the next cabinet meeting, which was due to be held in two weeks. We asked Dad to use his emergency powers to order the equipment, safety clothing, medical supplies and pit props we knew would be needed for the remaining ten mines we had to visit and to have them stockpiled, guarded, near to the mines in question. He agreed, and the order was issued next day. Finally, we presented him with our second interim report. This was the one compiled by our accountant. It showed that, from the ten mines we had visited, fifty per cent of the income accruing from the mines had been diverted into accounts owned by the former Vice President and his six cronies. That figure was greater than the amount that had already been identified as being taken from budgeted state revenues and the issuing of contracts. We were genuinely concerned by Dad's reaction. He was so incensed with rage that we feared he might have a stroke. Mum, as angry herself, urged him to calm down for his own sake, and we joined in. Jake, who, as usual, was having dinner with us, poured him a stiff brandy, and he slowly wound down. Afterwards, Mother said to us, "You'd better be careful how you present your final report after what we've just seen."

Next morning, at breakfast, we raised with Dad the issue of the management of the twenty mining establishments. We asked him to instruct the Minister for Trade and Industry to nominate twenty men or women for the role. The people appointed to the ten mines already inspected should take up their posts immediately, the others should join our team. We would allocate each one to a mine and introduce them to the two supervisors we've already appointed, so they could prepare for their roles together. Finally, they should join us on our inspection of their new responsibility and be ready to take over immediately. We asked that this should be done within the next two weeks, and, ideally, in the next week. We told him that we planned to resume operations after a two weeks' gap to allow us time to deal with the St Michael's Island situation, which had worsened. We had received a telephoned report from Longinus which alarmed us. Apparently, the male slave who had been sent to replace me when Father took us away, had been caught stealing a maize cob, which he had picked while doing fieldwork that afternoon. Maritza was infuriated and ordered that he and his partner should be flogged and then, in the presence of all the slaves, hanged. The flogging, done in the cellar was merciless, witnessed by Chloe and Colin, who had been dumped into cells and left while this was being dealt with. The news of the arbitrary and utterly out of proportion sentence reached the other slaves, who demonstrated their anger and demanded she should change her mind. Maritza called in the troops "to restore order" as she put it and ordered that the hands of the eighteen slaves should be tied to the bars of their cages and each should then be flogged, almost as severely as the other two had been. Following this, their wrists and ankles chained, they were marched down to the farm – and made to watch as the two condemned slaves were dragged down, their arms bound behind their backs, pushed up step ladders, and hanged from two of the trees in the farm. They died slowly by strangulation, not by their necks breaking, as evidenced by the length of time their legs kicked in the air in what the English used to describe as "the Tyburn Dance". Following this, the remaining eighteen slaves, their legs still shackled and their hands loosely chained, were made to work weeding the maize field through the night. As far as we knew, the bodies were still hanging from their trees.

For us, that Friday began a new experience. We had decided we needed to learn to shoot. Dad had decided it would enhance our standing if we were given a commissioned rank in the Army. We told him that if we were Army officers, even honorary ones, we should learn to handle and shoot a weapon. He agreed, pointing out we had become a target for his political opponents, and needed to be able to defend ourselves. Jake undertook to teach us. That day we had the first of a dozen intensive lessons on handling and firing a handgun. We quickly learned how to empty and load a pistol, and how its components worked. We also learned which part of the body to shoot at. We learned the rule that if we have drawn our guns when faced with a dangerous opponent, we should shoot to kill and not to wound. That part was easy. The actual firing was more difficult! It took us two days even to hit the target. Jake was very patient with us as always. He corrected our errors and made us try again and again and again! At times we wondered if we would ever be able to fire a handgun successfully. On the third day we actually got a few bullets to hit the target, which pleased us immensely. Jake said we were making reasonable progress. He told us many recruits took much longer to get near a target, much less hit one. Slowly and steadily, over the next few days, our ratio of successful to unsuccessful shots improved. By the time we set out with the expedition to St Michael's Island, in our new Major's uniforms, we were about ninety per cent successful. Jake was pleased with us and told us to remember to go to the firing range once a week, at least, to continue practicing. He said he wouldn't be really happy with us until we were one hundred per cent successful when we fired a pistol.

Longinus arrived at 17.00 hours on Sunday afternoon. He brought with him a recording, which he played to us. He explained that, while the monsters, as he termed them, were carrying out their executions and floggings, Chloe and Colin were left in their cells unsupervised. He was able to get in and get Chloe, the more confident of the two, to tell their story to him. He did not have enough time to talk to Colin, he explained, because he saw Maritza heading back to the house. He slipped out of the cellar and exited by the rear door. He played the recording to us.

"I'm sorry Mark and Judy," Chloe began. "We were stupid. Our escort told us not to do it, but we wanted to go back to Casa Isabella, because that's where we met you, and then to go on to the slave centre where we wanted to see our friends. He told us it was too dangerous and a visit to our former slave breeding centre would endanger the whole purpose of our role. As a result, he said, you would all be very angry with us. However, we were determined, and we forced him to take us. When we got there, the man in charge of the Army met us, told Eric to join the officers in the Mess and took us into his own quarters, telling us that the President's son and daughter deserved no less. He was nice to us at first and got our trust. We were taken into dinner and given wine to drink. We became very tired and fell asleep at the table.

"When we woke up we were naked, in chains and tied to a table with electrodes stuck to our bodies in all the most sensitive places. "Ah, my beauties, you're awake at last are you?" a harsh female voice said behind me, laughing as she did so. "You're not in the palace any more," she sneered. "You're both just common stinking slaves again now. That's what you'll be until you die. Well, now I think you both need reminding what it feels like to be a slave." That's when she flicked a switch and sent a wave of electricity through our bodies. The pain was excruciating and we both screamed. "Did you enjoy that?" she said howling with laughter. "Oh good, I'm so glad you enjoyed it. Have some more!" she continued, flicking the switch again. I don't know for how long she kept taunting and electrocuting us, but it felt like hours. They must have heard us screaming outside. When she finally finished, she said, "Well, now you can go and spend the night working in the cassava field. Letizia here will be keeping an eye on you and if you don't keep working hard you'll get a taste of her whip." It was cold and we were dirty because we had to use our hands to dig the soil. We worked as hard as we could, but by the morning our backs and thighs felt as though they were on fire. That morning we were tied to the tree and the woman who had electrocuted us was back. "I see Letizia didn't think you worked hard enough so I think it's time you tasted a bit more of my hospitality, don't you?" she crowed as she brought the whip down hard across my back drawing blood. She laughed as I screamed and she hit me again. I don't know how many times she hit me. *(We thought we can guess.)* Finally she stopped and a bucket of cold water was thrown over my back. You can stay there for a while Princess, while I entertain your partner. She then thrashed Colin too. After this we were taken down to a bitterly cold cellar and thrown into separate cages with a bit of food and water. "Don't think you're getting your cosy warm cage back, Princess," she told me as she shoved me inside, shut and locked the door. "Somebody else has it. This is your permanent home now." I had no more than ten minutes to finish eating and drinking before she put the lights off. It was pitch black in there and absolutely freezing cold: it was made worse by the fact that we couldn't even snuggle up together for comfort and warmth. I clutched my arms around my body and prayed to die. *(We understood what she felt because we had felt the same down there.)*

"Next day we were left there until the evening. We were taken to what you call the milking and harvesting room. Colin said he was sucked out until he was completely empty. I felt my insides were being pulled out of my body. This went on all night. We were used to being milked and harvested in the other centre – but never like this. I wondered what you had done to deserve such hatred. She never asked who we were, so we never had to lie. She assumed we were you two. That's why she mocked me with the title Princess and Colin with the title Prince. In the morning we were taken down given some food and water, and put back in the cells until the evening. It's always dark and cold. We never work in the daytime: only at night, and we're always beaten lots of times. And always on our own. We have never been allowed to meet or talk to the other slaves and no one is allowed to speak to us (only the two women) and we know they are slowly killing us. What I don't know is how long I can continue to hold out. I'm being punished because she thinks I'm you, Judy. I want to tell her I'm not. I want to tell her she's wrong. I think then she'll stop. But then, again, I think, she'd just kill me there and then. And I don't want to die.

"Captain Longinus is the first human being to speak to me, and he's told me they're coming back. Apparently they've hanged two slaves and flogged the others. I'm not surprised because the woman is a beast. Please come soon and rescue us, or you will only find what's left of us after we've died. Please forgive us; we were stupid and disobedient, but we do not deserve to die because of it. Please, please forgive, come quickly and help us. Save us from this inhuman monster."

Then the tape went silent. Judy cried. She felt guilty for agreeing to let Chloe be her – knowing, as she did, the risks Chloe ran. There were tears in my eyes too. Jake and Longinus saw how moved we were and told us it wasn't our fault. We all knew the risks and we had tried to limit them. This was the result of the failure of our precautions.

"That doesn't make it feel any better, " Judy sobbed. "you knew in theory, Jake. We knew in our bodies because we had experienced her hate and it had almost killed us. We should have warned her explicitly what to expect. We didn't! If those two are killed, as we nearly were, we will never forgive ourselves."

I looked at the two men.

"I know you're going to plan the attack," I said. "We intend to be there with you. No one must kill those two women. They must be taken alive, made to kneel in front of us in the presence of the slaves, the garrison, our troops and the other prisoners. Then we will take our pistols. At least, we can pull the triggers. We'll place the muzzles of them against their necks aimed towards what passes for their brains. Then we're going to make them plead to us for their lives, before saying, 'No', and pulling the trigger."

Jake began to say, No. But I cut him short. "That is what we are going to do. Nothing and no one is going to stop us. We need to do it for our own peace of mind, for the two slaves we never met who she hanged, for our two doubles and the other eighteen slaves. If we have to go to Hell for it when we die; let it be so. Surely God will understand our need and forgive us! May He help us. Because we can do no other. And if that damns us for all time – then Amen (may it be so). It will be a price worth paying."

Longinus urged us to reflect, "Remember the saying about revenge; that it is a dish best served cold."

Judy answered him coldly, her tears wiped away and replaced by a cold fury I had never seen in her before. "If it has to be hot – so be it. Like Mark, if I have to burn in Hell for doing it – then let it be so."

We stood up, asked Longinus curtly for the tape recorder, asked how it worked, and told them we were going to Dad to play the tape to him. I promised Longinus we would bring his recorder back, since I assumed he and Jake would spend the evening together in our flat.

After we left, Jake told us later, he told Longinus what had happened to us that last day on St Michael's Island at the hands of Maritza and her sidekick and its results. He told him of the long, so nearly futile, struggle to save our lives, and the two long months period of recovery we went through. "It's not surprising they feel that way," he said. "I fear for them. They don't know the effect what they plan to do will have on them. However, it's something, I fear, they will have to do."

Longinus agreed. "Louis, we both know how it felt when we shot and killed our first man. We, of course, did it deliberately. If a civilian did it to another civilian, it's called murder; when we soldiers do it to a soldier wearing a different uniform to ours, it's called war and doing our duty. But it's no easier because 'a man's a man for all that', as a famous Scottish poet once wrote. And it's true. They will find that out. However, they will have to find it out the hard way. You, Louis, and their parents, will have to help them cope with the guilt which will afflict them for ever afterwards."

Jake sadly agreed. Then they settled down to plan the attack.

We left them talking, and walked over to our parents' apartment. We entered and gave them (and received from them) our customary embraces and told them what we had brought with us. After explaining where it had come from, we told them we had promised to return Longinus's recorder, though not the recording. Then we played the recording without comment. Dad was still fuming over the near fatal assault on us and the fact that the assailants, at our request, were still in post. What we all heard on the tape confirmed him in his belief that we had persuaded him into making a mistake.

"It's all your fault," he grumbled, "Yours and Louis'. If I had stuck to my guns they would be the ones dead; not the two slaves I took there, and two total innocents would not be in fear of their lives."

Judy sobbed. "We know it's our fault, Dad! You needn't remind us! If there's one thing I've done I'd like to change – it's that! But I can't!"

"It is what it is, Dad," I said. We did it, as Judy said, and we can't undo it. It's something we'll probably both have to carry for the rest of lives. All we can do now is get them out of there as quickly as possible and pray the two bitches don't hurt them too much. (If God exists perhaps He'll hear us and stop them!) Louis and Longinus are planning the attack now. All we need to do is get the logistics and the men, select the landing site and transport our assault team to link up with the men already there, and kill those evil bitches."

"Do you want me to come with you?" Dad asked.

"No, Dad," I said. "It's enough that we're there. Give us uniforms and warrants for the two women's executions (they've killed two slaves without Government permission) that's reason enough. Judy and I will carry out the executions."

They both pleaded with us not to do it – but to leave it to Louis and Longinus. We repeated what we'd said earlier and what Judy had said to them a few days before.

"I've executed a man in the way you obviously intend," Dad said. "It's easy to do – too easy in fact. You can do it, and I did, with your eyes closed. But I warn you both – you'll never get over it. In our culture, young Judy, you would never be allowed to do it because of the fear that it might affect the character of your baby."

Judy remained silent.

I then did something I never thought I would ever do. I stood up, with my back against the ornate fireplace that now housed a radiator, and lectured the President and his wife, our Dad and Mum. This is what I said.

"Mother and Father, you're black and we're white. They're facts we can't escape. We can only live with them; as we are doing and will continue to do. We come from different backgrounds with different expectations. You looked on our people as natural rulers, longed to escape our control and rule, but expected that economic, social and political overlordship would still continue whatever the situation on the ground. We were taught to accept we once ruled half the world. We believed most of the world still spoke our language, respected our culture and recognised our morally leading position, even though it was no longer backed by military and political power. We no longer ruled half the world, but we exercised a generally benign influence on most of it. Neither you nor we saw any reason why this should change. In the USA black people still had to remind white people their lives were important too. They couldn't just be shot dead in the street because a white guy, either in a blue uniform or not, saw no reason why they should live and breathe the same air they did. In recent history, they had been slaves and were descended from slaves. They had to fight for everything they had, even for the right to breathe the air in some areas. That was then.

"Then came the Great Northern War. You know more about that than we do; even though it was our home and our country and our families that were destroyed and yours that were not. You saw your parents die, naturally, in honour, and full of years. You have lived with your siblings to support you, with your homes and your communities intact. We are orphans. Because we were here, we were not with our families when they died. We don't know how and when it happened – but, as we told you, we're sure it happened. We have no family…"

They tried to interrupt me to dispute this – but I raised my hand to still them and let me continue. They looked at each other and did so.

"We have no family, no home, no country. We had a job – in another country – that's all. Even that was taken from us. What was left of our past was taken from us. Our clothes were ripped from our bodies. Finally our freedom was taken from us. Fifteen thousand of us suffered these losses. Currently we are the only ones to have had them replaced. Yes, Mum and Dad, we have a new family, a new home, a new country, and a new status. You have given us that. You love us as you would have loved a son and daughter from your own bodies. Maybe, God, if there is such a being, and neither of us are sure of that, kept you for this purpose? We love you both as we once loved our birth mothers and fathers. But we are the lucky ones - although some now question that designation and, undoubtedly, in the future, some learned historians will repeat the questions. Who knows, or even cares? But we're unique – just two out of fifteen thousand.

"The truth is that the age of white supremacy is definitively over. Nelson Mandela said the twenty-first century would be the age of Africa in the year 2000. He has been proved right. Black men and women are now the masters of the planet – its life, its past, present and future, its politics, its society and its economy. Military and political power lies here and with you. For my compatriots, the future is bleak. All across Africa now, former Europeans are being enslaved, following the example set here. Soon we may be the only people of European descent able to walk freely and live as we did before. That's not true, of course, because you have raised us to a height few can scale at any time. Certainly we never dreamed of it. Soon, slavery and subjection will seem the natural fate of white people. Eventually, you and your fellow people will resettle the presently devastated lands of Europe and America. Black Kings, Princes and Presidents will refer to white people there as the natives, round them up, put them in reservations and pass laws to make them protected native tribes. The rulers' friends will visit the reservations, ply the natives with cheap booze, watch their traditional dances, listen to their traditional songs, buy a few trinkets, and say, 'How quaint!' Your historians will look at the ruins of their cities and speculate that some black traveller must have visited the area at some time in the past and shared his or her knowledge with the indigenous people. However, white young people will try to break out of their prison (anywhere in the world) and they will have to fight for recognition as basic human beings - as people. They will be the ones shot down by black men and women in blue uniforms because they are demanding an equal right to live. They will begin to say to black officials 'we white people have a right to life as well as you.' That is now and that is the future. That is what our child and future children may face and certainly what all those children being created as future slave labourers in the laboratories across the country and maybe elsewhere will face."

I sat down. Our parents were silent. Then both clapped – recognising the sincerity with which I spoke. Mum turned to Judy and asked if she agreed with what I'd just said. She said she did but felt I hadn't said quite enough. Dad asked her what she would add. She smiled, and said:

"Not a lot, Dad. It's something Mark didn't say, but we both feel deeply. We're aware of just how big a risk you took in seeking us, taking us away from that awful camp, saving our lives and adopting us. We know how much you love us. We didn't see it, obviously, in those long hours when you sat beside our hospital beds as we lay unconscious, with only the noise of the bleep, bleep, bleep of our heart beats on the life support systems. Without you we would be dead, and you would have wept for us and buried our bodies. I know that last is a fact; unlike those poor souls murdered by Maritza. If she had had her way, it would have been our fate too. You not only gave us back our lives and our freedom, you gave us hope and a future. It is impossible to say how much that means to us. Kisses and thank yous seem too little to pay for such a debt, but it's all we have and we give them to you gladly in exchange for such a gift. We will bring your grandchildren up to respect you and realize how much they owe you. We will teach them the culture and traditions of Austrasia as their culture and traditions. But we will also teach them what we know of the history and traditions of the country and families we've lost for ever. Because they can never be brought back. And we will teach them always to remember all people are human beings and every life is just as important as every other life. One of our poets once wrote 'a man's a man for all that'. It doesn't matter if a human being is a black businessman or a white slave working in his factory. Both are human beings, and both have to be respected as human. I heard you say that, Dad, on the jetty when you landed on the Island to take us away. That's when I stopped hating you for what I thought you'd done to us and started loving you for who I now know you are. I was confused when you spoke with us in the slave quarters. Everything you said and did contradicted what we were told about you. In the end we both learned to put what we saw, heard for ourselves and experienced above what others told us – and we came to the truth."

She paused, before adding, "Do you know who our main teacher was?"

Dad smiled, and said gently, "No, darling, tell us."

"Josiah Ndenge. We met him twice and I realized he was the true author of our misfortunes. We both suddenly realized that you both were always intended to be his next victims. We were simply added to the list when he met us and recognised we were a danger to him. I think he realized we saw through him and would cause you to break his stranglehold on power. As we did."

We were all silent for five minutes. We were silent because we had exhausted our emotions and had nothing more to say. Mum was silent because she was trying not to cry. Dad was thinking what he should say. He believed he should say something. Finally, he stood up and walked over to where I had stood and turned to face us.

"Mark and Judy, our son and daughter, and through your bodies, our as yet unknown grandchild, I have to make many speeches (that's the role of a President) to many audiences, but never one so short and to an audience so small but so important. I've been told I never use four words if I can use twenty! I will try to be succinct. Your words should be written down and studied and learned by every child in school (just as the American Black leader Martin Luther King's speeches are). I will be honest with you both. I have never really realized the differences between us because I believe them to be more apparent than real. They don't change anything in the relationships within our family. You're our children. As you said, Mark, the children we never had naturally. I fell in love with you two when, after you'd overcome your natural initial reticence, you relaxed and treated me like I knew you must have treated the men and women who gave birth and life to you both. But, Judy, it was you who sealed the deal with your cheeky question, 'Who will be the Daddy?' when I told you that your baby would be my grandchild. I knew you were asking whether it would be me who made you pregnant. I thought if you had the courage, in that situation, to ask the person who was offering to take you from it a question about whether he was going to force himself on you, you were the sort of people I was looking for. That's the moment you ceased to be slaves (things to be used and then thrown away without caring what happens to them in the future) and became our son and daughter, two young people who would share our lives for the rest of it and, as you put it, watch us become old in years and honour and die [hopefully] in peace.

"But you're correct. We are living through an age of revolutionary change in the real meaning of the word. The old world has gone (destroyed by the folly of its rulers). We must make sure that we do not repeat the mistakes of the old world. You're right, of course. Before long the only free white men and women in positions of power will be in Australia and New Zealand, and, of course, sharing power in South and Central America.

Everywhere else they will be reduced to either a condition of outright slavery or become second class citizens. Some will call them subhuman. Some will consider that the only good white man is a dead white man. And, others, so called liberals, will look on white people as historical curiosities (living in native reservations or living museums). Somehow, we have to remember our own past, not with bitterness, seizing with glee the chance to exact full and complete revenge for wrongs done to us in the past, but in a spirit of forgiveness and humility, hoping to build a new world where every man and woman living in it can take his or her full place in society and develop his or her skills to their full extent. We four have to lead that campaign."

He walked over to his drinks cabinet and poured out four glasses of Australasian sherry. He offered us each a glass and we drank to the future of our family and of our country. Then we embraced, before we all sat down, relaxed, and began talking about everything and nothing. The one thing I can remember was Mum asking Judy how she was feeling, and Judy saying she was feeling fine. Mum was persistent and asked her directly whether she had suffered from morning sickness, and she said she hadn't. Judy promised she would tell her if she did. Looking back while writing this, I realize that this was only the second time the four of us spent time together. For most of the time Louis was with us and later Chloe and Colin were also with us. So, it was also the last time. We finally left, with the recorder, at about 9 pm, and returned to our apartment, where we found the two men still deep in conversation, but we quickly picked up that it was typical old soldiers' talk of past campaigns and wars both fought in. I gave Longinus back his recorder and wished them both a good night. I reminded Jake to make sure the door was locked as they left, and we left them to continue drinking our brandy and enjoying their reminiscences. We have no idea when they left, because, after making love, exhausted by an emotional day, we fell asleep.

Next morning, Longinus joined the five of us for breakfast and discussed the plans for the attack on St Michael's Island with us, and especially with Dad. He agreed the plan, after making a few minor suggestions for modifications, with one exception – our intended role as executioners. The conversations and arguments of the previous day were repeated and rehashed by the four of them, and we repeated our position, in much the same words. In the end, and with great reluctance, they accepted that we would not change our minds. Dad summed up their acceptance.

"Very well," he said. "You've made your choice and you must accept the consequences. As they used to say in your former country, 'You've made your bed and you must lie in it'."

Jake added, "But, you don't have to do this. If, at the last minute, you decide you can't, we won't blame you or call you cowards. You'll still have as much respect from us as you have now. In fact, you'll have even more than you have now. Longinus and I will carry out the executions in those circumstances."

The other three nodded their agreement.

Then the conversation, much to our relief, turned to logistics and dates. In the end it was decided that twenty Palace guardsmen, under the command of Jake and accompanied by us, wearing the uniforms of major, would be assembled at Port Franklin at 12.00 hours on the following Saturday to await the arrival of the "Macrone". Once she had completed unloading, we would board her, our equipment would be loaded into her hold and we would depart at 16.00 hours.

H hour was fixed for 08.00 hours on Sunday. Given the situation, the landing would be made directly on to the jetty. With that, the meeting ended, and Longinus left us to return to the island and brief his troops and the boat's crew.

We continued with a discussion of the agenda for Wednesday's Cabinet meeting, which we'd brought forward, the main topic at which would be our interim report on the mines as well as Dad's report on factories and privately owned slaves. We expected the draft decree on the treatment of slaves working in factories and private homes and all slaves out and about in public places, which Dad and our team had prepared would be approved at that meeting so it could go for publication in the two main national newspapers on Thursday. Once that was agreed, we left with Jake for our daily stint at the firing range, followed by a meeting with our secretariat team. For the rest of the week, our days consisted of shooting practice and dealing with government documents, except for Wednesday when the Cabinet met.

There was shock and anger at the financial aspect of our report and dismay at the appalling conditions we found at the mines we had visited. The number of deaths appalled them. Dad's report cheered them up a bit, since what he had to say was much more positive. The decree we proposed was discussed, but there was no serious opposition. A few questions as to the meaning of some phrases were asked and it was decided to change the pronoun "it" for a slave to "he or she". Otherwise the document was approved unaltered. We held a news conference after the meeting to deal with the new document but making no reference to our interim report. We wanted nothing said until the inspections had been completed.

Dad was as good as his word, and twenty men and women met us on Thursday. We assigned them to the various mines as the new managers. The ten who were moving to take up their posts immediately received and signed their contracts and set out for their new workplaces. The other ten were introduced to their two supervisors and given copies of the documents we held about their mines. They were also told the new dates for their inspection and the date they would take up their posts. That done, they received and signed their contracts.

As our attention turned to the St Michael's Island Operation preparations, we received some grimly reassuring news. Longinus reported in with an update on the situation there.

"Maritza came down to visit me in my office with her mate, Letizia. She wanted to know my reasons for leaving my post. I informed her that my Commander in Chief, the President, had ordered me to report to Freetown for consultations. She demanded to know what we talked about. I told her that was no business of hers, but I had a message for her from the President. The President wanted his children returned and was prepared to pay any price she demanded. What was it? She told me to tell him that he and his wife had to resign and then she would (quote) return the slaves to the hutch (unquote). She assured me she had no plans to kill them yet. However, she would make them suffer until they begged her to kill them. Finally, she said this, and again I quote her exact words. 'The date and manner of their deaths is fixed. This so called President's birthday is on September 25th. If he is still in the White House at midnight on the 22nd his pets are going to be beheaded. Their heads will be delivered in a box to his door at midnight on 24th/25th with a birthday card from Josiah's friends.' She clearly meant it. We can stick to our plans knowing that the kids will be suffering still, it's true, but their lives are safe. Incidentally, last night one of my men who is a qualified electrician deactivated the generator which controlled the electrical device she used to torture the slaves. He also fused the milking and harvesting devices. Sadly, he did his work so well that neither they nor the electrical torture machines will ever work again. What a pity!"

We thanked him for what he had done to limit the amount of torture the two women could inflict. With that, we had to be content. We informed our parents, who were also relieved.

The assault party, comprising the two of us and twenty soldiers under Jake's command, left by helicopter for the airport at 09.30 on Saturday. We arrived at Port Franklin two and a half hours later at 12.00, to arrive at the harbour just as the "Macrone " entered it. We all worked with the crew to unload the boat and reload it, although there was little to put on except fuel and food under the circumstances. We loaded our equipment into the hold and, an hour later, we left for the Island. We all knew the plan, so there was little talk. We knew there was little risk to ourselves, but it was an execution party and all of us were reflective about that. Such conversation as occurred was inconsequential. Jake spoke to Longinus over the phone and asked for an update. He told us the eighteen slaves were working in the maize field, Chloe and Colin were sleeping in their cells and Letizia was also asleep. Maritza was in her office, apparently, in a foul mood. He commented that was fairly normal and boded badly for the two slaves' night. He expected they would be made to work through the night and would still be in the farm when we arrived.

The day passed slowly. Having never been in this area, we spent much of the time on deck with Jake who pointed out places of interest on the shore as we passed them and told us stories of how he and his dad, who came from this area, used to go fishing in the lake. It became dark, and the cook called us all down to eat dinner. He used a local recipe. We ate and drank some of the local wine. The soldiers organised a sing song afterwards. One of them brought an accordion with him to accompany them. Then we all tried to get some sleep, some successfully; others, including us, with less success.

We were too nervous to sleep. We went up to the bridge and spent the night chatting with the skipper, who we had come to like. He asked us about life in the Palace, and we asked him about how his life would change after this operation was over. He told us he would be relieved because he could go back to his old job of running tourist trips and trading with and carrying post to the villages along the shores of the lake. The hours passed slowly. The island eventually came into view in the distance, and the skipper asked us to go below and awaken the troops.

We landed earlier than planned while it was still dark. Longinus came on board to join us and we left him in command while Jake came with us and four of our men to rescue Chloe and Colin. Longinus told us they were in the cassava field in the charge of Letizia. We made our way quietly up the track to the farm, collecting the guards on the gate as we passed them. Entering the field, we formed a line, with two Palace Guards and one of the gate guards at either end, and the three of us in the middle. We moved forward in silence. We had covered a third of the field without making contact when we heard a sound ahead. "Get up you little bitch!" an irate female voice shouted, followed by the crack of a whip three times and a female cry. My hand went to my pistol, and Jake's hand dropped over it and stopped me moving it. "Don't!" he hissed. Jake issued final orders. We were to move towards the sound, circling around its source, so the people were surrounded. Two men were directed to seize Letizia from behind and handcuff her, while two more were instructed to search her. Their job was to remove any weapon and her whip. The other two were to act as cover. We were to collect Chloe and Colin and take them straight to the boat. The others would follow us with the prisoner. We moved forward and the work party came into sight. Chloe and Colin were kneeling down pulling out weeds, using their bare hands to dig in the soil to disturb the roots (as we used to have to do). Letizia stood a few feet behind them, watching them like a hawk and flexing her whip in a threatening manner.

"Get your backs into it, you lazy bastards if you don't want another feel of this!" she said, cracking the whip loudly. As she was doing this, we watched our men creep up on her, the slight noise of their approach drowned by her own voice and preoccupation with her victims. They moved swiftly forward and seized her arms, dragging them behind her and handcuffing her before she realized what was happening. As the other two men closed in on her from the front, she snarled at them, "Who the hell are you and what do you think you're doing. I'll inform Maritza. You'll hang for this. Let me go you bastards!" "It's over. Letizia," Jake said to her. "We're not from the Garrison; we're from the Palace, and I'm the Minister of Justice. You're under arrest. Search her, lads and disarm her." He turned towards us. "Mark and Judy you know your role. Now's your time."

We moved forward to the now obviously bewildered Chloe and Colin. Judy went to Chloe and I took Colin. We raised them to their feet. "It's all right now," I said to them.

"I'm Mark and this is Judy. You met us before You've been us and suffered horribly because of it, we know. We're terribly sorry this happened to you, but it's over. You're safe now. We've come to take you away."

They were reeling with tiredness and stiff with pain.

I called out to Jake.

"Jake, you only need two men to escort that harridan from hell to the boat. We need the others to carry these two down – they won't make it on their own feet."

The four Palace guards joined us. One picked up Chloe in his arms and another took Colin. They told us they were as light as a feather, and we wouldn't need all four of them. I nodded and told the other two to rejoin Jake's party. They left us and we led the way back to the boat, with the two soldiers carrying their precious loads following us. We carried their rifles for them. It was daylight by the time we reached the boat. We took Chloe and Colin on board and left them in the care of the crew. When Letizia was brought on board, she was secured in the hold.

We then left for the slave centre, in three columns of twenty men. Judy and I led a party from the garrison, followed by Jake leading the Palace contingent and Longinus leading the other garrison troops. We diverted from the track to go around the building and enter from the back, followed by Jake's party, while Longinus entered from the front door. Jake had given us his keys to the slaves' quarters, and we made our way quietly up the stairs to the top floor, unlocked the door, and entered the familiar room. The slaves, surprised, jumped to their feet and crowded into the corridor asking what was going on. I held my fingers to my lips, signing them to be silent and got them to assemble in the centre area.

I spoke to them, as ten guards went to each door to secure it against any attempt by escaping staff members to enter. We could hear the hubbub and shouting from the floor below. Happily there was no shooting. I spoke to the slaves.

"We're different from how you knew us; but I'm still Mark and this is still Judy. I know you thought we were prisoners here – but they were Chloe and Colin, our doubles. They foolishly allowed themselves to be kidnapped. As a result, we've been forced to act much earlier than we intended. But you're free now. We've come to take you from this hell-hole and punish those who broke the rules to persecute you."

There was a cheer, but Jack hushed them.

"It's all right for you two," he said, "but how can we be free? We're slaves still."

"This afternoon, we're taking you to the east, where you will be met by a group of partisans who will escort you to their base. There you will be safe, if not as comfortable as you would like, and live in freedom. For the moment, however, we want you to follow us downstairs to the dining room, where the staff and the rest of our party will join us. The roles have changed, you're free now, but if they're not already in handcuffs, they very soon will be."

As I finished speaking, the door burst open and an enraged Maritza forced her way through the barrier of soldiers, who were too much in awe of her to stop her. *(Apparently, she was in her office when the raid began. Longinus believed that she entered the slaves' quarters with the intention of seizing one or more of them as hostages to enable her to escape.)*

"What the hell's going on!" she shouted. "You slaves get back in your cages!" she snapped. "Who gave you permission to leave them?"

"I did," I said. "I'm in charge here, not you Maritza."

"Who the Hell are you?" she said. "I'm in charge here. This is a Government institution and you've raided it. Release my people and remove your soldiers from the island at once."

I laughed.

"You're not listening, you silly bitch!" I said to her, "I told you I'm in charge on this floor. WE represent the Government, not you. I'm the son of the President and Judy is his daughter. You probably recognise us ."

I took off my officer's hat.

"I wouldn't do that!" I said as her hand went for her gun. My pistol was already in my hand. "This is loaded and un-cocked and I know how to use it. I also have your death warrant in my pocket."

I motioned to Jack, who, with two other male slaves, seized her and disarmed her. I ordered one of the soldiers to call either Jake or Longinus to bring handcuffs. Jake arrived and handcuffed Maritza who spat at him.

"Traitor!" she hissed.

"No traitor, Ma'am," he said calmly, "I'm the Minister of Justice and I'm arresting you on the orders of the President for the unauthorised killing of two slaves and the kidnapping, torture and planned murder of two slaves you wrongly assumed were his son and daughter."

He turned to Jack.

"Jack, I'm giving you and your partner the pleasure of manhandling this piece of human excrement downstairs to the dining room. Don't be too gentle while you're doing it."

Jack grinned fiercely.

"Trust us, Jake, we don't do gentle with trash like this."

When we entered the dining room we found the remaining staff and the troops who had arrested them were already assembled there, the prisoners in the middle of the room and the troops standing around the room. The slaves and our soldiers joined them. Maritza was placed at the front, guarded by Jack and his partner. Shortly afterwards, Longinus led Letizia in, escorted by two of his men. She was brought to stand beside Maritza. I noticed that Longinus left the door ajar. I wondered why, but events prevented me from asking the

reason. Jake appointed twelve of the Palace Guards to be the jury –
and the trial of the two women began.

Jake gave evidence of their attack on us, the injuries we suffered
and how close we came to death. Longinus gave evidence of their
treatment of Chloe and Colin and Maritza's threats to the President
and plans for the two slaves' deaths. Jack gave evidence of their
treatment of the eighteen slaves and the murder of the other two. Jake
asked the other prisoners if they had anything to add to the evidence
and three spoke about how they had objected and been bullied and
threatened by Maritza and Letizia to keep them in line. (We noted
them and had them removed from the rest of the prisoners.) Jake
then allowed the two women an opportunity to make their defences.

Maritza spat at him.

"It wasn't my fault. She made me do it," Letizia pleaded.

"I don't recall seeing Maritza there when you were viciously
beating Chloe in the cassava field this morning," Judy said. "I cannot
begin to understand how one woman can treat another so cruelly."

"She's not a woman," Maritza yelled. "She's just an animal, a
dirty rotten slave."

Jake nodded.

"Have it your own way," he commented.

He asked the jury for their verdict. One by one they said
"Guilty" to all charges for both women. I handed the warrants over
to Jake who read them out. He asked if there was any reason why
the sentence should not be carried out. No one raised any objections.

My heart lurched as I realized what I now had to do. Judy later told me the same thing happened to her. Jake and Longinus both looked at us, hoping that we would step away: but we didn't.

"Prisoners, kneel," I commanded.

They refused.

"If you're going to shoot us you jumped up little pipsqueak you've got another think coming. I don't kneel in front of slaves – and you'll always be a slave whatever you think," was Maritza's response.

I wanted to strike her across her face, but restrained myself. I spoke instead of acting.

"I'm very tempted to slap you, you heartless bitch," I told her. "But I don't hit women, especially not defenceless ones. In any case I do not want to sully my hand with your foul face. Get ready to die and end your evil life."

I nodded to the four escorts.

"Push them down and keep them down," I ordered.

They kicked the women's knees to force them downwards and then used their hands to force them completely down on their knees. I spoke to the women.

"You've probably forfeited any right to plead for your lives, but if you have anything to say why you think you should be permitted to live, say it now."

"What! And give you murdering bastards the pleasure of hearing me plead for my life," Maritza spat, "dream on!"

Letizia screamed, "Go to hell!"

I concluded with these words –

"Very well, we give you five minutes to pray to whatever god you worship to forgive you."

We moved behind the kneeling women and stood, watching them. The room was absolutely silent. I looked at Jake and pointed to my wrist. He nodded to show he understood. He studied his watch. Four and a half minutes crawled past. We reached for our pistols with shaking hands. I looked at Jake for the signal. He shook his head gently. I turned my face away and looked at the hand on the butt of my pistol. I began to count silently to thirty, measuring the seconds. Later, Judy told me she did the same. We looked at each other. I nodded to her and we began to draw our pistols, trying and failing to remain calm while doing so. We felt, rather than saw or heard, the room hold its collective breath. We knew, without looking, that Jake and Longinus were staring at us, willing us not to do it. The silence in the room was deafening.

To Compositor: Please place a complete page between the end of this chapter and the beginning of the next so that the reader has to turn over a page to reach it.

"Now this is not the end. It is not even the beginning of the end. But it is, perhaps, the end of the beginning."

Winston S Churchill

CHAPTER 22

Justice!

We began to draw our pistols when the door was kicked open noisily. "Stop!" a familiar and commanding voice which demanded instant obedience said. I looked up, startled by the interruption, and then smiled as I saw Dad walk into the room.

"Put your guns away, children," he said gently to us. "You don't need to do this. I will. It's my job, my warrant, my responsibility."

We sighed with relief and put away our guns.

He turned away from us and spoke to Jake and Longinus.

"Form a firing squad from ten of my guards, Louis.

Longinus, you will command them."

"Yes, sir," they both responded. The President ordered the four escorts to clear a section of the wall, pull the two prisoners to their feet and push them against it. This was done. Longinus ordered that the prisoners be blindfolded. The firing party lined up. Longinus and Jake took their rifles, emptied them and reloaded them, so one rifle contained a blank bullet, before returning them.

In utter silence, everyone waited. The two officers stood at either end of the firing line.

Dad spoke to the two women.

"What you have done can never be excused. It is an example of pure evil unrestrained by any sense of morality or decency. You should thank whatever god you worship, because it is not one known to me or mine, for the mercy we are showing you by giving you a soldier's death. In all honesty, true justice would see your naked bodies, flogged to within inches of death, nailed to a tree and left to rot like the corpses of former slaves in Casa Isabella."

He turned away from them to address Longinus.

"Carry on, Captain," he said.

Jake read out the two warrants again. Longinus ordered the firing party to take aim, and, on command, fire. He paused for a further minute to give the prisoners a final chance to pray and then gave the order. "Fire!" The volley crashed out and the women fell to the floor. Jake and Longinus moved forward, drew their pistols, and gave the women the coup de grace. Their bodies were removed, and the trials of the remaining officers began.

It became clear that some were more guilty than others. In the end Father ordered the executions of an additional four, terms of imprisonment for a number of others and dishonourable discharge for the rest, except for the three who had given evidence in the trial of Maritza and Letizia. They were reassigned to work in three different centres elsewhere. Finally, he turned to the eighteen slaves and the garrison.

"My son and daughter have specially pleaded for you. I know you've done your bit for the Republic. You are now freed by my command. I understand that you're going to be taken from here to the east end of the lake and there set free. I'm not going to ask you or anyone where you go or what you do from here, but I understand there is a plan for you. I wish you luck. Soldiers of the garrison, I'm sending you on six months leave. You can return to your homes. Those who wish to remain with us should report in six months' time to my old regiment at Tolosa. I will be happy to see you there. The others will be able to start drawing their pensions." In the end, only five, the oldest, did not return to the colours.

The rest of the morning and the early afternoon was spent in tidying up. A squad of soldiers removed the six bodies and carried them to the barn, where they were buried in a pit they dug for the purpose. Once it was covered, they stamped the soil down and commented that it was the right place for them being under where the cows and pigs shit. The convicted and sentenced prisoners were taken (under military escort) by the boat to the landing place on the eastern shore where a helicopter, summoned by Dad, collected them. The "Macrone" returned to the Island. The prisoners were flown, under a police escort, to Port Franklin airport, from there to Freetown and then on to various prisons. The local guards, sacked officers, and former slaves boarded the "Macrone", which repeated its earlier journey to the east, where they disembarked and went their various ways – the soldiers and former officers to their villages and the former slaves, met by Jake's contact, were escorted to the "rebel" (according the CO at Casa Isabella) base in the mountains.

We were left with our party, Longinus, the three 'innocent' officers, and Dad. We ate lunch which had been brought up to us by the boat crew and we talked. I admitted we were relieved when Dad arrived and took the responsibility of executing the two murderers from us but did not understand how he had managed the timing.

"It's simple", he said, "Your Mum and I did not want you to be burdened for the rest of your lives by the blood of those lice. I arrived by motor boat from the southern shore while you were fully engaged in your operation, arranged for Chloe and Colin to be flown to the hospital you know so well, and arrived here after you started. I waited by the door, which Longinus deliberately left slightly ajar so I could hear, and selected my moment exactly, so that you could go through the formalities but not actually pull the triggers."

I looked at Longinus accusingly. "How did you know that Dad had arrived?"

He grinned, "Because Monica and Jake arranged it with him and informed me. We all knew that, at the last, the full enormity of what you intended to do would strike you and you would want to back out – but we also knew your pride and position wouldn't allow you to do so. They knew only your father could overrule you. He came on board the boat while I was collecting Letizia. We completed the plan together. They were right about you, weren't they?"

"Yes," Judy said. "My hands were shaking as I drew my pistol and I actually wet myself."

Jake grinned. "I didn't notice the second thing! However, I did see the first! Mark's hand was shaking too. I shook my head at you – but you both ignored me as I knew you would."

I asked what was going to happen to Longinus, Chloe and Colin. Dad answered that he was promoting Longinus to Major and appointing him to the Palace Guard, to serve as his ADC. As for Chloe and Colin he said he was going to do with them what he had done with us. He grinned at this and told us the people would think we were two pairs of twins. He was also arranging to marry them. We discussed the future of the island. I said they could make it into a tourist site. Dad said that might be for the future. What he was going to do now was to arrange for the cattle to be moved to the new centre on the south side of the lake but leave the pigs to roam and breed on the island. Jake pointed out that the disaffected rebels would move there as they were flushed out from their mainland villages. Dad said that is what he hoped they would do. If that happened, we would have them where we wanted them, he said. "And then we'll deal with the whole shooting match in one operation."

The boat returned in mid-afternoon, and we all boarded it to sail for Port Franklin, leaving the Island for the last time, and from there to fly back to Freetown. The St Michael's Island Incident was finally over, and the notorious camp closed down. We left the island unoccupied except by a herd of cows, and another of pigs, a field of cassava and a field of maize, all of which could bear mute witness to the amount of suffering that was inflicted there.

CHAPTER 23

The Inspections Resumed

We spent much of the week after our return from St Michael's Island, travelling to and from the hospital, sharing bedside duties with our parents and getting to know our new brother and sister better. Also, we were trying to get in our heads whether and when to add the words "in law" to our titles. When we weren't doing that, we were shopping with Mum, buying clothes for our new siblings. Dad opened up a second formerly disused apartment and had it redecorated and equipped with furniture for them. I asked Mum if that's what they'd had to do for us. She said they had done that – but they obviously had more time then. This was much more rushed. She told us, with a laugh, she'd put her foot down if Dad suggested adopting any more of us. Four rather wayward and determined twenty-somethings in a family was more than enough for any couple to deal with. She had told him so in no uncertain terms and Dad had agreed.

What we found was a grim picture of criminal neglect of safety procedures, failure to preserve internal mine structures or to enforce recognisable mining disciplines in the mines, deliberate underspending on the mines, under reporting of production figures, falsification of sales figures, and deliberate siphoning off of profits. The ten per cent casualty figure persisted where we could obtain the information. Eventually, we came up with a figure north of one hundred and sixty deaths out of eleven hundred workers and around forty serious (life changing) injuries. In the end, aided by our decision that all workers, regardless of legal status, should be paid, some of the original workers were brought back. They had been laid off by the VP's cronies in favour of slave labour. They were happy to get back and, by and large, the two groups got on well together. As we collated the information and the general picture became clear to us, we began to draw up remedies. Our eventual list is summed up in the headings below.

1. All workers, slave and free should be paid at the same rate, because they face the same dangers.

2. All workers should be provided with proper clothing and proper equipment.

3. Modern machinery should be installed in the mines, including transport for miners and mined ore.

4. Safety devices have to be installed to warn of danger – particularly in coal mines.

5. Shifts should be limited to eight hours a day, and no more than five days a week.

6. There should be adequate medical provision at all sites.

7. All records are to be kept in a safe place and made in duplicate – a copy to be held on site and a copy to go to the Ministry of Trade and Industry.

8. All senior appointments should be made by a transparent and fair system of competition.

9. The legally recommended provision of paid annual leave should be made available to everyone.

10. A complaints procedure should be agreed in each mine and all staff encouraged to use it.

11. If miners, especially slave labourers, live on site, proper, discrete accommodation has to be provided for them.

12. There has to be an agreed retirement date for all workers, including slaves and a pension plan for each worker.

Those were the specific points we raised – but also the general rules applying to slaves applied to these slaves as well.

We recognised there were many who would baulk at the cost of all this – but we pointed out that there is no way you can count the value of a human life in terms of hard cash. We hammered these points out in two days of intensive negotiation and debate, often involving outside specialists. For instance, the point about retirement rights was raised by the Mining Union General Secretary, who was pleased we were addressing the issues of the abuses with the required level of seriousness.

At the same time, we had a second document ready for discussion, labelled confidential. It was prepared by our accountant and referred to the new Accountant General. It covered the amount of cash siphoned off, or redirected from, each of the mines for which we were able to obtain exact figures (seventeen out of twenty) and estimates for the final three based on averages from the others. The figures were astronomical. The three of us called the two accountants who had prepared the report to meet us and made them take us through the figures, justifying each one in turn. They were absolutely convinced (and convincing) of the accuracy of the first seventeen figures but issued us with a strong warning about the final three. Basically, the statement there was, "enquiries are continuing." However, they felt, and we agreed, that they could present these figures to a closed cabinet meeting and defend them. I suggested a three stage process – first the President and Vice President, then the Senior Cabinet Ministers, and finally the whole Cabinet, thus expanding the group each time. They thought this was a good idea, and I left the meeting, to take it to Dad. He listened to me, asked to see the report, which I showed him, and, reading it, his face paled slightly. "My God!" he said, "how did he get away with this?" I told him I intended to find out and explained what I intended to do. (I will write about that later in this chapter). He agreed that I should do so and also the document should be labelled Most Secret, be given out at the start of a meeting and all copies collected after the meeting ended. "This must not get out!" he said urgently. I told him I knew, agreed and understood. He asked where our accountants were, and I told him they were waiting with Judy in our apartment while I spoke to him. He stood up, left what he was doing, and returned with me.

He spoke with the two men and asked them searching questions similar to the ones we had asked about their findings before agreeing to the time table and approving dates. So began a series of secret meetings at which the figures were digested, and the implications studied in ever wider circles, with the story kept securely under wraps. By the time of the full special cabinet meeting it had been decided that Judy and I would use all our best endeavours to find out how this gigantic fraud or simple theft, however you want to define it, came about and was so successful for so long. I told them this involved research into the life of Josiah Ndenge, and this was agreed. I also told them we might be talking to each of them in turn, to explore their memories and experiences of dealing with this man, to which they also agreed. Meanwhile, the accounting team continued their investigation into the remaining three mines, trying to find the full extent of the theft. This was proving to be extremely difficult as many of the records had been destroyed. With that, the meeting was adjourned, and all the papers were collected in. No one was exempted – not even the President. Indeed, Dad handed in his copy first, in order to set an example to the others. The same evening I attended an important ceremony. I finally got round to arranging a visit from the Palace barber who cut my hair so I no longer seemed to be a brown haired twin to the blond haired Judy. Judy, who had been pestering me about it ever since we returned from the hospital on the first day, expressed her satisfaction. "At last!" was her only comment when she saw the result.

Next day we attended another meeting. This one was a meeting of the inspection team, to which three people had been added – Ade, Longinus and Daniel (the former manager) from the St Michael's Island team. I told them our target now moved to the Slave Breeding Centres. We, however, were recusing ourselves because of our prior experience as a slave at a breeding centre. Jake, Ade, Longinus and Daniel (all with experience of this type of centre) were going to lead the team. We were going to conduct an additional but related piece of research – looking at the life and activities of Josiah Ndenge. Judy and I kicked off the conference by giving them a slave's eye view of a centre, outlining the basic programme followed and the feelings we experienced (all described by me earlier in this book), and stressing that there were few opportunities for financial exploitation in this type of institution, but considerable opportunity for personal exploitation and abuse of the slaves individually or collectively. Judy finished off our contribution by saying we had personally experienced this and preferred not to talk about it. She said they should be aware that many slaves at the centres might wish to say nothing or could be too afraid of retaliation to say anything. Finally she told them that our four colleagues, who were to lead this part of our work, would no doubt fill in details of our story and that of the two slaves who were doubling for us when they gave their addresses or in answering questions later. She said if any individual member wished to talk to us specifically about our experience, we would be happy to answer their questions on a one-to-one basis. Jake took over, thanked us for our work leading the mines section, and made it clear they fully understood and sympathised with our reasons for withdrawing from this phase of our work. We thanked him, wished them luck, and left.

Next day we led a team of police to the Ndenge house in the city. We spent the entire day combing through the multi bedroomed mansion, deserted following the arrest of the family and the sealing of the property. We removed boxes of diaries, photographs, address books, letters, school reports, company reports, and simple rough handwritten notes. We even removed a book of Sudoku puzzles! All this was in addition to passports, travel documents and laptops. On successive days we travelled to Casa Isabella and visited the family compound there – also now sealed by the federal police. Here again we removed every available document of any kind – together with two or three books which seemed to have been read a great deal and were full of annotations. The house was on the outskirts of the town, and so we avoided any possibility of coming into contact with the local military, who, in any case, were all away far to the north-west, allegedly chasing counter revolutionary bandits. Judy and I were not taken in by this designation of Jake's Partisans. We did risk asking if anyone had heard any news from St Michael's Island, and received a negative answer. After finally finishing at the house, we visited the local newspaper office and collected a file of stories on Josiah Ndenge which we had asked them to compile and photocopy for us. We had done the same thing with the national newspapers. Returning to Freetown (before the Casa Isabella garrison could return from their excursion) we turned to the political structure. We asked for details of the former Vice President's career in the United Independence Party, the only political party permitted to operate in the Republic. It was currently, suspended because of the on-going State of Emergency. We were allowed to take his file and those of his six associates, from the office. Finally, following my instinct, I looked for material related to the life of Maritza. We were surprised to receive three files on her: one each from the United Independence Party; the Federal Police; and the Security Service.

When we had collected everything, we spread the boxes we had collected across the floor of our living room, we realized they virtually covered the whole floor as well as the chairs and table. I asked Dad to come in – showed him – and he laughed. "Rather you than me, son!" was his decidedly unhelpful comment. I told him we needed two things – a large office and a trained team of detectives or historians to work with us. He nodded, suddenly serious, and said he would see what he could do. While he did so, we went off to the firing range and worked on our shooting. When we returned, we found our living room empty and a key and a note on the table. It just said come to Room 26. That meant the sixth room on the second floor. We went down and found everything had been laid out in a medium sized conference room, and ten young men and women were wading through it. They turned around as we entered, and an older man, I had not noticed, came forward to greet us. He explained he was Professor Nwamarkwa from Freetown University Department of History. The young people were his students who had volunteered to take part in the project. He asked me to explain to them what we were looking for. I called them to form a circle around us and sit down on the boxes, since we did not have enough chairs. (That was something we sorted out as soon as we had finished speaking). I told them we had uncovered evidence of financial irregularities of considerable importance. We needed to find out how they were carried out and why it took so long to catch up with them. We also wanted to know the motivation behind the actions of the man we were investigating.

"Everything you see around you concerns the life and actions of this man and his friends. The man was Josiah Ndenge, who until ten weeks ago was Vice President of the Republic and head of all the Mining Companies in the country after he had nationalised them following the Revolution. We intend to build up a complete picture of the man from his birth until his recent death. Will you help us?"

They all agreed, and we left them in the hands of their Professor, as they worked out how they would proceed with the task, while we went on a chair and table hunt for eleven people. I started, as I usually did, at Dad's office. He was expecting me and had already begun the search. Within half an hour, palace staff had found us five large tables and thirteen chairs. When we returned to the conference room, we found the tables had already been labelled with figures; 0-10, 11-20, 21-30, 31-40, 41+. The professor explained that these referred to Josiah's age and his students were now reviewing every document and photograph to place it in the right age bracket. Once we understood the system we began to work with them, taking a box each and going through it. Once a box was emptied, we collapsed it and piled it up in one corner of the room. We worked on this preliminary stage for a week, until every box and file had been emptied and the tables were all stacked with assorted papers, books, photos and other documents. We looked at the piles and talked with the professor and sought his advice. He suggested that we needed a larger team to sort the documents into chronological order and thereby construct a timeline of the main events in the man's life. We agreed, and he found another ten students to help us, while we found additional chairs for them. We set four to a table; setting them three tasks to be accomplished in sequence. The first was to arrange the documents; the second was to produce a timeline; the third was to produce a mini biography. I looked at the professor. "Do you have four more of your excellent students we can beg, borrow or steal?" I asked. He looked surprised, but nodded, made a phone call, and, like magic, four girls appeared an hour later. Meanwhile we had gone from table to table collecting diaries and address books. We put slips in the books indicating what table each came from and promised they would be returned as soon as the students had processed them. I took the girls to our living room, so they could use the table there. I gave them a laptop and told them to create a spreadsheet. They should start with the first diary or address book. I told them to ignore the diary entries and just look at the addresses and phone numbers, etc, of his friends and family. That's what we wanted them to put on the spread sheet. For each entry there should be a date, name, address, phone or mobile number and e-mail address if one existed. Once a book was dealt with, I told them to put it on our desk with the slip in it, so we could return it. I pointed out that, as they moved from one book to another, certain names would recur. They should enter the new details under the date in the row allocated to that name. They nodded and started work.

Meanwhile, we began the laborious process of creating a family tree. We discovered African family trees are not like British ones were (relatively simple). Instead, they are incredibly complex, due to polygamy and extended family systems that go back through generations and extend over multiple levels of kinship. We went from table to table collecting information on family from the four researchers and writing it down. Our problem was that there were obviously individuals alive who knew the information we were seeking to find, but it was unlikely that they would assist us, in view of what they perceived to be our role in Josiah's death. Above all, I hoped that one of my researchers would stumble on one family member who he'd offended or who just didn't like him. Eventually, one turned up – a distant cousin who had been sacked by him after he'd complained about Josiah's business methods. We took his name and address – in Freetown – and went to see him. We told him what we were doing and why we were doing it – and he expressed approval. He asked how he could help.

"By doing two things," I said. "The first is by compiling his family tree as far as you can, as it exists at the moment – or, at least, up to this year. The second is to tell us more about your sacking and what you know of his business methods that concerned you as well as anything else that might help to explain his character and his behaviour."

"Leave the family tree with me," he answered. "I'll bring it to you at the palace by the end of the week."

Then he spoke to us about the quarrel. He told us he was suspicious of the amounts of money that seemed to pass through his cousin's hands. He knew about the turnover of the company where he worked and the profits never seemed to match up to what he had seen go in and out of the factory. He had asked Josiah about this and Josiah became very angry, told him to keep his nose out of his affairs and sacked him instantly. I noted this, took the name and address of the company, a fruit and vegetable canning operation on the outskirts of the capital, together with the date. We thanked him and left. We then began to work our way through the cabinet members, picking up odd bits of information, which we entered on the computerised record we were building, but none of which really led anywhere.

Something had been bugging me since we had begun this document chase. It was a while before I put my finger on it. I realized it was the way the town of Casa Isabella kept cropping up. I looked up the number of the town hall and telephoned the Council Chief Executive. I asked if they had a local business directory and a list of people registered to vote and live in the area. He told me they had, and I asked for a copy of each. They arrived by express post three days later. For the moment, the names meant little to me, but I had a gut feeling that they might mean a lot more later. Meanwhile, the meticulous research went on. The piles of documents on each table reduced in size and the timelines with annotations grew in length and complexity, as did the chart of contacts. Two days later, the Josiah Ndenge Family Tree arrived – a massive document, which, when opened up, covered an entire wall in our living room. On a hunch, I began to cross check the names on the family tree with the names on the register. I noticed that name after name appeared on both. I pulled one of the girls, Julia, off my mini team, giving her a marker pen and the register. I asked her to look for names in the register on the family tree, and, if she found them, to mark them in both documents. A few days later, while looking at the family tree to see how Julia was getting on, I noticed Musaveni's name on it. I looked further and picked out the names of the six Ministers who had supported Ndenge on the Cabinet and were involved in the fraud with him. At that point everything clicked into place in my mind. I mentioned my discovery that evening after dinner. Dad nodded. "That explains why he was able to do it so easily and for so long," he commented.

One evening, Dad came in to see how we were progressing. We explained how we were working and showed how our team had nearly completed a timeline of his life. Then, I told him, we were going to construct a basic biography. We were planning to add interviews to get extra colour and a clearer understanding of this man. We went to our living room and I showed him the spread sheet of contacts we were building up. Judy had been working on this and we had a list of English names and addresses from his early years and teens. I gave them to Dad. "Could you help us?" I asked. He asked how. "Could you take these names, check them against the names of people who were enslaved and see if any are on that list?" He said he would and eventually came up with two possible names. The first was a male slave worker at a factory on the outskirts of Freetown, and the other was a female slave in the household of a wealthy banker in the town of Ancora on the south-western border. We visited both of them. The man was of little help. He said they'd been friends at University, members of an African Society. "Josiah," he said, "was very serious and frankly, boring." He only seemed to be interested in money-making schemes. He broke with Josiah, at the end of the second year, when he had real reason to suspect that Josiah was involved in stealing from the Society and in some sort of financial fiddle with other foreign students.

He had, however, no proof either way. It was just a strong hunch and persistent rumour.

The owner of the female slave was suspicious of our motives and insisted on sitting in on our interview with her. He thought we were trying to take her away or find out something detrimental to himself. He was surprised when he found we were asking about events in England thirty years earlier and involving the former Vice President. She told us she had been Josiah's girlfriend for a few months when he was a sixth former at Eton. She lived in the area and was in her fourth year at secondary school. She said he seemed quite a glamorous person, but the glamour was illusory. He was not really interested in her as a girl, but as a sort of trophy. He almost carried her around as an exhibit for his African friends – "look, I've got a white girl friend." She got tired of him and dropped him. He was very angry and considered that he had been humiliated by her because he was black. She heard he had hated white people ever since. We asked her some more questions, but that was the most important thing she told us. She did say that she was frightened he might come to the town as Vice President, see her in her new situation, recognise her and try to take his revenge on her for his perceived humiliation. I assured her that she had no need to be afraid of him any more as he was no longer alive.

It was while we were interviewing the cabinet members that Professor Nwamarkwa asked to speak to me. When I met him he showed me a hand-written document, explaining it had been found and brought to him by one of the students who was part of the team building the 41+ files. It was an informal note of what might be called a family meeting. It consisted of Josiah and his six cabinet allies and an additional name, otherwise unknown to us. It took place during the planning of the coup, after the outbreak of the Northern War. I read the note and realized that this was the smoking gun. It comprised two elements. The first was what they planned for Dad. He was to be a figurehead President, cut off from all real power, but useful (in the short term) to carry the blame for the unpopular policies deemed necessary by the group at the outset. At the appropriate time the President and his wife were to be assassinated. They intended to replace him with Josiah Ndenge and pack the cabinet with relatives and associates of his. The same section also included the intended murder of President and Mrs Igbokwe and their children. The other, included the detailed instructions for our enslavement and our subsequent use as slaves (the part they were authorised to investigate, and which was reported and approved by the overall group of plotters later). *(See chapter three)*. Interestingly, there was no mention of the issues which most angered and humiliated us slaves – that of our compulsory nudity and vulnerability to assault from the public without recourse to legal protection. That confirmed what Dad had told us. I showed it to Judy later the same evening.

This document made us understand that Ndenge and his associates, among whom had to be included Maritza and Letizia, had intended to degrade us to a point where we weren't even seen as subhuman, but as little more than animals. It partially explained why Maritza treated us (and, by extension, Chloe and Colin) as objects or playthings, to be used and hurt or damaged without any concern for our emotional or physical well-being. We were less important to the two women than the beds they slept on were.

I photocopied the notes and took them to Dad, who was less angry than I expected. He had realized the truth some time before, as had we. That was not the reason I took it to him though. I showed him the list of participants and pointed to the extra name. I asked if he knew who it was, and he said yes, grimly. He told me it was the CO of the regiment garrisoned at Casa Isabella. He told me that Musaveni had commanded the assault on the Palace, leading units from his own regiment, that subsequently formed the Palace Guard we had eliminated and replaced by members of Dad's regiment. We looked at each other. It was clear that Casa Isabella was the centre of the armed opposition to the Government. I asked Dad to come and look at the Ndenge family tree. He came with me and I asked Julia, the student who was working on it, to explain it to him. Seventy-five per cent of the names were underlined in red, including that of Colonel Musaveni and the six former ministers. He looked stunned. "So," he said to me, "Colonel Musaveni is now the leader of the Ndenge group." He left me, looking deep in thought.

Meanwhile, the first two slave breeding centres had been visited, and the reports reached our desks. They contained no surprises, and the main recommendations comprising outdoor clothing and recreational clothing for slaves, time limits on milking and harvesting, regular medical checks of slaves, an end to non-punishment floggings, careful checks on staff behaviour and attitude and a complete ban on making slaves work on fieldwork or on the milking and harvesting machines overnight, were in line with what we had come up with following our experience on St Michael's Island. We sent the reports to the Secretariat for printing. The regular fortnightly cabinet meeting approved our final report on the mines and a decree was issued regarding the care, conditions of work and supervision of mine working slaves. Dad also published a decree freeing the St Michael's Island slaves unconditionally, and a press statement announcing the freeing and adoption of Chloe and Colin.

The sub-team completed their recording work at the end of the first week and we set the three girls a second task; to read and review the diaries, warning them to look for references to Maritza or Letizia. I told them to note any references and pass the notes to us. I also recalled the accounting team, realising that there were financial transactions of some kind recorded at the end of the diaries, and they joined us in the detailed diary research. The meticulous work of comparing the family tree with the residential list at Casa Isabella was also close to conclusion. I gave the girl doing it the business directory and asked her, once she had finished her first task, underlining relatives in red, if she would compare names in the directory with those on the family tree as well and underline common names in blue – adding the name of the company underneath. After further consideration, I detached a second member from the main team, and told her to use our phone and talk to all the people she could identify from the spread sheet, working backwards, so long as they lived in Austrasia or elsewhere in Africa. If she found anyone of real interest, she was to invite them to come to us for interview, and, if they agreed, make an appointment. Finally, I asked them to pass anything they learned from the phone interviews or diaries about Josiah to the main team dealing with that decade.

In the main hall, some teams had reached the third stage, writing an outline biography. The teams dealing with Josiah's first ten years had least to do and were nearly finished. I asked the Professor to split them and move two members to the team dealing with his years in government, the most complex area of investigation.

Judy and I divided our forces. She took over leading the work of the office – becoming quite busy with cabinet papers, reports from our inspection teams, and now documents from the research group, while I continued to work with the Professor's team. We ate together, went shooting together, and, of course, slept together – but otherwise worked separately. We both realized how important the research work was, but also how big an exercise it was proving to be. Our evening meals in the Presidential apartment became almost a nightly conference, reporting progress. The number of people involved had grown from 5 to 10, including Chloe, Colin, Longinus, Daniel and Ade. Dad became anxious to track down the Musaveni regiment, as he termed it, and Jake became concerned for the group based, I had learned, in the caves behind the Ngugi waterfall in the mountains. We sent out a reconnaissance group, using members of Dad's old regiment not incorporated in the Palace Guard. They confirmed that the "Partisans" had not been troubled. They also informed us the Musaveni regiment was still scouring the forests of the north-west, but that Musaveni had obviously heard of the events at St Michael's Island, because he had sent a detachment to occupy it. Dad said he was not surprised, although he was surprised that Musaveni had learnt so soon and acted so quickly. Judy said the explanation was obvious. Dad looked at her quizzically. "It's obvious, really," she said, "and we should have realized it as soon as Chloe and Colin were kidnapped. Maritza and he were in regular contact. She either sent a panicked message as our attack developed or he realized when the contact stopped suddenly and sent someone to investigate."

Spurred by this revelation, I opened my Maritza files, and found the documentation we had removed from the Island. Amongst the official documents that comprised part of our post action report, I found her diaries for the previous two years. I read them and was sickened by what I read. Had she been alive, they would have formed the basis of a prosecution. As she was dead, they were not relevant, except as a warning about the dangers of racism and the need to vet applicants for posts dealing with racial minorities very carefully. Because of this, I authorised some extracts from her diary to be included in our report and circulated to the press. However, I also found evidence of her affair with Ndenge and her connections with Musaveni. I found out, quite quickly, that they were siblings, as was her relationship with the woman who had been imprisoned for the first attack on us. Musaveni was the oldest and Maritza was the youngest of the three. I realized he now had three reasons to hate us and want to kill us. I told Judy and we resolved that we would only meet him if and when he was arrested and disarmed, and in our office with two armed guards behind him. As I commented to Dad earlier, if you are dealing with a venomous snake, you ensure you keep a thick pane of glass between you and it. Incidentally, it also seemed that Letizia was distantly related to the Musaveni family. It appears that our contact who drew up the Ndenge family tree was unaware of it.

One afternoon, while we were in the middle of the investigation, Dad called me to his office and asked me to go to Tolosa to find out the truth about the disappearance of a B Class slave from the local slave breeding centre. He felt the other slaves might talk to me and tell me what they knew since the Governor could not get them to speak to her. I asked Jake to come with me and we travelled to Tolosa on the following day. On our arrival at the centre, which we saw resembled the one on St Michael's Island, we went to meet the Governor. She told us the male slave had disappeared one afternoon about three weeks before during their Sunday recreation period. His female partner, treated according to law as a suspected escapee, was awaiting execution. However, she had delayed this because she was not convinced that the man had actually absconded voluntarily. She wanted us to try to get the truth from the other slaves.

We found the eighteen slaves gathered in their seating area. I introduced myself, telling them who Jake and I were and why we were there. There was silence for a few moments before one of the female slaves spoke.

"What will you do to Louise if I tell you what happened?"

"Do you know the law?" I asked.

"Yes. That's why I asked."

"We will try to save her life."

She looked relieved and then told us what she knew.

"It's actually quite simple. He was kidnapped. Two local men signed for him to come over to them while we were relaxing during our Sunday afternoon recreation period. He walked over to them and, before any of us could interfere, one of the men pulled a sack over his head and the other bound his arms to his side by tying a rope around the sack. They bundled him into their car and drove off. He never returned."

I asked if anyone could confirm this story and several did so.

We thanked them and returned to the Governor's office in order to report to her. She thanked us and told us she had heard of similar happenings elsewhere. Apparently B and P Class slaves were being kidnapped quite often. They were then put up for sale in illegal and unlicensed slave markets.

"My problem," she said, "is that I don't know what to do with the slave girl involved. It seems wrong to hang her when her partner didn't try to escape and was taken away against his will. However, I can neither keep her here nor free her."

We told her we would take the girl with us and employ her in the Palace as part of the domestic staff. The Governor took us down to her. When we entered her cell she stood up and backed away from us, her eyes showing her terror. We assured her that we were not going to hang her. Instead, we planned to take her away and find her a job in the Presidential Palace. We took her from the cell and the Governor found clothes for her and she flew back to Freetown with us. Sadly, we never discovered the fate of her former companion who she told us was named Marcel.

Jake followed the issue up with police chiefs throughout the country. We were told it was a bit like cattle rustling used to be. He managed to recover a few slaves and arrested and imprisoned a few thieves. However, the majority of cases were not resolved. Arising from this case, Dad persuaded the cabinet to repeal the law that ordered both partners to be punished in the same way if one of them broke the law. This case made Judy and I wonder whether Antonio and/or Maria had suffered in this way.

Despite our absence, the work went on. As the groups finished their sectional biographies, so Josiah Ndenge came back to life in front of us. The bare bones of his life began to be filled in by extracts from the documents, dairies and the interviews we were able to obtain (not everyone proved willing to talk to us). The final stage was to illustrate the story with photographs, chosen by the individual teams in consultation with the Professor and ultimately approved by the five of us. Once work on the written content of the diaries was finished, they were handed over to the accounting team, who were able to use the figures in the later diaries to complete their analysis. We found no other evidence. It was clear to us that some evidence had been destroyed by the Ndenge family (and we drew Dad's attention to this.) Again, he was not surprised. "I expected it," he commented. Our sub-team finally completed their work, and the family tree was now a mass of black lines connecting the family members, red lines indicating individuals living in Casa Isabella, and blue lines showing family ownership of businesses in the town. It presented an alarming picture, showing that the Ndenge family, secure in their Casa Isabella (and now St Michael's Island) bases were still a major danger. Thanks to I.T., the different sections of the biography were easily put together. We sent the text off to the Government printer and told them to print and bind it in fifty initial copies – for the team and the Cabinet. We entitled it 'Josiah Ndenge, thief and traitor, a life.'

The team concluded that the evidence we gathered showed that Josiah Ndenge had had two basic motivations behind his actions. The first was a love of money and a desire for the power it gave him. This seemed to have been caused by his father's physical abuse of him as a child and the family's relative poverty. He believed this was partly down to European (and especially British) colonial exploitation. That was the origin of the second driving force which impelled him – a hatred of white Europeans and especially white Britons. That hatred was only intensified when Rosalyn (the slave I spoke to in Ancora) dumped him. His diary confirmed Rosalyn's belief about his attitude and suggested she was right to fear his vengeance if he found her. His craving for money and power was the basic cause of the coup against Frederick Igbokwe. Josiah was one of his Ministers and President Igbokwe discovered he had been purloining monies allocated to the armed forces. He warned Josiah to stop and return the money he had stolen, or face dismissal and arrest. The coup was to pre-empt this. However, once in power, he was able to nationalise the twenty mines and take them over, sharing the spoils with his relatives (the six Ministers and Colonel Musaveni). He had to kill President Igbokwe in order to allow him to kill the other Minsters, whose properties and bank accounts he then appropriated for his family and associates. We, the fifteen thousand, of course paid for his obsessions, and especially the eleven hundred slaves in the mines.

We finished our work as the inspection team finished theirs. As a result, our secretariat was kept very busy producing reports. The final report on the Ndenge mine frauds was also made ready at that time. Marked 'Top Secret' it was also printed. As a result, cabinet members had three reports to consider – the Ndenge life report; the Ndenge fraud report; and the Slave Breeding Centre report. To complete our inspection work, we arranged a visit by our entire team, including ourselves, to one of the two AI (Artificial Insemination) laboratories, which we found very interesting, but, as we saw no issues needing our intervention, we merely noted the visit in our final report without comment. I did, however, ask Dad, what plans he had for the individuals given life by this process. Typically, I'm afraid to say, at that stage he had no plans at all for them.

The cabinet accepted our reports. The first and third were authorised for publication, together with a decree bringing together all our recommendations arising from our inspections, and setting new regulations for the care, use, legal definition, status, and consequential rights of slaves. The work of the inspection team was over. They received thanks and appropriate remuneration from the President. The former Governor of St Michael's Island, suitably sobered by the realisation of how his errors at the island had enabled the abuses there to flourish, was reassigned to another management position. The fraud report was passed to the police, the intelligence service and the Accountant General in an effort to track down and recover the stolen money. This was destined to take decades and will probably only partly succeed.

Mark goes on to discuss other issues, most notably the schools and the nascent simmering rebellion, so I thought it appropriate to sum up this major section of his book. I've read all three of the reports he described. He has given a full account of what they found, and the remedies proposed, so there is no need to repeat them. The slavery decree referred to the problems found and set out new regulations for the care of slaves. The following is the most important part.

"Most slaves are employed in homes, small businesses or factories. Slaves involved in meeting the public must be, at least, basically clothed (loincloth or breech cloth and suitable footwear), but preferably suitably or fully clothed, even if it is a clearly identifiable slave tunic.

"Slaves must never be naked in public – but can be naked in the homes of private owners if the owners so decide. Slaves in mines must always be properly fully clothed in protective clothing. Slaves in breeding centres must be necessarily naked for milking and harvesting, but otherwise basically clothed.

"Owners and users are entitled to punish slaves, but punishments must be for infringements of rules or other misbehaviour, not as exemplars or warnings, or as a result of capriciousness, and must be proportionate to any offence alleged or committed. Owners who cause the death of a slave deliberately will face the same punishment as if they had killed a non-slave, as will owners who cause such a death by reason of neglect. If a slave is killed accidently, it will be independently investigated to ensure there was no foul play involved. No person may hurt or abuse a slave who does not belong to them."

There were other issues referred to, but they're the most important.

The Ndenge book is a devastating indictment of the man, more impressive in that it was independently written and published under the University's authority. The fraud report is absolutely shattering, and the amounts involved were nearly ten times the annual GDP of the Republic. It's no wonder they kept it quiet – both Ndenge reports are also, if unintentionally, indictments of President Ngangi's early rule.

CHAPTER 24

Renewing Old Acquaintances

Once the inspections and investigations into the Ndenge clique and plot were completed, Mum and Dad took us aside, looked us up and down, and he said, "You both look exhausted. Go away somewhere and have a holiday. You can go anywhere in the Republic." Judy interrupted Dad, "...except Casa Isabella or St Michael's Island," she added. Dad nodded, "except those," he said.

"The Secretariat team is very good, and Emma is an efficient leader in your absence," Mum said. "You can leave everything in their hands. They can come to us if there are any problems."

We looked at one another silently for a minute or two, both thinking, before we both nodded and turned around. "Okay," I said for both of us, "We'll go to Concordia to visit our old school. Dad, please will you let them know and make clear the sort of reception you expect them to give us. Tell the local Party Secretary to organise it." "Of course, son," he answered, and I'll send you a small military escort to make the point. Be sure to wear your uniforms and go armed." Mum underlined the point, saying she felt we should do so wherever we went at the moment. However, they both said the school visit would not be enough. I told him we were going to ask Jake to take us with a strong military escort on a safari to Ngugi Falls when we returned from the school. We said we would not go anywhere near Casa Isabella. They agreed and said they would talk to Jake.

So three days later we set out for the northern border town of Concordia where we had been based before we were enslaved. Jake insisted on coming with us and selected a group consisting of half of the party which went with us to St Michael's Island. We travelled by plane and were met at the airport by the Party Secretary and a welcoming party of civic dignitaries, headed by the Mayor and an honour guard drawn from the local garrison. The National Anthem was played, and the oath of loyalty recited. We were invited to inspect the guard of honour before the Mayor formally greeted us in a speech in which he expressed the honour the town felt that we had chosen them for our first official visit.

I answered the greeting.

"Mr Mayor," I said, "We feel gratified that you and your colleagues now feel honoured by our presence. We noticed you've sent cars to carry us to the town hall and the school. I'm sure our official portraits now illuminate both buildings and I'm equally sure they're festooned. round the town. I'm certain you'll forgive us when I tell you we still remember our last mode of transportation between the school and the town hall and what happened on the steps of that building." I saw them look at each other and grimace. "You and we were dressed somewhat differently then, weren't we? And what touched us was not a friendly handshake but something altogether different and decidedly warmer!

"However, that was then, and this is now. Things have changed, and we have to change with them. Then we were young, stateless foreigners, orphaned by actions over which we had no control thousands of miles away. Now, we are citizens of the Republic like yourselves, but unlike yourselves. When the United States still existed they had special titles for Presidential children. I would be called the First Son, and Judy, the First Daughter. We're also commissioned officers in the Army. These handguns are not for decoration because we've been trained to use them. We're senior members of the Government. Once, we were your helpless victims; now we're your masters. It behoves everyone here to remember that. Several times, over the last few months we've been told it's our Christian duty to forgive those who offend us. Ignoring the assumption that we're Christians for the moment, we need to see evidence that anyone here sees a need for forgiveness, so let me help you.

"We came here at the ages of twenty-three and twenty-one, full of enthusiasm and with a desire to help you and your children. Because of this, we were not with our families when our and their world and their lives were destroyed. Instead our care became your responsibility. You took away all we had left after the destruction of our homes – our possessions, our clothes, our dignity, our freedom. We were branded in two places and placed in chains. Then, presumably tired of carrying us tied to poles and on your shoulders, you put us in cages piled on the back of a lorry and sent us away. That's not the complete tale of what was done to us, but you know that. We were designated as breeding animals and sent to a centre where I was placed on a milking machine, like a cow, and Judy had her insides almost sucked out on what was called a harvesting machine. We were made to work, naked and barefoot on a farm, pulling out weeds with our bare hands and moving dirt in the same way. We were flogged for no reason regularly and raped in every way physically possible, sometimes in several different ways at the same time and by different people. I was once raped in three different places at the same time. You're all men – so you know and understand what I mean.

"That was the consequence of your actions that day – and we have been asked to forgive you. Really? The only reason we're here was because another intended victim of the Revolution, the President (and his wife), saw us, liked us, and decided to adopt us. They did so, but in order to adopt a living son and daughter they had to save our lives first because a vengeful woman tried to kill us and very nearly succeeded in beating us to death. Instead, she is now dead. That's the forgiveness we showed her. What sort of forgiveness do you and your townsfolk seek – the forgiveness we showed Maritza or the forgiveness we have shown all those in the government who were deceived into voting us into slavery? I can offer both." I pulled my handgun out. "As I told you this is not a decoration. This is one kind of conclusion to the issues presently between us. There are two more handguns and ten rifles behind me to add to it." I put the gun away and put my open hand out. "Or this? On the whole I prefer the second option – but it's your choice and you must make it."

There was silence as I stepped down from the podium. I knew my words were broadcast over the local radio station and relayed from speakers in the street. We waited, and then the Mayor ascended the podium for a second time.

"Mr and Mrs Ngangi, Mark and Judy, you have spoken fairly of the terribly bad wrong we all did to you. We are all guilty – doubly so, because we knew you were orphans and what our customs told us was our duty to orphans, however old they are. We did not do what we should have done. We should have embraced you in our arms and comforted you in your distress and nurtured you as our future fellow citizens. Instead we stripped you of everything and treated you like, but worse than, our animals. We were wrong, very wrong. We did wrong, very wrong. We could make excuses – but they would be excuses. We knew our duty to you. We deliberately and wilfully failed to do it. We should have protected you from harm. Instead we inflicted it. Personally speaking, I have never forgiven myself or understood what drove me that day. It was I who drove the heated branding irons into your skins and the skins of your two companions, not once, but twice; not twice, but eight times!" He knelt on the podium. "I know I don't deserve your forgiveness, but I beg you to forgive me and my equally misled companions."

We looked around and saw that the councillors and the Party Secretary had also knelt. I looked at Judy and nodded to her. She walked over to the Mayor, while I walked to the Party Secretary. We held our right hands on their heads and Judy spoke for us both.

"We forgive you and all your companions for the wrong you have done to all of us, and through you, for all who were involved in our enslavement and those of the other fourteen thousand, nine hundred and ninety- eight foreigners living and working in (or just visiting) the country. We obviously cannot speak for the others, some of whom sadly will never be able to say the words of forgiveness because they're dead and some will never wish to. Nor can we forgive everyone involved, because some of the crimes committed can only be forgiven by God, if there is such a being as a god. None of you here are like that. So, for us and for you the past is past. That was what it was. This is the present. It is what it is. But we have to live together for the future. Let that be what it will be. We, the First Son and First Daughter (and through us, our future child and any who will come to us later) call on you all – those here, those in Concordia, those in our old school and those of you listening to us on the radio or watching us on television: let us all forget the past. Let it go. Let the enmities and hatreds which caused an otherwise good people to do what they did to fifteen thousand foreign orphans die. Let us come together to build a new future for this country and our world. Our world was destroyed because of mutual enmities. Let us learn from the mistakes of the Northern rulers and peoples and not let it happen again. We, in Africa and the South are all that's left. A huge responsibility rests on our shoulders. Let us prove ourselves worthy of it."

She stepped down from the podium to spontaneous applause, and we were then given a warm and heartfelt greeting, which was echoed by the crowds who lined the street as our procession made its way to the school, consciously retaking the route followed by those who carried us down to be branded and chained once we reached the town hall. At the school we were greeted by the Head, staff and children. They were waving flags and cheering us. We smiled at them and were given chairs and invited to sit and watch them as they performed a local dance of welcome and sang a hymn to welcome us, followed by the National Anthem. I walked forward to the microphone.

"Headmaster, our former fellow staff members, pupils and, I see, some parents. I'm sure you've heard what we said at the airport. I'm not going to repeat it. I still remember, Headmaster, that you tried to warn us, and we took no notice. Unfortunately, that cost the lives of Mr and Mrs Gooding, and we have not been able to find any trace of Mr and Mrs Maulucci. We alone are able to come back here and are pleased to be here. None of you had any part in what happened to us except for two (I must assume to be) student teachers, who we will speak to afterwards. I suspect the senior pupils who were responsible for attacking us have left, and we have a good idea where they might be. If you're listening, and I feel sure you are, wherever you are, remember this saying – you can run, but you can't hide. Some time, somewhere, we and Nemesis are going to catch up with you – and then you will answer for your crimes. Be assured, we will not forget you, however long it takes. I have been reminded several times of the saying that vengeance is a dish best served cold. You were ordered by others – and I know who they were (and some are no longer in our world) – but that does not excuse you. You knew us and you knew who and what we were. The young people here took no part in what you did – you should have done the same. When you next meet with Colonel Musaveni, tell him I said so and warn him he needs to constantly look behind him because he will never know who's there." I smiled at them all and added, as I drew my handgun out, "some people think this is just a decoration, but it's not. We, like you, have both been taking lessons. You've been reading your books; we've been shooting our guns."

I pointed to a tin lying on the ground about twenty feet away. "Watch the tin." I pulled off the safety catch, pointed the pistol and fired at the tin. The tin jumped into the air and moved a few feet. I blew the smoke from the barrel theatrically, put the safety catch back on and put the pistol in its holster, the children clapped and cheered. We walked into the staff room where food and drinks awaited us. Judy said she couldn't drink beer or spirits and asked for a soft drink instead. One of the female staff asked if she was pregnant, because she had never previously refused alcohol. Judy smiled and answered, "What do you think?" The woman knew she had her answer. I went over to the two student teachers to put them out of their misery. I told them they were not involved in what happened to us. I asked them a simple question: "Did the five students come from Casa Isabella and have they returned there?" They nodded and we left it at that.

From there on the visit was largely ceremonial. We met and spoke to the students, much older now, who we had taught, and answered their questions – about what it was like being a slave and what it was like now being a First Son and First Daughter. We told them. Later the three of us were entertained by the Head and his wife. They brought us up to date with events at the school. They told us what they wanted us to do for them. We promised to do our best. Then, after thanking them and the staff for their hospitality, we left for the town hall where we met the council members and listened to their requests. We both addressed them briefly, were entertained by them to a cocktail party, and finally left, returning to the Palace at about 21.00 hours.

Our parents greeted us, and the three of us were treated to a late supper. They told us they had listened to our three speeches at Concordia.

"I was taken aback at first by the way you spoke to the Mayor, son," Dad said. "I wouldn't have dared to speak that way, no matter how they'd treated me. Listening, though, I felt you had struck the right note. They certainly reacted dramatically."

I asked them if they thought our action and Judy's words were over theatrical. "Like your pistol shot," Mum smiled. "Exactly!" I replied. Dad conceded it was sometimes necessary to use theatre to convey a meaning. Jake agreed commenting that actions were often more valuable than a thousand words.

I told Dad we had realized we could not sensibly undertake to visit every school; there were simply too many and suggested we should set up an inspection service such as they used to have in England. Dad asked us to explain how it worked. We explained as best we could. Mum told us she had some books about the old British education system and she promised to look up inspections and see what she could find out. Judy told her to look up the word Ofsted – meaning Office for Standards in Education. She said she would, and, eventually, they did set up an Austrasian version of Ofsted.

We went on to discuss our intended safari. Dad an Mum had been working behind the scenes while we were at Concordia and had made all the arrangements.

"Chloe and Colin are coming with you. Louis will be in charge and your St Michael's Island squad will accompany you. One of them's a cook, so you'll be fed properly. We have hired mules to carry food, water and tents, etc., and you will carry your spare clothing in rucksacks. Louis will explain."

Having said this, Dad pointed to the map of Austrasia on the wall.

"We'll fly you all to here," he said, pointing to the town of Fort Augusta which is about fifty miles east of Casa Isabella, "and a coach will take you to here," pointing to an obviously largish village. "The mules are here, and their owners will act as muleteers for you." He and Jake looked at the map. Jake nodded. He knew the area and the village. He also knew the route from there. He told us it it was a six day trek from there to the cave (about one hundred and twenty miles). We were due to start two days later. I asked if Chloe and Colin were up to it. They assured me the two of them were fit enough and our parents thought the journey would be good for them. Judy asked what clothing they would wear. Mum told her not to worry; they were going to wear military uniform – but not as officers. "And they won't carry weapons," Dad added. "Otherwise they might be tempted to use them, and heaven alone knows what or who they would hit if they tried that!" I crossed myself, and they all laughed. "I thought you said you weren't Christians!" Mum pointed out. We grinned, thanked them for our late supper, and left to go to bed.

Two days later, standing on the edge of the wilderness, we did not feel so sure of ourselves. I looked at the long column behind us as it formed up. The five of us were at the front, accompanied by ten soldiers. In the middle came fifteen heavily laden mules and muleteers, with the other ten soldiers bringing up the rear. Four other soldiers had joined us from the troops based at Fort Augusta. They were to act as scouts, go about a mile ahead of the column and find a suitable place to pitch camp each evening. Jake spoke quietly to them, giving them instructions and checking the intercom system they were both using. Finally, he turned round, looked down the column, looked at his watch, and said, "Okay let's go!" He grinned at us. "You're lucky, we're only doing fifteen miles today because we've started so late!" I was tempted to reply – but my only thought was an extremely rude one, so I kept silent, as did Judy, although we looked at each other in a meaningful way. Jake grinned at us. He told us he knew what we were thinking, and a two fingered salute would have said the same thing. We laughed as we set off in good spirits, chatting idly as we went. The land was fairly open here. The track was very clear and quite wide. It was certainly wide enough for two to walk side by side. On a sunny day, visibility was clear too, so we were able to just spot our scouts moving ahead of us. I told Jake we should really have brought a flag with us. He grinned and pulled some coloured cloth out of his pocket. The colour and pattern seemed familiar but different from the flag we had become accustomed to. He told one of the troops to attach it to his rifle barrel, using two small metal rings in the fabric. He did so, and we were surprised to see we were flying a Union Jack. Jake noticed this and grinned. "I thought you'd be surprised," he said. He explained he did it to honour the four of us, our lost families and country. I thanked him, but, looking closely at it, I pointed out it was upside down, explaining that meant we were in distress. Jake told the soldier to turn it around and we were happy. What he didn't tell us, and what we learnt later, was that it was a signal, identifying us as a friendly force to his men and women who would be watching us from the woods before we reached the caves.

That night we camped near a stream. The mules were tethered and unloaded. The tents were erected. A foraging party collected wood for our fire. We helped the cook, and we refilled our water bottles from the stream in order to save the water we were carrying for later. The muleteers took out our bedrolls and arranged them around the fire for us to sit on. We used the metal plates and cups which hung from our rucksacks for our supper. We used bread to clean the plates between the two courses. All in all, we enjoyed our first barbeque meal. We noticed Chloe and Colin looked tired and asked how they were feeling. They had been very quiet during the walk. Colin told us they were okay, but I knew the meaning of that word spoken in that weary way. I told Jake I thought they might struggle tomorrow. He went over to them and spoke to them quietly before telling us that he agreed but he thought they would cope. However, he also spoke to two of the soldiers and placed Chloe and Colin in their care, asking them to take their rucksacks off them if they were obviously struggling too much. When he returned to us, I asked him where he got the Union Jack from. He told us he'd salvaged it from his local town hall on Independence Day before they could burn it. He kept it for a souvenir, but he had also found other uses for it.

The days succeeded each other as we got ever deeper into the wilderness. The terrain changed becoming hillier and the vegetation increased. The trees steadily grew more in number, growing closer and closer and steadily taller. They closed in on the path which reduced from a double track to a single one. Sometimes it was even narrower than that. At such times extra care was necessary because we could not be sure what we might step on. Fortunately, we didn't suffer any casualties. Jake was right. Chloe and Colin did need help on the second day. The two soldiers gave it to them, shouldering their packs as well as their own. However, they grew steadily stronger and on the last three days of the trek Colin and Chloe were fine. Each evening we camped by a stream, and once by a small lake. On the final two days we followed the bank of a river. On three evenings one of our soldiers, a hunter in his days as a civilian, shot an antelope. This was skinned and cooked for our evening meal. Our muleteers knew the forest and knew the fruits which could be eaten and those which couldn't. They foraged in the evening. While the soldiers collected the wood, they collected forest fruit. As a result, every evening, we were well fed, which strengthened us for the next day.

On the sixth and final day of the trek, one of our scouts returned to us after only two miles of walking. He brought another man with him. He was dressed in army uniform and seemed familiar to me as he came nearer. Judy and I both recognised him at the same moment. "Jack!" we called out and ran to meet him. We embraced him and he told us how pleased he was to see us. He grinned at us. "Your security isn't very good," he commented, or you would have seen us before." Bill and I were tracking you all day yesterday. We're the outer guards and we began to follow you from the moment you turned along the river. Two others have remained to keep watch in case you were followed. We knew you were friendly from the British flag. Jake always uses it as a signal to us. Jake came up to us, leading the column, and Jack fell in with us. Jake smiled at us. "You may not have seen them, but I did!" he commented. "I expected them and looked for them. Because I looked, I saw them. They've come to lead us in." He explained we had a shorter than usual walk outside (only about ten miles) but another ten miles in the cave system before we reached the main cave where we were expected, and a meal would be waiting for us. I asked about the animals. Jack explained that the donkeys would be coming in with us. "You're going to live with us for a week, so they can't stay outside." This came as a surprise to us. We expected to stay overnight and begin the return journey next day, but Jake told us Mum and Dad had told him he had to make us rest. We should only leave earlier if the cave was attacked.

The rear entrance to the cave was carefully disguised. The land suddenly rose up in front of us as the path turned away from the river. As we approached, what seemed to be a narrow cleft in the rock revealed that it was wide enough and high enough for a single person to go through or an animal to squeeze through. We entered into a dark tunnel, which we soon realized sloped downwards. Jack and Bill presented each group of us with torches, which they lit. As we continued, the passage gradually became wider and every so often we found more torches in sconces in the walls. They were lit from the torches we carried, and the first torches were extinguished in buckets of water kept at the spot. Then the old torch replaced the new in the sconce. As we went along, every so often we had to pick our way across low walls. Jack explained they were defensive and could swiftly be built up from the rocks we saw apparently haphazardly lying along the tunnel to either block the tunnel completely or to make a defensible firing line. We found evidence of small excavations on the sides of the tunnel, usually behind one of the walls. He explained these were rest areas for workers involved in wall building. Finally the tunnel opened right out, and the sides disappeared from view. We could see a fire blazing about a mile ahead and we could hear the roar of water in front of us. Within a few minutes we could see that the roar of water was formed by a screen of living water falling consistently down across the mouth of the cave – Ngugi Falls. We saw a crowd of people gathered near the fire to welcome us. We had arrived at our destination.

We were too tired to rush the last half mile, but, eventually, we joined our new hosts, and, as we did, we heard the noise of an engine starting. I looked around, since the noise came from one side and behind us. I should have looked up, because suddenly, along the sides of the cave light bulbs came alive and the cave lit up. Jack laughed at our astonished faces. "We acquired a generator," he explained. He told us the village was basically their base camp and supplies were sent to them by mule train every week. Those supplies included fuel for the generator as well as tools, electric wire and food. He explained they intended to extend the system along the tunnel, supplemented and maintained by a number of small sub generators. Jake and Jack took the four of us to the water curtain. I put my hand into the waterfall and withdrew it quickly. It was freezing cold and my hand felt as though it was being pricked by a thousand needles at the same time. Jack saw me and laughed. "We all did that when we arrived," he confessed. "We know what you felt and none of us did it more than once! However, after looking through what at first appeared to be a solid wall of water, we were able to see through it to what lay beyond." I was surprised. "We must be two hundred feet up", I commented. Jake told me it was nearer one hundred, and the falls were about one hundred and sixty feet high. Judy thought it was impossible to climb up, but Jake corrected her. He said it was possible, but difficult, even for an experienced climber. Only one person could do it at a time. If hostile, they would be killed before they could enter the cave. Jack said the only time when an attacking force could effect a lodgement was at night. Because of that, they always mounted armed guards there at night. Judy asked about the way we'd come. Bill, who'd joined us said it was almost as difficult, especially the first section, assuming they'd spotted the entrance in the first place. Anyone who assaulted the cave system against a determined defence – especially when it was as strongly manned as the caves were, with over sixty defenders, would suffer crippling losses. They both concluded that no sane enemy would attempt it and the only way to get in would be to starve them out.

"It's not an easy place to mount a siege," Jake pointed out, "that's why I chose it."

Jack told us they had a short wave radio and mobile phones and could summon help if they were surrounded. I asked who they expected to come to their rescue. He smiled at me and answered in two words. "You would!"

There was no answer to that, and I did not try to give one, but a thought did cross my mind. I left it for a more appropriate time. As we walked back, I felt a hand on my shoulder. I looked up and saw Bill. He spoke to me.

"You've changed, young Mark. Both you and Judy. You were both as quiet as mice in the cages, but now you..." he paused. "I'm what?" I asked. "You and she have suddenly become confident, authoritative people used to issuing commands which they expect to be obeyed. I saw it that day on the Island when you collected us and when you beat down Maritza. Would you really have shot her?"

"Yes," I said simply. "Yes, I would. I would have been sorry I'd done it, but I would have done it and so would Judy." She heard me and nodded her assent. "We were both relieved when Dad took that decision from us though. They warned us before we left Freetown we would want to back down but feel unable to do so and he was determined to save us from ourselves. But don't misunderstand us. We were thirty seconds from pulling the triggers when Dad ordered us to stop, or we would have done it."

"I believe you," Bill said. "I'm glad you didn't though. You're both too young and too naively good to get into the trap of self-flagellation over something like that."

There was no answer to that, and we didn't try.

Our seven days passed quickly. We renewed our old friendships and made new ones. The women quickly discovered Judy's pregnancy, and this became a matter of conversation. Our hosts, seeing us and Chloe and Colin together, as became very common in later years, asked if we were a pair of twins. They said they understood why Chloe and Colin were confused with us. We told them that was what we intended – but it had turned out differently from what we planned. We explained what we were doing and why, and how they fitted into the plan. They admitted they had messed it up by their own obstinacy. We all admitted we had underestimated the extent of Maritza's hatred for us and the lengths to which she would go in order to make us suffer. We told them what we had discovered of her family relationships and how this explained Maritza's and Musaveni's attitude towards us.

Things changed on our last afternoon. We were called to the screen by the watchmen on duty and silence was called for inside. We went to join the leaders of the group. A small group of soldiers had emerged out of the forest at the foot of the Falls. They were looking up at it, directly at us, if they could have seen us. Our hosts were not concerned because they knew we could not be seen. They also knew the only scalable route up was hidden by the falling water at this time of year. We watched as a soldier went back to return later, accompanied by an officer we recognised as Colonel Musaveni. There was a lot of talking and pointing. A soldier edged gingerly around the edge of the curtain of water and returned shaking his head. The operation was repeated on the other side, with the same lack of effect. Finally, the Colonel shrugged his shoulders, and the party withdrew from the Falls. We did not see them again. Jack told us he would send out a reconnaissance party in the next few days, but, meanwhile, ordered the watch on the rear entrance to be increased. That night the guards at the front of the cave were doubled. However, the men did not return – not even to collect water, so a very sober group had a last meal with us, using torches augmented by the fire instead of the generator to light the cave.

Next morning we left, and, over the next six days, retraced our steps without incident. As it turned out, it would be a while before Musaveni and his men again came as near to the Falls as he did then, and he would never get so close to the four of us again until it was too late. On arriving back home Mum and Dad warmly welcomed us and told us how well we all looked. We said nothing of our experiences in the cave but talked about the trek we made and how wonderful the Falls were. Jake, we knew, was closeted with Dad and Mum after we left, but they never told us what they discussed: we never asked.

CHAPTER 25

Anna's Story

It was during this time that an unusual incident occurred which illustrated to us the dangers of targeting a group identifiable only by the colour of their skin caused. Judy and I had left the Palace to visit a school in Freetown, the main secondary school which was situated near the city centre. We had completed our visit and were standing by our car talking to the Headmaster when someone blundered into me, almost knocking me over. I turned around to see who it was and saw an obviously terrified young slave girl. She was naked, but without collar or cuffs and had no identifying marks. She had clearly been running for her life and was almost on the point of collapse. Apologising to the Head, I opened the door of our car and told her to get into it. Acting on instinct, I told her to lie on the floor and ordered our driver to lock the doors, which he did. "If anyone asks about her, Reuben, you haven't seen her, okay?" I said to him. He nodded, and I returned to our conversation.

Ten minutes later, a middle aged man, puffing from what appeared to be unusual exertion, and carrying a whip, appeared, asking if we had seen an escaped slave girl. All three of us denied seeing anyone. I asked about the girl. He told me she was obviously white, brown haired and with grey eyes. Judy asked how old she was, and he replied she was eighteen. I asked about her condition. He didn't understand the question, so I exemplified what I meant.

"Was she cuffed and collared and wearing either a loincloth or a breach cloth? Was she branded, and if so, what was the brand? Was she designated a P slave, and did she wear a disc with your name and address on it? Finally was there some form of personal identification on her body?"

He answered 'no' to all the questions. Judy pointed out that he had broken the law on several counts and if the police picked her up they would confiscate her and put her up for sale in the slave market.

He was extremely angry at this.

"That's theft!" he shouted, "she's my property. I bought her and she belongs to me and to no one else."

I pointed out that the law required slaves who are in the public with their owners' consent to be basically clothed (loincloth or breach cloth and sandals), clearly marked with a letter, brand mark, and personal identification, ankle and wrist cuffs and collar with a disc identifying him as the owner. If not the slave would be taken to the market and sold, and the previous owner would be fined if he or she could be found. "That's the law," I concluded. "Didn't you know it?"

He shook his head. Judy asked him how he had acquired her. He told her he was a personal friend of Colonel Musaveni who had given the girl to him as a gift for informing him of our arrival in Casa Isabella. I advised him to return to Casa Isabella and forget the girl. "You've lost her," Judy added. He was not mollified and stormed off, obviously intent on resuming the search. We bid the Head farewell, told him how pleased we were with his school, and returned to our car. We raised the girl from the floor and sat her between us, but told her to hunker down until we were clear of the school.

When we reached the Palace, we agreed I would remain with the girl while Judy ran inside and fetched some clothes for her. She returned with some underclothes, a dress and sandals, and helped her put them on. Then the three of us left the car, thanking Reuben, our driver. We took the girl to our apartment where we fed her, gave her tea and then spoke with her. She told us her name was Anna Browne and she was eighteen. We asked where she was born and she replied, "Here, in Freetown." We were surprised at that and asked her to explain.

"It's really quite simple," she began. "Dad and Mum were farmers. They came out here in their twenties, like you did, and bought land near Casa Isabella. There were several farms owned by white men and women in that area. I was the youngest of five children – three boys and two girls. I was the last and the only one born after independence – but we were all born here in the Freetown Hospital – because that was (and still is) the nearest one to Casa Isabella. Mum and Dad stayed on after Independence, but the other farmers sold up and returned to Britain (three of them) or Germany (two of them). My sister married one of the British farmers and went back with him. My brothers all returned home as well".

Judy asked where home was, and Anna replied it was Bradford in Yorkshire. She told us she had visited it once and stayed with an uncle and aunt before returning to Austrasia. I asked her where she went to school. She said she attended a boarding school near Pretoria in South Africa. Judy asked how she became a slave.

"It was after the Revolution," she said. "Some of the local yobs came to the farm. My Dad shot and killed one of them when he became violent. They attacked him and Mum, beat them up and killed them. I tried to run away but they caught me, stripped me, gangraped me and then beat me up so savagely that my back was almost cut to pieces. You must have seen the scars."

We nodded.

"Then they took me to the Barracks in Casa Isabella and sold me to Colonel Musaveni. He was fairly kind to me, but his wife didn't like me. She didn't trust her husband's motives in keeping me and told him to dispose of me. That's why he gave me to that man – who wasn't kind to me. He beat me every time I made a mistake and kept me locked up."

I asked if she often made mistakes and she admitted she did. She said that she had been spoiled as a child and didn't learn as much from her mother as she should have done. Judy asked how she had managed to escape. She explained that her owner came to Freetown to shop once a month and always brought her with him. She was left outside while he went into the big supermarket. She realized this was her opportunity to escape, because he was usually inside the shop for over an hour.

"I had to screw up my courage before I could do it. I chose today because I heard someone say you were visiting the school nearby and I knew you would help me if I could reach you. Luckily I could and did. And here I am!" she concluded triumphantly.

Judy and I discussed the situation. We agreed that she could not be returned to her 'owner' because she wasn't actually a slave. She wasn't a foreign worker and so could not legally be enslaved. However, because of her skin colour we knew that no one would believe her when she said she was born here. In the end we took her to our parents and sought their advice. They saw the problem immediately. Dad said that the first thing we had to do was prove her story, so he rang the police, told them that we had an alleged escaped slave whose 'owner' had broken all the rules. As a result we (Judy and I) had confiscated her and requisitioned her under the Emergency Powers Act. Therefore we were now legally her owners, but we had learnt she claimed to have been born in Freetown. He gave the police her name and date of birth, asking them to check the register of births, deaths and marriages for her birth certificate, and also any evidence of a legal sale. They came back two hours later to confirm that she was born in Austrasia, and, after another three hours, that there was no evidence that she was ever sold as a slave legally.

When we learnt this we told her we were no longer her legal owners, because she was as free as we were. We were not freeing her because legally she was never unfree. However, legally, she was still a minor and it was patently unsafe for her to be allowed to wander the streets of Freetown unescorted. We kept her with us for a while, acting as her legal guardians, until Dad came up with the answer. He suggested that we should take her down to the new town we had founded for freed slaves and other refugees. We discussed this with Anna and got her agreement. As a result we took her in a helicopter down to the south and introduced her to Jack and Clare, who happily took Anna under their wings. Several years later, she returned to us and we appointed her to a post in the Ministry dealing with the rehabilitation of former slaves. In the course of time she married a local man and became the mother of four children. Eventually, we appointed Anna as Minister for Rehabilitation. *Later still Judy and Mark appointed the slave son they adopted to be her Private Secretary.*

Her story did have two consequences. The furious 'owner' sued us for theft and demanded compensation. The case was heard in the High Court. We presented the evidence of Anna's Austrasian birth and nationality and the case was dismissed, as was the claim for compensation, since, among other things, he had not bought her as a slave but had been given her as a gift. The second consequence was a clarification of the original law which had been used to enslave us. It stated that anyone born in Austrasia, except through the slave breeding programme, could not legally be enslaved.

CHAPTER 26

Towards the End

The day after our return, the five of us met to discuss the implications of what we had learned from our visit to the Ngugi Falls cave complex. I told them (and Jake especially) that I was worried about the Ngugi Falls Community. I told him they could easily be trapped there and, "If there are children," I added, "it could be a disaster. They're much too close to Musaveni and Casa Isabella." Dad asked us to describe what we saw and explain what we meant. We did so, at some length, working together. Judy concluded, "The basic problem is there are sixty of them there. That's too many if they are cut off to hold out for long and far more than they need to conduct an effective defence." Dad asked Jake for his opinion and he was forced to agree with Judy.

Dad asked us what we recommended. I said he should arrange to evacuate at least forty of the inhabitants to a place of safety, in, preferably, a different, more settled, part of the country." Judy agreed and Jake made no objection. "The problem is where," Dad agreed. For the next few hours we discussed different possibilities. Finally, we selected a relatively lightly populated area beside a lake on the south eastern border of the country. We agreed to send a building team to the site to create a village, using traditional methods, to hold up to sixty individuals. The following day we commissioned three architects to design a new native style village. *After the fall of Casa Isabella the Ngugi heads were recovered from the Army Barracks and united with the remains of the crucified victims taken from the trees in the Town Square. They were taken to the new town and buried in a mass grave. The grave was eventually marked by a memorial unveiled by Chloe and Colin. (I added the remains taken from the cave complex to the grave later [JO])* A week after receiving all the design proposals we made our choice. A month later it was built by troops drawn from the nearest garrison.

It was during this procedure that we experienced our first example of the all too common use of bribery to gain contracts. One of the company representatives offering tenders asked to meet us to present their application in person. We met them in our office and listened to their outline of their planned development of the chosen site. When Judy asked him about the cost, he grinned and pushed a briefcase across the desk.

"The details are in there," he explained.

I opened the bag, looked inside, and passed it across to Judy, who did the same. We looked sternly at him.

"We don't accept bribes," I commented, as I returned the bag to him. "We'll still present your company's proposal, but it has to stand on its own merits. You would be better using that money, if you've got so much that you can afford to spend it on corrupting public servants, on increasing the salaries of your workers."

"If you've nothing else to say about your proposal, you might as well leave." Judy added, "Thank you for coming."

We told father that evening. He congratulated us on resisting temptation. Needless to say, his application was rejected. It turned out to be the first of far too many attempts by Austrasian businessmen to bribe us to support their applications for contracts. They all received the same treatment. Eventually the message sank in and the attempts to bribe us ended.

Two weeks after the village was completed, we evacuated fifty of the cave dwellers, loaded them on to helicopters as near to the cave as we could get them, and flew them all to the new village, where they are still flourishing. The ten who remained consisted of six former soldiers, two former miners and one of the breeding couples – Tessa and George. Sadly, six weeks later, according to his report, Musaveni's men found them, attacked in overwhelming numbers overnight and shot the defenders. Tessa and George fled down the tunnel, were followed, cut off on both sides, seized, stripped, bound, shot and beheaded. Their headless bodies were left, and their heads were removed. Two local children who had found their way into the cave system two days before, were taken and killed and their bodies were dumped in one of the caves. The other bodies were thrown down the waterfall, after their heads were taken off, and washed down to the Lake. All nine heads were taken back to Casa Isabella and the hunt was ended. Musaveni and his men returned to their base and reported to us that the rebel nest had been wiped out and the cave entrance blocked up.

He was wrong, because one of the men told us he was not in the cave but on guard in the woods outside the cave complex. Unable to warn the people in the caves, he watched the attackers storm the complex and later watched them leave, carrying the nine heads on sticks. He then made his way to the village and was sent on to us. He told us of the attack and we were able to complete the picture from the Colonel's report. I decided I would honour the community by one day returning there, when I knew my days were drawing to a close (or if we were driven into hiding by a coup against our parents) and place this book there where I hope it will be found and our story told. Sometimes you have to be dead before you can be heard clearly.

Of course, as you will see, it was a different circumstance that caused Mark to return to the Caves.

We had done what we could for Ndenge's victims, and especially our fellow victims from St Michael's Island. We now began to consider the problem posed by the dissidents and armed rebels in Casa Isabella. Dad commissioned a report on the situation in that province and town from Longinus and we left further discussions about the Casa Isabella situation and that of St Michael's Island aside until after the report. We did hear, though, about a constant drift of dissidents from the north-east towards Casa Isabella Province. One evening we mentioned it in our after dinner discussions. Dad expressed grim satisfaction. "Let's get all the sods in one place so we can deal with them in a quick surgical operation," he repeated. The skipper of the "Macrone" had begun to call on the Island once more, and he kept us updated with developments there. He reported an increase in the size of the garrison, but said the increase was largely composed of untrained peasants who had come down from elsewhere. More significantly, he reported on the construction of defences on the Island and the weapons deliveries he was asked to make there, including light artillery pieces and their ammunition. Subsequent reports suggested that the fields we had tilled and weeded so assiduously were expanded considerably, following the removal of the farm fence, and large quantities of tinned food had been imported. We concluded they were preparing for a siege. We let them get on with it.

We prepared for an election. Our Secretariat staff had spent considerable time working on a new draft Constitution, incorporating the changes we had previously suggested and dealing with the

National Assembly; the rights and duties of slaves and citizens; the role of the judiciary and the military; and the setting up of a Supreme Court. We placed that before the Cabinet, who, as is the wont in such cases, discussed it at length, but approved it unanimously and recommended it to the public in a referendum. The vote was held in October and received approval from eighty-three per cent of the ninety-one per cent of the electorate who voted. Armed with this approval, the new Constitution was put into immediate effect. The State of Emergency remained in effect (it would remain so until the rebellion was finally suppressed). However, we saw no reason why the provisions of the Constitution could not be activated, so we appointed seven judges to the Supreme Court and set out a timetable for the first Legislative Assembly elections which we scheduled to be held in the following July. We created the Austrasian Ofsted, appointing a female Professor of Education from the University of Austrasia as the first Chief Inspector, empowered to appoint as many other inspectors as she deemed necessary. The first school inspection took place after Easter the following year. Thereafter, they took place weekly, without notice. We hoped standards would improve but knew it would take time. Acting on her advice, we reformed the school examination system. We copied an examination system then currently in use in South Africa. It has proved to be very successful and a major factor in driving up standards in teaching and learning. It was in this period that our first child, a daughter, was born, Chloe and Colin were married in Freetown cathedral and we had our marriage blessed by the Bishop in the same service. I will write about these two events later.

All six of us began a series of official visits, to towns, cities, military and civil installations, schools, the universities, and even our sports clubs. Looking back, as I am in writing this, my greatest and happiest memory, after the birth of our three kids, was attending the Africa Cup Final between the Austrasian Eagles (our national emblem) and the Green Buffalos (the Zambian Army team). The

Eagles beat the Buffalos 3:1 after extra time (after drawing 1:1 at full time) . We've never felt so proud as we felt that evening when we presented the Cup to the Eagles' Captain and the winner's medals to the players and coach. My condolences to the Buffalos Captain and the Zambian President who was our guest lacked a little in sincerity! Except for Casa Isabella Province, the country was settling down and beginning to make progress. The only things that really saddened us were that we could do nothing to end slavery completely because of our own connection with it and we found no trace of Antonio and Maria. As a long search only succeeded in drawing a blank, we concluded they were regrettably both dead. Nothing has happened since to cause us to change our minds. We remembered that conversation so long ago in Concordia and suspected they may have attempted to run away and were either killed by wild animals or kidnapped and sold back into slavery somewhere else by renegades. We find it difficult to decide which would be the worse fate.

The report of Longinus about Casa Isabella Province suggested any military operation against the rebels might prove costly in materials, cash, men and collateral damage. He said that success was certain. However, he thought we might consider the cost to be too high. He suggested we might look for a political solution and exhaust the possibilities of achieving one before adopting a military answer. We presented the report to the Cabinet. They were uniformly sceptical that any political solution acceptable to one side would be acceptable to the other but agreed it should be tried before battle was joined. We set a period of twelve months for those negotiations and agreed if no solution was found in that time, we would break off the negotiations and attack the rebels. As a result, we began what we all knew would be a futile dance, and a complete waste of time. The result could only be to strengthen the rebels and make our task of suppressing them harder and more costly.

We sent a message to Colonel Musaveni advising him we were prepared to discuss with him and his delegates proposals that might bring the present stand off to an end. For a month there was no response. Then a document setting out what his people demanded was handed to us by a solicitor acting for him 'without prejudice'. The document made the following demands. They were addressed to "Matthew Ngangi" not "President (Matthew) Ngangi".

1. "The clique of four slaves surrounding you must be dismissed from your presence and handed over to us to face trial for their part in causing the death of Austrasian citizens.

2. The new constitution must be immediately scrapped and the old one restored.

3. The elections must be indefinitely postponed.

4. You and your wife must resign in favour of Colonel Musaveni.

5. The new laws and regulations concerning slaves must be immediately scrapped and the laws established immediately after the Revolution be re-established.

6. All those involved in the judicial murders of Vice President Ndenge and Maritza and the arrest of the Vice President's family members should be executed for murder and the book defaming the name of the late VP be withdrawn from publication and all copies recalled and burnt publicly."

Our response was a single simple sentence. 'Its six noes from us.' We made the following counter proposals:

1. "Colonel Musaveni must resign, be arrested and charged with kidnapping and the murder of eleven people, including two native children, at the Ngugi Caves.

2. St Michael's Island must be evacuated and demilitarised.

3. The Musaveni regiment must be disbanded and all militia illegally recruited must be sent home.

4. All documents still in the possession of the Colonel and/or any member of the Ndenge family appertaining to the charges of embezzlement against the late VP and his associates must be turned over to the prosecutors.

5. Financial compensation must be paid to the former slaves who were victims of Maritza and her clique on St Michael's Island from the Ndenge Estate. The exact amount to be calculated later.

6. The citizens and all the soldiers in Casa Isabella must take part in a ceremony of public penance ending in each citizen swearing an oath of loyalty to President Ngangi, his family, and the Constitution."

We, of course, got the same reply. There the "negotiations" stuck for six months, while we got on with governing and preparing for the final offensive against the rebels, and they got on with strengthening their defences. Then quite suddenly, the rebels declared independence. They termed themselves the Republic of Casa Isabella. Two of our neighbouring Presidents offered to mediate between us. Dad rang them, thanked them politely for their offer, but said there was nothing to mediate. The elections were held, won by the United Independence Party, with the new Austrasia Party forming the main opposition. They united to condemn the attempted breakaway. We asked the two main Parties to appoint Members of the Legislative

Assembly (MLAs) from Casa Isabella Province to the Assembly on a pro rata basis, based on the national election result, until the situation there was normalised, and a proper election could take place. They did as we asked. We then presented the facts to the cabinet who rejected the declaration of independence out of hand and ordered that the outrageous demands of the rebels be printed and circulated. We did this and the clock slowly ran down to the end of the twelve months period as both sides stepped up their preparations for the inevitable military showdown after Christmas.

CHAPTER 27

The End

As the deadline for the end of negotiations approached, we closed the airport at Casa Isabella, withdrawing the military aircraft which were based there, together with the Air Force personnel, none of whom were involved with the Musaveni/Ndenge group. We did this shortly before the illegal declaration of independence. It is, of course, possible that our doing this triggered the attempt to break away. Dad appointed Jake, Longinus and Major General Okpara – an Austrasian of Nigerian descent to command three assault forces. In an exceptional move Jake and Longinus were promoted to the rank of acting Major General for this operation. "I don't completely trust any of my other generals," Dad told us. Major General Okpara commanded the Palace Guard and had succeeded father in command of his old regiment.

Longinus was sent to Port Franklin where he assembled the southern strike force, designated the 1st Army Corps, consisting of a quarter of the Austrasian Army which was about ten thousand men and women. They were mainly infantry but were supported by heavy and light artillery. The light artillery was sent to Port Franklin, and the heavy artillery was assembled within striking distance of the Lake south of the Island. His target was to be St Michael's Island and the landing place at the east end of the Lake.

Jake was sent to Concordia where he assembled a somewhat larger, again mainly infantry force supported by light artillery, comprising forty per cent of the Army (about sixteen thousand men and women). His role was to appear to be threatening Casa Isabella. This was the 2nd Army Corps.

Major General Okpara remained at Freetown with the balance of the fighting forces, fourteen thousand men and women, of whom seven thousand were earmarked for the operation. This force contained all the Austrasian tank corps and was highly mechanised. It was designated the Freetown Force and officially listed as the Army Reserve Force. In fact it had a different role. The Air Force was concentrated at the Air Base north of the state capital.

Thus positioned, they waited. As Christmas approached, Jake moved his forces west towards the border of Casa Isabella Province in what seemed to be a show of force. Musaveni, confident in the strength of his St Michael's bastion, moved the bulk of his forces east, to confront Jake. He left only light forces to defend Casa Isabella, which he did not consider to be in any immediate danger. Dad reacted to this move in a manner designed to reassure Musaveni that he had read our intentions correctly. He sent part of the real reserve (three thousand five hundred men and women) along the Freetown - Casa Isabella Road to set up defensive positions there, as though we feared a Museveni counter- attack on the capital.

We celebrated Christmas at the Palace with a party for the staff, ministers, and foreign ambassadors. It was a glittering occasion, designed to distract the public from the other aspect of our "celebrations" a secret high level meeting between Dad and the three generals at which the details of the upcoming campaign were hammered out. We were not present at this meeting, since we and Mum presided over the official reception. We announced that the President was indisposed. The Zambian High Commissioner spoke to me. He said rumours were flying around the city that military action to crush the rebellion was imminent. He asked what I knew. I told him I could answer in one word, "Nothing". He looked knowingly at me. "You're British by birth," he said, "so you'll understand this English idiom, 'Pull the other one - it's got bells on it!'" "I do, indeed," I replied, "but I fail to see its connection with the present situation." He laughed before telling me I was turning into a diplomat. That puzzled me until he explained a diplomat was a man or woman sent out to lie for their country. I asked him if that was what he did. He didn't answer but instead put his hand on my shoulder in a friendly manner and guided me to the bar, where he ordered drinks for us both and changed the subject. Judy later told me the Nigerian High Commissioner had attempted to corner her in a similar way. She had also fended him off. Mum shielded Colin and Chloe from any similar approach, since we were not sure they would be able to deal with such enquiries. A number of other ambassadors, most notably the South African High Commissioner and the Egyptian Ambassador also tried to draw us out without success. The South African High Commissioner offered us the help of one of his country's Air Force Fighter Squadrons. I told him I would pass the offer on to Dad and did so. He accepted it and the planes were used in a supporting capacity to our forces.

Jake and Longinus returned to their commands on January 2nd, after celebrating New Year in the Capital. We heard Musaveni had decided our mobilisation of forces was in the nature of a feint and he believed we were afraid to attack him. Accordingly, he returned to Casa Isabella and was still there when our offensive opened six days later on January 8th. He missed the significance of the fact that the "Macrone" and "King Carlos", the two boats which regularly plied the Lake routes, remained in Port Franklin after the Christmas and New Year celebrations. He also plainly failed to grasp the reason for, and significance of, the "accidental" fire which destroyed the jetty and the two warehouses at the eastern end of the Lake on the night of January 5th/6th. They were raided by troops guarding the artillery south of the Lake opposite the Island. Dad ordered the raid and the destruction of the facilities there to prevent any reinforcement getting to the Island. Final orders were given to the troops of the 1st and 2nd Army Corps on January 7th, and the operation began at 06.00 on January 8th.

The two assaults began simultaneously, but there was a significant difference between them. Jake began his assault with a heavy artillery bombardment lasting several days, as his infantry moved up to attack positions, in a manner reminiscent of battles in World War One in France. His purpose was to fix Musaveni's men in position far to the east of Casa Isabella. For the time being, it worked. Musaveni left Casa Isabella to hurry back to what he considered was the main battle front. Jake's troops, after the bombardment ended, began to launch probing attacks on the Musaveni front line, but seemed not to make any progress. In Casa Isabella, the news service trumpeted their "victories". The national newspapers were more nuanced in their coverage, partly because we did not give them much information about the progress of the 2nd Corps. Our reticence was intended to enhance the impression in Casa Isabella that they were winning the battle there.

In the meantime, the 1st Corps began a quiet but steady and largely unopposed advance eastward along both shores of the Lake, supported by the two lake boats. The "Macrone" supported the northern force while the "King Carlos" supported the southern force. Both boats were equipped with machine guns and light artillery pieces. There was some sporadic resistance on the northern (Casa Isabella) shore, but it was easily brushed aside. There was no opposition on the southern side. By the end of the sixth day (January 14th), the whole of the lake shore was secured. Rebel troops had withdrawn to the east or north (melting into the forests to begin guerrilla warfare). with some nuisance attacks developing from time to time on our troops on the northern side. The heavy artillery was moved forward to within range of the island on the southern side and more batteries were transported by the river boats to the northern side. On the eighth day of the campaign (January 16th), the Siege of St Michael's Island began with a heavy and continuous bombardment of the Island's defences from both shores of the Lake, supported by gun fire from the two boats. The garrison was completely cut off and Longinus settled down to starve or bombard them out. He had no intention of attempting to land his forces on the island until the defenders were either too weak to mount any effective resistance, or they surrendered. In the meantime, the approach from the east was sealed off.

The garrison on the island was left to its own devices. Musaveni was trapped in the east and dared not send or take forces west because he knew the 2nd Corps would pursue them all the way to Casa Isabella.

In the town itself, morale was good. They believed all was going well on the eastern front and they were told nothing at all about events in the west. Our air force had been busy strafing the defending troops on the eastern front and on the island, reinforcing the artillery and pointedly leaving the town of Casa Isabella alone. We did not want Musaveni's eyes to turn on the town until it was too late. On the tenth day of the campaign (January 18th) Dad redesignated the Army Reserve Force as the 3rd Army Corps and sent it north, led by the tanks, to seize Casa Isabella. On January 19th, they crossed the provincial border and closed in on the town, which then suffered its first and only air raid. One day later they swept into the town, driving the few demoralised defenders and many of the residents into flight from it. Faced with shelling from the tanks and bombing from our aircraft, the few troops left by Musaveni in his capital had no choice but to withdraw or surrender. At the same time (January 20th), the feint attacks in the east were changed into a real offensive. Too late, Musaveni saw the trap into which he had fallen. The 3rd Corps infantry, including the "defenders" sent earlier to apparently block the road south, followed the tanks into the town and secured it. Part of the force moved west to strengthen our hold on the Lake, while the remainder, including the tank corps, established a defensive line to the east of the town. We sent armed police to ensure peace within the town. In practice, those who remained were not supporters of the Musaveni rebellion, and therefore presented no trouble. By January 22nd the town was secure and the airport was once again in operation..

Judy and I took the opportunity presented by the fall of Casa Isabella and the reopened airport to fly to the town on January 23rd, to search the home and head-quarters of Colonel Musaveni. We seized all the documents we found there and, later, in the offices of the local government. We sent them to Freetown for examination. Acting under Dad's instructions, we appointed a new Mayor and Chief Executive, and a new group of councillors before returning to the capital on January 25th. Examination of the seized documents by our Intelligence officials enabled us to draw up a final list of those involved in the various stages of the Ndenge and Musaveni coups. We also removed the heads and crucified bodies we found in the town of Casa Isabella and sent them reverently to the new town on the lake for burial.

The campaign reached its second decisive moment at the end of January. While the main rebel forces were fighting a rear guard action in the east against the 2nd Corps which was now pressing its attacks vigorously, the 1st Corps pressed its siege of the island. We travelled down with Dad on January 28th to join Longinus as the siege was obviously reaching its climax. We could see that the defences and the main building itself had been largely demolished. Longinus began assembling fishing boats along both shores opposite the vulnerable eastern end of the island. It was done in such a way as to enable the defenders to see them and draw their own conclusions. To help them the troops on the southern shore practiced embarking and disembarking from the boats and then attacking the village nearby, knowing the garrison could observe them. The ploy worked. On January 31st, a rowing boat, containing an officer waving a white flag, left the island and was rowed across towards the south side of the Lake. We sent a motorboat across to meet it and took the emissary on board with a promise of safe conduct. Once on shore, he met Longinus and the three of us and told us he had come to negotiate the garrison's surrender. We acknowledged that and Longinus told them the surrender had to be total and unconditional. It had to include all those on the island. The only thing they asked (and we agreed to) was to be treated as prisoners of war and not rebels. We agreed we would accord that status to anyone who surrendered. However, if anyone insisted on continuing to fight us after the garrison's surrender they would be considered to be rebels and treated accordingly. They agreed. We drew up the surrender document, and the emissary initialled it. The actual surrender was fixed for mid- day on February 1st, but we agreed a ceasefire would begin twenty-four hours before that. The agreement was adhered to, and the surrender duly occurred next day. We evacuated the surrendered garrison over the following week and reoccupied the island with a small force of two hundred soldiers on February 7th. The 1st Corps now began the second phase of their campaign, pacifying the area to the west of Casa Isabella. That consisted of a series of sweeps into the forest to move the remaining rebel troops further away from the combat area and to degrade their ability to fight us. In effect they were driven towards the Ngugi Falls area. Eventually, what was left of the rebel forces in the whole of the province west and north of the provincial capital took refuge in the cave complex. Longinus left part of the corps to keep them blockaded within the caves and moved the remainder, about four thousand troops, to replace the 3rd Corps in the occupation of Casa Isabella town also on February 7th, freeing the 3rd Corps to move east to envelope the main rebel army from the west.

Musaveni was now trapped between Jake's 2nd Corps, driving westwards and Major General Okpara's 3rd Corps driving east. Facing the destruction of his army, he had no choice but to withdraw his men, or as many as he could disengage, to the north – following the route we had taken to the caves . In the end, about three thousand men escaped the trap. Led by Musaveni, they retreated (fled is a probably a better word) to join the other remnants of his army in the Ngugi Cave complex on February 10th. What remained of his army was crushed in the Battle of Engadi, which began three days later and ended on February 15th, when eight hundred men, all that remained of the defenders, surrendered. Jake and Okpara met after the battle ended. Jake left Okpara's 3rd Corps to clear up in the east, while he led the 2nd Corps in pursuit of the fleeing Musaveni. He knew exactly where Musaveni would be holed up. On arrival at the Cave complex on February 22nd, Jake's men sealed the rear entrance to the cave system, driving the few defenders away from it into the caves, but not making the mistake of following them into the tunnel as the defenders hoped they would do. In front of the Falls, Longinus's 1st Corps prevented any escape. The situation I had once feared could develop for our own people that day when Judy and I were there, had now developed for Musaveni. He was trapped without any hope of relief and would be starved out. He either had to surrender or try to fight his way out. Either option meant probable death for him and possibly for his men too. Faced with these unpalatable options, and before it was too late to have any choices left, Musaveni opted to negotiate with us.

On March 1st, Musaveni radioed to us that he was prepared to talk to Judy and me. He asked if we would come to meet him. We had moved with Dad to Casa Isabella on February 7th to keep contact with the rapidly changing course of events. The message reached us there. Before Dad could say anything, I responded to the message with a single word, "No." Dad looked relieved. He said he thought we might accept the invitation in an attempt to save lives. Judy, for the first and only time I can remember, was angry at Dad's comment.

"Dad," she said forcefully, "neither of us are fools. We would never make the same mistake that Chloe and Colin did. He doesn't want to talk to us. He wants to kidnap us and hold us as hostages so you will exchange our lives for his, letting him go free in the probably vain hope he will free us in exchange. There's no chance we would risk that!"

Dad apologized to us for the thought and asked us how we intended to reply. I told him we would give a nuanced reply. I spoke to the radio operator.

"We do not have the time to travel to Ngugi Caves, but if Colonel Musaveni will send us a message with any proposals he has to offer he should radio them to us, and we will consider them and give him our response."

He did so. His message said, provided we were prepared to guarantee that Musaveni would be permitted to leave the country for any other country, in exchange for renouncing his claim to be President of Casa Isabella, he would order his men to lay down their arms and surrender. We replied the only offer we would make, and they would have to accept, was that they should all surrender on the same conditions the other troops had accepted: unconditional surrender and guaranteed treatment as prisoners of war except for individuals identified by the government and the intelligence services as guilty of war crimes who would, of course, face prosecution. Musaveni responded by asking whether we regarded him as a war criminal. We discussed our answer with Dad before we sent it. This is the message which ended the conversation.

"Colonel Musaveni, you asked to meet us to talk with us. We are prepared to meet you to discuss your position, in Freetown, after you've surrendered with your men, like them, unconditionally. That is the President's (and our) final offer. Accept it and lead your men out of the rear entrance waving white flags and without any weapons or refuse it and take the consequences."

There was no reply, but two days later on March 3rd, we received a telephone message from Jake, telling us the war was over because the last enemy force had surrendered and Colonel Musaveni was on a plane, under military escort, on his way to Freetown. Jake remained at the caves for a week organising the collection of weapons and other military equipment left behind by Musaveni's troops after their surrender. One of Jake's men found some human remains in the area and Jake ordered them to be buried. Following this, his men sealed both entrances to the caves on the grounds that they were both a burial site and a potential hideout for criminal gangs. We plan to return to the caves one day, as I have already written. I realise that we will have to break down the barrier to gain entrance to the complex and restore the barrier afterwards. That means we won't be able to travel there alone.

Two days later on March 5th after his arrival in Freetown, Musaveni, handcuffed and closely guarded by two of our men, was brought into our office. Judy and I were working on papers for the cabinet, giving them full details of the conflict, intending the information should be released to what remained of the world press. We put the papers aside, motioned to Musaveni to sit down, and asked the guards to remove the handcuffs. I looked for the papers we had received the day before from our intelligence unit outlining

Musaveni's culpability. I found them, opened them, and we began the interrogation.

"Colonel Musaveni, why did you kidnap Chloe and Colin, drug them, strip them, chain them and send them to your sister, knowing you both thought they were us, that she'd once nearly killed us and intended to do so if she got hold of us again? " I asked

"Because you were both responsible for the death of our oldest sister. One life needs another. That's our proverb."

"Or" Judy said, "in our case, two lives. Do you consider that a fair exchange?"

"Certainly, you're only slaves. Your only value is commercial. My sister was a human being. You can't put a commercial value on a human life."

"Is that so?" I asked. "But you consider we have a commercial value. Are we not human beings as well?"

"I don't care what titles you claim or what uniform you wear. You and your girlfriend…"

"My wife."

"If you say so. You and your so-called wife are still slaves. You're not counted as human beings. You're sub- humans at most."

"Then why did you ask to talk to us, Colonel?" Judy asked.

"Was it because you intended to kidnap us and hold us as hostages?" I added.

He did not answer. I left him enough time to answer before resuming my questions.

"Did you or Maritza realise that you had the wrong two individuals? If so, when?"

"Maritza realised when she and Letizia stripped them and saw that the numbers on their wrists were wrong. She rang me to tell me."

"So why, realising this, did you allow her to keep Chloe and Colin and torture them in the way she did?" Judy asked.

"We knew the CO was an Ngangi man and we expected him to tell you what was happening and so we tortured them really severely to lure you into trying to rescue them. When you did, we planned to capture you and kill you both."

"And you thought that was right!" I commented in disbelief at his callous and calculated cruelty.

"Of course! As I said before, all four of you are still slaves, so your lives didn't matter. They still don't matter."

Judy was shocked.

"So, Colonel Musaveni, if you had us in your hands now, you would still kill us! Is that right?" she asked.

"Yes," he replied. "Absolutely. I'd crucify you. I'd hammer the nails in myself."

I sighed and changed the subject to the attack on the caves, pointing out that we had received two conflicting accounts. I asked Musaveni to explain what happened.

"How did you find out where the refugees were hiding?" I asked.

He told us they had noticed the regular convoys of mules from the village we had visited, became suspicious and seized one of the muleteers. Under torture the prisoner offered to lead him and his men to the cave entrance. I asked if he did lead them there and Musaveni confirmed it.

"What happened next?" Judy asked.

"We shot and killed our guide and entered the caves. We found two children there and I ordered them to be strangled to ensure their silence. Further on we discovered a pair of male and female slaves asleep. We dragged them to their feet, stripped them, bound them and tortured them to learn where all the others were and how many of them were left. Once we had got all we could from them, I ordered them to be bayoneted and their heads to be cut off. Their screams did not last very long, but we found them very satisfying. We dumped their bodies in the tunnel and took their heads with us. We made our way to the main cave and attacked the rest of the gang. There was a brief exchange of fire. I lost five of my men, but we killed all seven of the terrorists, cut off their heads and threw the rest of their bodies down the waterfall into the river.. We blocked the cave entrance with rocks and returned along the tunnel, taking the nine heads with us. We left the four bodies of the slaves and the children in the tunnel because it was too much effort to drag them to the waterfall. We buried our own men in the main cave before we left and took away all the weapons and ammunition we found in the caves. I left a small garrison there to ensure that you lot could not reoccupy the complex."

"Did you attack the village that kept the caves supplied?" Judy asked.

"We visited it on the way back to Casa Isabella. I summoned the elders, showed them the defenders' heads, and warned them that we would return if they showed any other signs of disloyalty. They didn't!"

I nodded and turned back to my papers.

"We took your papers when we gained control of Casa Isabella.," I continued after a couple of minutes. "Among them is an account of your role in the coup against President Igbokwe. That document makes it clear you shot and killed the late President and his family. General Ngangi had ordered their lives to be spared. Why did you disobey him?"

"He was never our leader. Josiah Ndenge was. I obeyed his orders."

"You were present at the meeting that planned the coup and our enslavement. It also planned to overthrow and kill Matthew and Monica Ngangi when they were no longer useful to you all. Were you involved in planning the final stages of the coup against them?" Judy asked.

"No."

"Did you know about it?" I asked.

"Yes."

"But you took no steps to warn the President?" I continued.

"No. Of course not."

I turned to his recent rebellion.

"Who ordered the illegally declared Casa Isabella Province declaration of independence?"" I asked.

"What concern is that to you? You're foreign slaves, with no interest in this country. It's my country – not yours – and your interference in affairs you don't understand was ruining it."

Judy stopped me from responding. Instead she leaned forward.

"Colonel Musaveni, we're no longer foreigners. We're Austrasian nationals. We were slaves; it's true. But we're now citizens. We were teachers; but we're now senior government and army officers. We were orphans; but we're now the son and daughter of the President and Vice President. You, on the other hand, renounced your Austrasian citizenship and became the first citizen of a now defunct and always illegal enemy or rebel republic. We have far more right to talk about this nation than you do."

He was again silent.

I asked him if he had anything more to say. He did not answer. I gathered the papers together, put them in the file, and closed it, before looking up at Musaveni and speaking.

"Colonel Musaveni, you wanted to talk to us, and we have given you the opportunity to do so. All you have done is to confirm your guilt. You murdered President Igbokwe and his family. You were part of a plot to murder us and were almost responsible for the murder of two other Government employees who were acting on our behalf. By your own admission, you ordered the murder of ten adults – all free citizens of Austrasia and two Austrasian children. You led an armed rebellion against this country and President Ngangi, and you have plotted to kidnap the President's son and daughter. The case that you are a war criminal and, therefore, exempt from the surrender conditions, is overwhelming. We are therefore handing this file back to the Prosecutors and you will stand trial charged with murder, attempted murder and treason. You will have every chance to defend yourself then. We had a saying in England, Colonel. 'You've made your bed, now lie in it.' That's our answer to you."

I turned to the two guards.

"Put the handcuffs back on and take him away. Deliver him to the Central Prison and ask the court to appoint him a public defender. We'll send the charge sheet and supporting documents to the Prosecutor when the Minister of Justice has signed them."

With that, the guards took Musaveni away and we never saw him again, except to watch his trial on television. This took place in the High Court three months later in June and lasted two weeks. At the end of it, he was found guilty on all counts and, after his appeals were rejected by the Supreme Court and the President, he was hanged on September 28th. With that the war and the failed coup was finally over and the State of Emergency was lifted so life could begin to return to normal. Following the interrogation of Musaveni and what that revealed to us about the attack on the caves, Judy and I travelled back to the village that had supplied the cave dwellers to thank the villagers and to discuss what we can do to help them in the future. I am pleased to say that that community has developed into a flourishing modern town and has acted as a third mixed ethnic community (after Ngangiville and Freetown).

Life did return to normal as peace returned to the country. Our first child, a daughter we named Monica Judy was born just before Easter in the year before the war (as I noted earlier) followed by a son three years later. We named him Matthew Mark, causing Dad to joke that he would have to be a priest, because he was doubly holy, being named after two evangelists. He was followed two years after that by our third and last child, a daughter we named Concordia

June because she was born in that month. The first Easter after our liberation was doubly important for us. It not only marked Mum's birth, but also saw a double marriage. Chloe and Colin were married in Freetown Anglican Cathedral, but Dad insisted that we should be too. We could not legally be married there because we were already married, but the Bishop made us go through the official vows and blessed our marriage. The ceremony did, however, mean we can now wear wedding rings and Judy was able to dress as a bride for her special day after all. We invited Daniel, the former Governor of St Michael's Island, to be our guest at the service. Soon after this, following both parents' insistence, we had our daughter Monica Judy baptised. (We would baptise our other two children shortly after their births.) After our frequent comments avowing our agnostic status, we were criticised by the press for being hypocritical. Following Dad's advice, we made no comment. "Let them say what they like," he said, "the public love you and will ignore them. Anyway," he added, she's my granddaughter and I have the right to have a say in what happens to her." We couldn't really disagree with that.

As our family grew, so our accommodation became inadequate. Dad and Mum recognised this and ordered that a house be constructed for us within the grounds behind the main building. We moved in there. Later a second house was built for Chloe and Colin for the same reason.

When we were away from Freetown on a visit, as we were quite often, Mum would add to her Vice Presidential duties by taking on additional parental ones.

Chloe and Colin sadly could never have children. The excessively brutal and abusive treatment suffered by them at the hands of Letizia and Maritza had rendered them both infertile, but the love they had for one another was a model for married couples throughout the country. They also helped us by relieving Mum of parental care of our later children whenever we were away. They were, after all, their godparents and, according to African tradition, surrogate parents.

We six members of the Ngangi family commissioned two memorials. The first was a memorial to all the victims of the Ndenge/ Musaveni Coup as we called it, including the fifteen thousand slaves and especially the nearly eight hundred who we finally calculated had died before we tightened the laws and protected them from assault. That was erected in the new growing town by the lake where we had settled the St Michael's Island/ Ngugi Cave refugees and survivors in what was a mixed racial community, the first real one in the country. We added the names of the twelve Ngugi caves victims to the memorial on a special panel later. Copies were made and built in other parts of the country over the years, the most important one, and one which Judy and I unveiled, being on St Michael's Island itself. We were accompanied by Colin and Chloe on that occasion. The island was redeveloped as a tourist holiday centre and small national park, as was the area around the Ngugi Falls, although the caves remained closed to the public. On the first anniversary of the final surrender in the Casa Isabella War we unveiled two memorials to the victims of the war. The President and Vice President unveiled the memorial in Freetown while we four "children" unveiled the one in Casa Isabella. As an act of reconciliation, with gritted teeth, we permitted the citizens of Casa Isabella to erect statues of Colonel Musaveni and Josiah Ndenge (their local heroes), so long as they also erected one to President Igbokwe, which they did, probably with equally gritted teeth. However, as we said to them, reconciliation is a two-way street!

Dad and Mum asked us to look again at the slave breeding programme. We told them they should cancel it, but Dad said the scientists wanted it to continue. We visited the centres and eventually came up with three recommendations to make it more palatable. These were accepted and implemented. We appointed an Inspectorate to oversee the work of the centres. We initially reduced the hours on the machines from thirty minutes per day to fifteen minutes, three days a week. (Eventually, we closed the machines down totally.) We improved the living conditions and accommodation of the slaves, and let nature take its course. The two A.I. laboratories remained open, but we had them in our sights for abolition and closure as the Matthew Ngangi Presidency drew near to its close.

The final thing we did to close the door on the past was purely a private affair for the four of us. Just before the swinging doors of life changed for us once more, we took Chloe and Colin, together with our Monica, Matthew and Concordia, and a party of former Concordia school children from our classes, hired a small cruise liner and sailed from Cape Town to what had been the United Kingdom. We visited the ruins of London fourteen years after its destruction in the Great Northern War. Remembering London as it was then, it was eerie walking through what used to be busy streets, crammed with cars and the noise of cheerful shoppers. Now it was a silent, derelict set of ruins, overgrown by brambles, convolvulus and other climbing or spreading weeds. It was as though life had never existed there. There was no sign of its previous inhabitants. We had no idea what had happened to them or where it had happened. We left the shattered city and travelled to our home village twenty-five miles outside of London, carrying provisions and tents for a three-day outing. There was no sign of it except for the ruins of the parish church standing on its hill above the former village, and the piles of scattered (and shattered) bricks which were all that remained of the houses. We also found evidence of human bones and skulls scattered around the site. We had no way of knowing who was who. We searched for the ruins of our old homes and eventually found them. Judy found her old teddy bear under the rubble and I found a few toy soldiers, part of a group of World War Two British and German troops. We took them back with us to Austrasia. We still have them and plan to have them buried with us when we die. We camped overnight amid the ruins.

Next day, we found some spades in the under croft of the church and some of the former students, knowing how we felt, dug a large grave in the former church grounds, while others collected the bones and brought them to the burial site. We buried the bones there. On top of the grave we followed an old Celtic tradition. We gathered stones and bricks from the ruins and piled them into a cairn. It was about two feet high from base to top. They picked some of the flowers growing in such profusion in the area. It did strike us how odd it seemed that human beings are so easy to destroy for ever yet flowers always survive! We said the Lord's Prayer over them. We didn't know any other prayer, but we believed God (if He existed at all) would hear it and honour it. We turned to our companions and asked them to leave us for a few minutes while we said, "Goodbye, thank you and we will always love you," to our parents. Next day we left, feeling tearful, and retraced our footsteps to the devastated former capital, arriving there the following morning and then leaving for Africa. We had closed the gate on the past.

When I reached forty, the minimum age to be elected President, Dad took us aside to warn us that in two years' time, when Judy had reached the same age, he was going to announce their decision to stand down. He told us they would nominate us to be their successors. This wasn't what we wanted. We told him so. However, he told us the Party wanted us, we were very popular with the people, and would win any election hands down. We reluctantly agreed on condition that they continued to help us with advice, based on their experience and knowledge. They promised they would do so for as long as they were able. Therefore, I decided to carry out my earlier decision. We had achieved much and done much since we arrived here at twenty-three and twenty-one years old seventeen years earlier. We were dragged down to the earth before being raised to the skies. We were humiliated and denied even human status and now we are about to be raised to the pinnacle of the state. We have worked with Mum and Dad to lead the country in peace, then at war and finally back to reconciliation and peace again. Now they want us to finish the job we all started together. Neither of us are enthusiastic about undertaking it, especially as we can see the difficulties we might face. We both know that Musaveni and Maritza were not unique and that some Austrasians would be unable to see past the colour of our skins and consider that we were really foreign slaves with no right to rule. In our former country they used to talk about people having a cross to bear – that is the cross we have to bear. We can do nothing to change those peoples' minds, but, our consolation is that they form a minority. Most Austrasians bear us good will and we are sure will give us their support. If they don't want us, they can always vote against us after all. If enough do that, we won't be elected President and someone else will have to take on the burden. That's democracy!

I have written about our lives, especially our hidden lives, telling you things not known to the public. What I haven't written about (the last fifteen years) are matters of public knowledge. What is to come in our lives and our deaths, and, of course, the deaths of our beloved and often unfairly maligned parents and our foster siblings, will also be known to you, the reader, though naturally not yet known to us! The time has come for us to close the final door on the past - on our past as slaves and victims - and to honour all the victims of slavery. We're going to leave in a few days' time with a now elderly Jake, our children, and our siblings and what's left of the old St Michael's squad and travel gently back to the Ngugi Caves to place a wreath, say a prayer and place this book there. We (and especially I, the author) leave it to you the reader to make of it what you can and will (if and when you read it). As I said to the miners, "Au Revoir and Bonne Chance" (Goodbye and Good luck).

Colonel Marcus (Mark) Ngangi (Cabinet and State Secretary)

AFTERWORD
BY JOHN OKONKWO

As you will see, I wrote to Mark to send him a copy of what you have now read and asked him if he would care to update it. He politely rejected my suggestion but suggested I could do so if I wished .I have done so here.

The second Ngangi Presidency lasted for over twenty years, covering five elections. (Matthew Ngangi had been elected three times.) It was marked by a continuation and a development of what was done during Matthew's Presidency. This was not surprising in view of the major roles played by both Mark and Judy in it. The two of them continued the policy of reconciling the various communities in the country under the title, "One Austrasia, many tribes, one united nation." They made a conscious effort to mix groups from different parts of the country and different tribes, most notably in education where boarding schools were established throughout Austrasia, with children being bussed from one end of the nation to the other. The Cabinet was chosen carefully to reflect all the groups, including the former slaves, "new Africans" (as Mark and Judy called them), who were represented by Jack and Bill. The Cabinet members appointed Chloe and Colin to replace Mark and Judy as their Secretaries. New Universities were also established to supplement the work of the two already established in Freetown.

At the local level, they spent a great deal of time, effort and money on rebuilding communities. This was especially important in the areas affected by the earlier civil war and the Casa Isabella rebellion. Mark referred to the work done on the village that acted as a base for the Ngugi Caves community and which is now the township of Monica. The temporary structures in the new village established for former slaves and soldiers were slowly replaced by modern (and permanent) buildings. It is now the town of Ngangiville. Considerable sums were spent on the country's infrastructure: upgrading existing roads and building railways and new roads, especially in the less developed areas on the northern border. This effort was extended to the development of new airports and internal and international routes.

Mark made contact with India, which, following the collapse of the Northern giants, is now the dominant political and economic power on the planet. Indian technicians were recruited to help develop new industries based on I.T. and also the entertainment sector, developing a native film industry. Our mines were modernised following the Ngangi Report's recommendations and became efficient and productive parts of the economy.

The slave breeding programme began to produce results, with the government divided on how to deal with the individuals created by this, (fortunately) inefficient programme. As the children grew older they became a problem, as Marcus suggested in his book they would, because they never knew what it was like to be part of a loving and stable family. Judy, of course had predicted this. An inspectorate was set up to ensure the orphanages in which these children were placed were very carefully monitored. Regulations were laid down to ensure the children were not mistreated, but these orphanages were no substitute for a proper family. A boy and girl were eventually adopted by Chloe and Colin and were given all the love a child could possibly wish for. I learnt from talking to Colin that they named them after Mark and Judy. Judy and Mark also adopted a boy to be a brother for their own son, Matthew. They decided to name him after his new godfather, Louis Jake. A handful of kind owners allowed their slaves, if they were a childless couple, to adopt one of these children, but most could not be placed. Some were drafted into the mines to replace former slaves who had become too old for this work or had died. Others were sent with the colonists to the North Atlantic Islands (the former UK), where unfortunately, the colonists treated them as slaves (which was sadly not what Mark and Judy intended) and some were sent to develop the new village and the village that had acted as a base for Louis' "partisans" into mixed community towns.

Mark's first act as President was to close down the Slave Breeding Programme, arguing it was cruel, immoral, unethical and inefficient. Both he and Judy said publicly that it was a complete waste of money and they ordered the destruction of all unused genetic material. There is no sign of the programme ever being restarted. The slaves involved in it were freed and given a choice; to move to the two new towns or stay where they were and develop the areas around the former centres. Most took the second option. They also emancipated all the state slaves working in the mines, which, of course, were Government owned. They said they would like to end the new slavery all together but did not think they were the right people to do it. However, they did put a stop to the branding, collaring and cuffing of slaves (in future the only mark they would carry would be the tattoo on the wrist).

"Only an indigenous Austrasian can end slavery in Austrasia; not a white Austrasian who would be seen to be self-serving," Judy explained.

Outside of the country, both of them were strong advocates of equality between people from different ethnic groups, arguing that the very existence of the new slavery was creating problems that could afflict society for decades if not centuries. They pushed other Presidents to tackle the problem of the devastated northern lands before the new colonial rivalry created another war. As a result a colonial conference took place in Abuja (Nigeria). Mark and Judy attended and, as a result of their *persistence, Austrasia was allocated the North Atlantic Islands as its area of development. Mixed groups of white ("new-borns") and young black Austrasians were sent to four centres – Southampton, Dover, London and Edinburgh. Marcus appointed an experienced administrator as Governor and hoped the mistakes seen elsewhere in the history of colonisation were not repeated.*

Sadly, he and Judy quickly learnt their hopes were in vain. Where survivors were found, they were either killed, enslaved or driven into poorer (more distant) areas, or into dedicated native reservations, as foretold by Mark in his speech to his parents which he described earlier in the book. In other respects, their foreign policy was a success as they built good relationships with other African leaders and, by dividing the devastated Northern areas up between the various African and Asian nations, prevented another war. Africa colonised Europe, while South America colonised North and Central America and South Asia colonised North Asia. The old world and its history was turned upside down .

Looking at the Mark and Judy administration overall, the period was one of steady consolidation and improvement. The most dramatic event of the "reign" was the state funerals of first Matthew and then Monica Ngangi in Freetown Cathedral, events marked by genuine sorrow among the people. Interestingly, it was after this that the attitude of the two younger Ngangis towards religion seemed to soften as they became close friends with the Anglican Archbishop of Freetown. Perhaps they were always really Christians after all despite their frequent utterances to the contrary! Who can tell?

John Okonkwo

EPILOGUE

Dear John,

Thank you for your letter* and this very interesting copy of your book. You probably don't realize that I appear in it. Professor Nwamarkwa wasn't just one of my predecessors in my chair. I was one of the students who was part of that party. I was one of the four handling the 40+ section. In fact it was I who found and handed the Professor the vital document which conclusively proved Josiah Ndenge planned to use Matthew Ngangi to carry the blame for the controversial policies Josiah created and forced through against Matthew's will or despite Cabinet opposition, thus proving his intention was always to overthrow and kill the late President and Vice President.

I noticed and felt deeply moved by the last few paragraphs the present President wrote. I've met and spoken with both of them on many occasions and I know he and Judy feel really cut up by the fact that they have failed to end the condition of slavery imposed 39 years ago now on those unfortunates who've lost family, country, freedom, and even the status of full human beings. Black militants have criticised them for <u>wishing</u> to do so and white rights campaigners have criticised them for <u>not</u> doing so or for not doing enough. I think your and their book makes the reasons for their actions, and the dilemma the issue put them in, clear and, in the context, understandable. They simply can't do it because they are the wrong people, but they have done what they could to ameliorate the conditions of these unfortunate people.

Their action would be misrepresented and misunderstood and, by the beneficiaries, unappreciated. They are being criticised by both sides for different reasons. If they did what they want to do, they would be damned by both sides. For one side it would be the act of a guilty conscience and an example of a national leader favouring his own group over the interests of others. For the other side, it would be too little too late. They can't win, whatever they do. I feel really sorry for them. As Mark wrote, they did not want this honour and it has proved a heavy burden to them.

As to your question: should you publish it? You read how the Josiah Ndenge book came about. I think they would both say yes – but you should write to them and ask them for permission. However, do pick a nice title won't you? The Ndenge book title was (and is) a terrible one although fully understandable at the time. Since it was a book published by this department, I'm thinking of republishing it under a different title; perhaps, "The Life and Times of Vice President Josiah Ndenge."

Good luck and well done, whatever you decide

Your friend,

Nathaniel Ajayi.

-0-0-0-0-0-0-0-0-0-0-

See PROLOGUE

Dear President Ngangi

I have recovered your book and have added a little to it. I enclose a printed copy that I would like to publish. It's clear you expected it to be published eventually, but in view of one of your comments in the book, you probably expected it to be published after your deaths. Would you allow us to publish it while you and your children are still alive? Also would you like to include an update that we can add as an epilogue together with my letters to and from your friend Professor Ajayi who told us he was part of your team and found the crucial Ndenge document?

Best wishes,

John Okonkwo

-0-0-0-0-0-0-0-0-0-0-

Dear John,

Thank you for writing to us and sending us a copy of what you have done with my book. It was interesting reading at the age of sixty-four words I originally wrote when I was twenty-six. Reading it through again with your insightful additions has made us both relive the past. Thank you for your hard work on it and the work of your team in reopening the Ngugi Caves to the public. Judy has asked me to pass on her thanks too. She laughed when she read some of the cheeky comments she made then and remembered the expressions on the faces of those who first heard them. I fear she traded on the love people had for us and always got away with it. We couldn't do that now. It's sad that youthful exuberance has to give way to what we console ourselves by defining it as the wisdom of old age and the responsibility of our exalted position.

Thank you too for giving us the option to say yes – publish now; no – publish when we're safely lying below the ground; or no outright. I have spoken with my beloved wife and life partner, Judy, as well as with our four children. They all agree to let you go ahead. I don't feel the need to write about the doings and decisions we and our government made over the twenty-four years since we became President and Vice President. They're a matter of record. If you feel you need to write an addendum covering our Presidency please feel free to do so. I leave decisions on whether we were wise or foolish to the historians. It's amazing how wise one can be judging a decision fifty years later! Mistakes are impossible then! The one decision I do defend is our decision to include Jack and Bill in the Cabinet. We also included Erica and Lancelot, two former supporters of Josiah Ndenge, as well as the best of the tribes and regions. I believe that this has helped bring the nation together after the tumultuous events following the coup against President Igbokwe. We were delighted when the Cabinet, on its own initiative, freely chose to offer our previous jobs to Chloe and Colin. They've done a good job as our secretaries, and we all owe them a great deal for what they endured at the hands of Maritza and Letizia.

You have noticed, and I presume Nathaniel, who I'm planning to nominate as my successor, has told you our greatest regret is that we cannot emancipate the remaining slaves. We really want to do so, but we have done as much as we feel we can and dare do as white former slaves to ameliorate their condition. We simply cannot end slavery totally. Representatives of the oppressed group cannot end the oppression. Instead of an act of delayed social justice, it will appear as one of the group helping the rest of the group. You push me up and I'll pull you all up. That's what Ndenge was doing. It's why he had to go. We have worked on it, though, and we have produced a fully worked out scheme for Nathaniel to announce on his inauguration, so he can get it out of the way quickly. It involves three strands:

1. Emancipation of all slaves including laboratory produced slaves, with compensation being paid to all owners and former slaves. The exact figures for both types of *compensation could be worked out by negotiation with the interested parties later.*

2. *Repeal of all laws on slavery and the treatment of slaves, and their replacement by a law forbidding the description of white Austrasians as slaves.*

3. *Granting citizenship to, and a designation of, all former slaves as a new discrete Austrasian tribe.*

Nathaniel has discussed the plan with us (and yes I did remember he was the one who found the document which finally damned Josiah Ndenge) and he has approved it. It will be our final gift aimed at the reconciliation of all peoples and the closing of the door finally on that tumultuous period in the history of Austrasia.

We are planning to retire at the next election and are going to live in a modest house built for us by the people of Concordia, whose citizens have been kind enough to forgive us for what we said to them when we returned for the first time. They have built a statue of us as a young couple in Major's uniforms outside of the town hall. I forbade them to depict us as slaves being carried through the town or with my firing a pistol at a tin! Our children, as well as Chloe and Colin and their children are staying on in the South. Monica, Matthew and Concordia have been offered places in Nathaniel's first cabinet and Chloe and Colin are planning to retire to live in Ngangiville. Louis has joined Anna's department. We understand that Colin and Chloe's children are planning to open a business running tourist trips along Lake Nkrumah. Anna has used part of her budget for developing new industries by former slaves to enable them to purchase a boat of the "Macrone" class for the purpose. Judy and I intend to join their parents for the first cruise in about a month's time. Why don't you come and join us as our guest? It would be good to meet you and have a chat. We need to talk about the plans to open up the Ngugi Caves to the public and the finance you need for that purpose. You must let us know the date of the opening and we'll put it in our dairies. Judy and I will certainly come to make speeches and cut the tape for you.

There is one final thank you which I need to say to you, John, and it is the biggest of them all. Thank you for correcting an "error" for which Judy and I have been heavily criticised over the years — that is not removing the remains of the last four victims in the Ngugi Caves for burial. To be honest with you, neither Judy nor I could bring ourselves to come face to face with the mutilated remains of two of our friends and companions in the hell-hole that was St. Michael's Island. We flunked it. Thank you for putting this right for us and giving final rest and justice to four innocent victims of a sadistic monster.

Good luck with our (your and my) book

(President) Marcus Ngangi.

(Incidentally, not covered in the book, three of the boys, including the Head Boy, who attacked us in Concordia, were killed during the Battle of Engadi and the other two served ten years of a life sentence in prison. Judy and I persuaded Father to pardon them and reduce their sentence, believing they had suffered enough for mistakes made when they were young, easily influenced and their blood was hot. MN.)

Milton Keynes UK
Ingram Content Group UK Ltd.
UKHW012133110624
443988UK00001B/134